Silenced Cry

Marta Stephens

BeWrite Books

Published internationally by BeWrite Books, UK.
32 Bryn Road South, Wigan, Lancashire, WN4 8QR.

© Marta Stephens 2007

The right of Marta Stephens to be identified as the author has been asserted in accordance with sections 77 and 78 of the Copyright, Designs and Patents Act 1988. All rights reserved.

A CIP catalogue record for this book is available from the British Library

ISBN: 978-1-905202-72-0

Also available in eBook format.

Produced by BeWrite Books
www.bewrite.net

Cover photograph: Dawn Allynn Photography & Creative Design
www.dawnallynn.com

Cover design: Scott Parkison

To Rick, Jessica, and Tracy for your love, encouragement, and amazing patience.

In loving memory of Nicole

Acknowledgements

Silenced Cry was two years in the making. In that time, family, personal friends, and professionals have offered the valued guidance and the motivation I needed to finish this manuscript. Although it is impossible to list everyone who has offered their support, you each have my deepest gratitude and sincere appreciation. I would like to further acknowledge and thank these friends who were more directly involved through their readings, feedback, and selflessly gave of their time.

M. Christina Ruggiero, Mari Lyons, S. W. Vaughn, John Sullivan, Mike Reed, Jason Ryan, Pat Brown, Warlen Bassham, Police Officer Reba Grass, and Police Sergeant John Foster.

A very special thanks to my publisher and editor, Cait Myers and Hugh McCracken.

© Jessica Stephens

Marta Stephens, a native of Argentina but a life-long resident of the American Midwest, began her career as a fiction writer in 2004. The desire to journal her thoughts evolved into a life-changing passion that has led to the birth of her Sam Harper Crime Mysteries and her debut novel, Silenced Cry. She also has several short stories and flash fictions to her credit.

Stephens lives in the Midwest with her husband, their daughter, son and three very spoiled Boston Bull Dogs. She has a degree in Journalism/Public Relations, is a member of Sisters in Crime, Deadly Prose Critique Group and The Midwest Writer's Workshop.

Aside from her writing, Stephens has earned several awards in local competitions for her oil paintings, enjoys gardening, antique collecting, graphic design, and sharing moments with friends. She is an avid reader and believes that learning is a life-long adventure.

www.martastephens-author.com

Silenced Cry

1

The hour-long sessions started at nine in the morning, twice a week, whether narcotics detective Sam Harper liked it or not. The only good thing about this damp and cold Massachusetts morning was that it marked the midpoint of Harper's commitment. Internal Affairs had drilled him for three days in a row. Now the police shrink wanted a piece of him. He was sick of her dogged questions. *That was his job; to wear the other guy down.* Three sessions left, three hours of digging into his past, into the events of that night – that goddamned night.

Neither the mild vanilla scent floating up from a flickering candle on the doctor's desk nor the subtle gurgle bubbling from a tabletop fountain were doing their job to relax him. Harper rubbed the arms of the leather chair with his thumb as he calculated his next move. He stared at her and finally broke the silence.

"You ever kill a man, Doc?" A subtle twitch of her brow told him he had her attention. "A split second. That's all it takes, pull the trigger, and whoosh! He's gone."

Dr Brannon lowered her gaze and resumed her scribbling. The navy overstuffed chair seemed to swallow her small frame.

"Why did you go there?"

"Mellow was our only link in the case. At least that's what Gillies thought. He told me every damned thing hinged on getting to Mellow before homicide got their hands on him."

"And you had reservations?"

Harper looked away as the Chandler Police Department (CPD) psychiatrist took notes of his crumbling life.

"Does it matter?" His glance swept up to the dark paneled wall behind her desk. Framed certificates hung in an orderly row like crows on a wire. They mapped out her qualification and gave credence to her ego.

He didn't need her to question his motives or to dig into his past and drag the memories of that night to the surface. They were there, frozen in Harper's mind – the second he got off his round. He'd never forget the blast or the hammering rain beating against his face. The look of Frank Gillies' lifeless eyes had scorched itself into his memory. Harper leaned forward and dropped his head. Fists jammed against his eyes as if to rub out the intruding images. He had spun the moment any number of ways, but the outcome never changed.

Brannon crossed her legs. She folded her hands and tapped her fingertips. She watched in silence, waiting to analyze his next thoughts.

"You do realize you don't go back to work without these sessions." She picked up the notepad again. The sound of her pen striking twice against its surface made dull impatient clicks. "Look, Detective. No one said this was going to be easy, but you have to open up. You are the only one who can do it."

Harper didn't buy her attempt to bring him back into the conversation. He didn't know if he could, as she said, open up. He pursed his lips and glanced out the window.

"Damned wind's picking up again, Doc." He buried his mouth in the *L* of his thumb and index finger touching the outer corner of his eye. He rose and turned his back to hide the familiar burning that blurred his vision. Apprehension had become his unwelcome companion, a reminder of the failings he refused to accept. Anger crept in. It bubbled and seared holes into his sense of reason.

"Should've been me." He closed his eyes, pinched the bridge of his nose, and cleared his throat. "I was right in Mellow's line of fire. The damned piece was inches from me." The thrust of his fist made a hollow sound against his chest. "You don't get it, do you?"

"Yes, I do. Let's start there."

"What's the point? You know what happened. We've been over it a million times. Don't you get tired of listening to this crap?"

"It's the only way."

"We can talk all you want. Won't change a damned thing. Won't bring him back." He dropped back into his chair and swept a hand across the stubble he hadn't shaved in three days. "What're you going to do? Tell me to think happy thoughts? Will that do it? Is that going to stop the dreams?"

"Tell me about them."

"Not today." He wrestled between his grief and growing suspicions of Gillies. *What really went down five days ago in front of the Roving Dog Saloon?* He jabbed a white knuckled fist onto the arm of the chair and looked away. Every sordid detail came rushing back without prodding. "It was past eleven that night when Gillies got the tip that Mellow had violated parole."

"Come on. Gotta go." Detective Frank Gillies rushed to Harper's desk and slammed an opened hand against it on his way to the elevator. "The big guy just answered our prayers."

Harper caught his partner's grin and his thumbs up gesture. The gray had gone beyond Gillies' temples to the mass of short locks that covered his head. Harper's glance dropped to the new spot that had landed on his partner's tie six hours before from a greasy burger. One of many meals that had settled around Gillies' middle.

"Let me guess, Stewart Martin's leaving." Harper turned to the next page in the file. He prayed every day that Detective Martin would transfer.

"Yeah right. Soon buddy, real soon, but not tonight. Word is Mellow blew a guy's brains out." Gillies struggled to slip his arms through the narrow sleeves of his overcoat.

"Wasn't he just released a couple of days ago?" Harper was unmoved by the news. Mellow was nothing to their case against Jimmy Owens. They were after the supplier, not the low-end dealer. "When was this?"

"Few minutes ago. Over on Calvert near the Trenton overpass. Homicide's on their way. Come on." Gillies shook his head. "Will ya put that crap down already?"

Harper turned his head in time to see a bolt of lightning crackle and spark across the eastern sky followed by a quick clap of thunder. He adjusted his sight on the windowpane and the ribbons of rain flowing down the glass. "We don't need him."

"He knows where to find Owens."

"Di Napoli is on it."

"Di Napoli can't find his ass with both hands. Move it, Harper!" Gillies rushed toward the fourth floor elevator and jabbed the down button.

Harper glanced at his watch. It was exactly eleven twenty-five p.m. He grabbed his coat off the back of a chair and motioned to Gillies he would meet him downstairs. His partner was a master at spewing out insults. Harper wondered how he had managed to measure up to the man's expectations when Di Napoli, the eight-year veteran undercover assigned to work with them, couldn't. He took the steps two at a time and reached the lobby as the elevator doors opened.

"He's out, what, four days and breaks parole?" Harper pressed Gillies. "It's a waste of time. The guys in homicide aren't going to let us anywhere near him. Hell, you know what they're like. Bunch of assholes."

"No shit. That's why we're going someplace else."

"Where?"

"A dive over on Howard and Third. Just got a tip the fucker's sitting in a booth there right now."

Harper pulled his coat collar up and looked out the glass doors. The March rains were pounding down for the fourth consecutive day. The odds on staying dry weren't adding up in his favor. He swept a glance over to Gillies' and caught a similar sense of hesitation before the two of them made a run for the car.

Another bolt of lightning lit the sky followed closely by a clap of loud thunder.

"Harper?" Dr Brannon leaned her head to one side. "Where did you go?" The light of a small Tiffany lamp on the corner of her credenza illuminated the right side of her face.

"Want to let me in on your thoughts? It's just you and me here," she said, tapping her pencil on her notepad again.

He threw back his head against the back of the couch and closed his eyes. His left foot dangled over his knee while the restless right tapped on the floor.

"Right. You, me, and that thing." He motioned toward the tape recorder on the coffee table.

She glanced at her watch. "Cut the crap, Harper. This is your third session and you have been defiant from the very beginning. Let's get one thing straight. I'm not out to get you, understand? The bad guys are out there." She pointed toward the door. "You want to fight them, fine. Go ahead. But walk out that door and I'll make sure you don't come back." She stared at him in icy silence. "You don't have a choice, Detective."

"The hell I don't. I risk my life every goddamn day. That's my choice just as much as it was my duty to follow my partner to the dive that night. I didn't do anything wrong. And there's not a damned thing you can do to change it." Heat rushed to his face. "Who do you think you are, anyway? All you do is sit in your office and analyze the hell out of us. Where do you get off ordering me around?"

"You have a problem with authority?"

"Just you."

"Interesting. Let's get back to what you were thinking a minute ago."

He hated her self-assurance. He frowned – wished he could run. He glanced at the door then turned to focus his sight on the wet bark of the maple tree in front of the window.

"It's spitting snow."

"Damn it, Harper. I'm sworn to secrecy. Nothing you say leaves this room." She paused for a moment. "I am not going to risk your confidence unless you give me reason to think you are capable of hurting yourself or others." Again, she waited for a response. "Did you hear me?"

"Guess it's only rain." Guilt continued to eat at him. *If only he'd shot sooner. If only he had known. If only.* The questions outweighed the number of plausible answers. He rose to his feet again and paced.

"No one was supposed to get killed. Not Mellow, sure as hell not Frank." His fingers sliced through his hair and spiked the blond strands with the random pass of his hand. The knot in the pit of his gut tightened like a vise. The sessions, the job; he had to get through one to have the other. "I just wanted the truth. What the hell was Gillies thinking?"

"He knew the risks," she said, without taking her eyes from him. "Let's talk a minute about you. What have you been doing with yourself?"

"What difference does it make?" He knew the drill. Sure, the shrink time was mandated, but he didn't want to talk about himself and the baggage he had swung over his shoulder.

She remained straight-faced and waiting. There was no way around it that he could see. The doc seemed as determined to make him talk, as he was to remain evasive.

"I finished a fifth of Scotch, and when I was good and drunk, I watched soap operas. Only damned thing I know more depressing than me these days."

"You do that often?"

"I'm fine. All right? I can handle the booze."

"How do you know I was asking about the booze?"

She caught him off guard with that remark. *How damned stupid was he anyway?*

"Do you think you have a problem with it?"

Harper sized her up with a seasoned glance. Her dark green sweater set off the red tones in her hair that curved slightly beneath her chin and framed the curvature of her face. She was easy on the eyes but too damned clinical for his taste. Nothing worse than a scrutinizing shrink to kill the moment. He assumed she was in her thirties, like him, but obviously twice as smart and a lot more obnoxious. Part of him wanted to tell her about Frank Gillies, how he died, and the thoughts that had haunted him since that night. He could still hear Gillies' voice as they ran out to the car. He fingered the change in his pocket, leaned his forehead against the cool windowpane, and tuned her out.

Harper rushed into the car and slammed the door. He wiped his face and secured the straps of his bulletproof vest.

"What's Mellow doing in a bar?" he asked Gillies. "Is it near the scene?"

"Nah. It's down in Avondale." Gillies switched on the siren and cut through traffic. "Hole in the wall place smack in the middle of slum lord row."

"That's clear across town. How long ago was the shooting?"

"What do I look like, some fucking information sign?" Gillies growled. "How the hell should I know? Idiots in homicide can figure that one out."

"You sure your informant has it right this time?"

"What the hell's with ya and the million fucking questions? All we need to do is talk to the guy about Owens before homicide gets to him."

"Doesn't make sense," said Harper. "Most shooters would run like hell, not stop for a drink. Besides, what makes you think he's going to talk now when he wouldn't before?"

"No one accused him of having brains, ya know what I'm saying, college boy? You and me, we'd be out of jobs if little shits like him had any brains."

"Who called in the shooting?"

"Shit, Harper. Here, let me get my crystal ball out." Gillies sneered. "That's homicide's problem; I could give a rat's ass about it." He shook his head. "All right, look, someone in dispatch called up about the shooting. Thought we'd want to know. That's all. Just following a lead, all right?"

Harper knew about Gillies' connections. Not who they were or how he managed them, but that they existed. They didn't always pan out, but the grin that split Gillies' face and the urgency in his voice implied this one was a sure thing.

"Seems stupid of Mellow to screw up right after making parole."

"Yeah, well, like I said, if little shits like him had brains we wouldn't be here."

Harper had seen anger take over people's minds. It shoved them over the edge without saying how far or how hard they would fall. Maybe Mellow hadn't figured the distance yet.

Gillies turned off the headlights and nosed the unmarked patrol car into position across the street from the Roving Dog Saloon. The deserted street and the rain thumping against the car roof gave a false sense of tranquility.

Harper glanced across the way at the tavern door and the red neon lights shaped like a dog just above it. The dog's legs and tail appeared to move back and forth making him seem to rove for a good mug of beer. The sign's light cast an eerie red glow and shimmered off the wet objects beneath it. Harper pulled up his collar, cupped his hands around his mouth, and blew warmth into them.

"What now? You're sure he's in there?"

Gillies winced as he watched the windshield wipers slap the water from side to side. "Only one way to find out. It's your turn, rookie."

"The hell it is. I ran after the scum in the Capelli case, remember? Chased the guy five blocks through a foot of snow before you cut him off with the car. You can be so damned smug sometimes. You and that stupid grin of yours. This wasn't even my call."

"Ah, come on. Rookies aren't allowed to say no. Besides, you're younger. What are ya, thirty-one, thirty-two now?"

"Cut the jabs."

"What? What'd I say?"

"Cut the rookie and college boy bit."

"I'm just joshing with ya. Don't go getting sensitive on me, all right?"

"It gets old." It was almost midnight. Harper was tired and in no mood for Gillies' mindless humor. "Haven't been a rookie in years."

"Is that so?" Gillies chuckled and threw him a playful punch. "All right. Listen. Ya don't even have to talk to the asshole. Just see if he's in there. Don't want him running out the back or nothing and have to chase the little creep in this shit."

"That's it, huh?" Harper leaned his head against the window and watched the rain. "It's not letting up."

"Go on. It'll take ya two minutes. We'll wait him out. Ask him a few questions and go home."

"Was that a typical surveillance?" asked Brannon. Expressionless eyes studied him from behind a set of silver framed reading glasses.

"No. We always worked together before. That night." Harper shook his head. "Nothing made sense. One minute we're just going to talk to the guy. Next thing I know I've got two fatalities to answer for and I don't know what in the hell happened."

"What do you mean, you don't know?"

"We didn't need Mellow to get Owens. Gillies knew it as well as I did. He acted as if we were the only ones on the case. There was a whole team of us including some undercover. But Gillies, he was so bent on going after Mellow that night. It was almost as if …"

"What?"

"He wouldn't take no for an answer. What the hell was I supposed to do? He was the senior partner. Had to trust his judgment."

"Did you?"

"That's what we're supposed to do, trust each other." Harper lowered his glance. "That night, after it was over, I checked with dispatch." He swallowed hard. "There was no shooting reported anywhere on or near the Trenton overpass."

2

The Roving Dog was a typical joint. Dark walls and sparse lighting managed to hide the stains, but couldn't mask the stench of what might have slipped through the cracks in the floor. A couple of old men at the bar were too engrossed watching the small, suspended television to notice Harper as he walked through the door.

Harper scanned the room from his perch on a stool at the far end of the bar while he searched for the face of a killer. Across the room, two others were shooting pool. The crisp, crackling sound of billiard balls hitting against one another; the plunk when they sank, a slight pause followed by another clink, were familiar sounds to him. A handful of patrons sat in the booths along the back wall. Each was at a different stage of inebriation. No sign of Mellow. Harper grabbed a napkin from a nearby stack on the bar and wiped his face.

"Hell of a night, huh?" The old bartender feigned a smile without looking up from the glass he had polished. "What's your pick?" he asked, carefully placing it on top of the set of clean glasses on the counter.

"Coffee. Blond and sweet."

The bartender returned with a mug brimming to the edge. Hesitation washed over his face at the sight of Harper's badge visible beneath his coat. He slowly pushed the mug and the packets of cream and sugar toward Harper, leaned on the counter, and whispered: "You here on business?"

"Depends, did you call?" Harper blew into the mug then took a sip.

"Where's Gillies?"

"Outside. What about Mellow?"

The man nodded toward the back of the room. "Got here about an hour before I called. Say, Gillies said he'd handle this himself."

"An hour?" Harper flashed a look into the old man's eyes. The words tumbled in his head in search for some logic. He raised his mug again and looked over the rim. Mellow came into focus. He was tucked away in the shadows of a corner booth, sidetracked by the woman sitting next to him and the freedoms she allowed him to take. "You sure he's been here an hour?"

"Yeah, positive. See that?" The bartender thumbed over his shoulder at the Miller Beer clock above the phone. "I'm sure."

"Doesn't seem to be causing any trouble. What made you call?" Gillies' haste and the old man's delay to call didn't add up. So far, nothing had.

"I wouldn't have, except I heard him tell her a thing or two when I served them their last round."

"Like what?"

The old man shrugged his shoulders. "Couldn't tell you exactly." He explained he only got the gist of the conversation. "Sounded like someone ripped him off. I heard him tell her, '… won't be bothered by that mother again.'"

"You called us on that? How do you know he didn't buy the guy a ticket out of town or something?"

"Anyone else, I wouldn't have thought twice. But him? Not about to take any chances. You know what these bums are like. Just out of jail; temper's as hot as his record is long. I've known him since he was this high," said the man, raising his hand to his waist. "He was a punk then, now he's nothing but a worthless piece of shit. Never hurts to think the worst." He paused for a moment then whispered again: "So what'd he do? Kill somebody? Heard about the shooting near the overpass. Was it him?"

Harper took a drink. The bartender with the raspy voice knew more than his customer's taste in booze and arrest record. "What do you know about the shooting?"

"Me? Nothing."

Harper heard the denial but caught the man's sideward glance.

"Someone heard the shots. A couple of the guys were talking about it. That's all."

"Which guys?"

"Ah, I don't know. They weren't regulars – left already."

"What happened after you served Mellow that round?"

"Nothing. I acted like I wasn't paying attention. Came back here. Made the call. Look, news in this neighborhood travels fast. I don't want any problems. Don't want him to know I'm the one who called either, understand?"

Harper nodded. "Who's the woman?"

"Couldn't tell you her name. She's in here with a different john every other night. As long as she pays the tab, what she does is her business. The rest of them," he nodded toward his clientele, "just want to sit around, have a few drinks, and forget their problems. All I'm asking you to do is get him the hell out of here. So go on. Get Gillies in here and do your jobs already."

"We'll be waiting outside." Harper reached into his pocket, pulled out a dollar, and tossed it next to his empty mug. "You've got Gillies' number. Call the minute he starts to leave."

"What? You're leaving?" The man thumbed over his shoulder again. "What about him? Aren't you going to arrest him?"

Harper pulled up his collar. "On what?" He waited for him to say the wrong thing. He wanted to catch him at a lie, to know what he knew. Anything to satisfy his suspicions that he and Gillies were in cahoots. When he didn't reply, Harper said: "You just make sure he walks out the front door. Got it?" He was near the door when he heard the bartender call out to him.

"Hey! Hold up. Here." He held out a capped Styrofoam cup for Harper to take. "This'll take the chill off the old man for now."

"Hey Skip." One of the gents at the bar waved his empty beer bottle. "Need another."

"Well? Is he in there?" Gillies held out a towel in exchange for the steaming cup of coffee.

"Yeah. You could have told me you knew the bartender." Harper jerked the towel from Gillies' hands.

"What the hell are ya pissed at? I've known Chuck a while."

"I'm your partner, not your damned stooge. The guy knows more about what went down tonight than I do."

"Don't take it personal. We got the call. That's all that matters. What's Mellow doing?"

"Getting drunk with a whore," Harper said squeezing the water from his hair.

"Shit, don't need him drunk tonight."

"Your friend claims he overheard Mellow telling her he got robbed."

"That a fact?"

"Yeah. Here's another news flash. He claimed Mellow was in the bar an hour before he called you. How do you figure that? How the hell does a guy kill someone two miles away while he's sitting in a goddamned bar?"

Gillies took a drink of his coffee and pressed his lips. He stared straight ahead in silence. Harper could see it, even in the dark. How Gillies froze while the wheels in his head turned and the gears screeched into reverse trying to find another way out. Harper had seen that same look on the faces of criminals when the walls of incarceration closed in on them.

"Must be mistaken," said Gillies.

"Did you tell him about the shooting?"

"No."

"He knows. How the hell does he know about a shooting clear across town minutes after it happened?"

"Mellow must have told him," said Gillies.

"Shit. Mellow shouldn't even be in there."

"Don't start assuming nothing. He's mistaken, that's all."

"I'm not assuming a damned thing." Harper shook his head. "Gotta hand it to you, that's one hell of a coincidence."

"It happens."

"It's bullshit and you know it." He slapped the towel on the seat. "Start talking."

"There's nothing to tell. I told Chuck to keep his eyes open for Mellow and Owens. He said Mellow knew where Owens was keeping himself and I'd have to talk with Mellow for the details. Called to let me know about the shooting; said he'd keep Mellow at the bar until we got here. End of story."

"I thought you said dispatch called you about the shooting? What the hell's going on, Frank?"

"Nothing. What?"

"You're lying. What kind of mess are you in this time?"

"What the hell are ya talking about? I just got confused is all."

"Since when? Next to my dad, you're the sharpest cop I know. Why did Chuck wait an hour to call?"

"How should I know? Tell ya what, I'll ask him next time we talk, all right?"

"You do that. And while you're at it, make damned sure you leave me the hell out of whatever is going down tonight."

"Would ya settle down? Nothing's going on that ya don't know about. We just need to see what he knows about Owens. That's it!" Gillies rubbed his hands together. "Damn this rain." He raised his wrist and rolled his eyes at the hour. "Man, the old lady's going to be pissed again tonight."

Harper stared at the tavern door. His partner was good at changing the subject whenever it suited him. He listened, but didn't intend to engage in the irrelevant conversation.

"Late nights," Gillies continued, "she hates them. I'm sure she'd be happier if I had turned out to be a goddamned bean counter or bank teller. Ya know, the old home by five, bored to tears. Can't remember the last time we didn't have a fight the minute I set foot in the door. It's bad enough when I'm not there for supper. On nights like this, she goes through the roof. I can tell ya right now, we won't be sleeping together tonight. Bet ya a twenty she has my pillow waiting on the damned sofa."

"Right, let's hear another one."

"Ya hear me laughing? It's getting worse every day. She must be going through the change or something."

Gillies' comment made Harper think of his fiancée, Deanna. *How often had they argued over his late hours at work too?* "My mother used to worry about Dad all the time. Wouldn't go to bed until she heard him walk through the door."

"Not Ruthie. Hell, she's locked me out more than once." Silent minutes dragged. Gillies looked at his watch again. "Damn.

Almost one. How the hell long is he going to be in there?"

"You never said what your plan is," said Harper. "You do have a plan, don't you?"

"We grab him when he comes out. We question him, simple as that." Gillies gave him another playful punch in the arm. "You just keep your eyes wide open, hear? If he pulls out a weapon, be careful. I hate breaking in new partners."

"He was soused two hours ago. I say we go in and get it over with," said Harper.

"Nah, have to assume he's carrying a piece. He's a loose cannon. Now he's drunk and about as predictable as a skunk in heat. You're asking for a shitload of trouble. Last thing we want to do is rouse him up in a room full of people. We'll just wait him out. He won't give us any problems."

"And if he does?"

"What do ya think?" Gillies rubbed his eyes. "We shoot first ask questions later. Ah, come on. What are ya worried about? We've been up against bigger problems than this guy, right?"

"I'm not worried. I'm tired."

Water rose to within an inch from the top of the curbs, pooling in front of the bar at a clogged drain. Harper swept a glance at the dashboard clock. "One eighteen. I can't believe I let you talk me into this. Should be home in my warm, dry bed."

Gillies yawned and stretched then bolted straight up in his seat. "There he is!" he blurted. He reached for his Glock and the extra cartridge he shoved into his coat pocket.

"Damn. I told Chuck to call the minute he saw him leave," said Harper. "Why the hell didn't he warn us?"

The men watched as Mellow and the woman staggered out of the bar. He stopped and teetered as he turned up the collar of his jean jacket. He reached an arm around her shoulders and tried to stay on his feet.

"Shit." Harper braced himself for another drenching and turned to say something when he caught sight of Gillies' shirt beneath his coat. "Where's your vest?"

"It's in back. Look at him. He's stumbling over his own feet. Won't give us any problems now."

"Damn it. Get it on!"

"A lot of good it'll do if I get shot in the head. In the meantime, he's getting away."

"Don't be an ass. It's regulations. Put the damned thing on."

"Ya know, I'd love to have this conversation with ya, college boy. Maybe later – at tea, real proper like," he sneered. "Come on will ya, I don't wanna be in this crap all night." Gillies slammed the door and scuttled across the street.

"Son of a bitch." Harper clenched his teeth and ran.

"Hindsight's the pits, Doc. Should've never let him leave the damned car."

"He was a grown man," said Brannon.

"Yeah. A grown man with a death wish." He leaned forward again and folded his hands. "We drew our weapons and ran. So much for the element of surprise. Mellow didn't see us at first. Gillies yelled for him to stop. That's when Mellow took off like a jack rabbit."

"Freeze! Police!"

Startled, Mellow turned and pushed the woman away from him. She shrieked and fell to her knees. Pools of water had gathered along the ruts in the sidewalk and splashed up around her. She scrambled to get out of the way of the men and their drawn weapons. She cowered against a building and covered her face.

Mellow stumbled and fell; struggled to his feet and ran.

"I said freeze!" Gillies yelled again.

Harper hustled to narrow the gap between them. He charged past Gillies and yelled the order: "Freeze!"

Mellow made a half turn, drew his weapon, and took a blind shot. Harper returned fire. With both hands on his .357 Magnum, he aimed for the heart. Squeezed the trigger. Reverberating blasts from the shot rang out above the sound of rain thumping against the metal awnings. Mellow buckled then stumbled backwards into a cluster of trash cans. Their rank contents flew out and scattered along the sidewalk. A lid rolled down the street, the driving rain muted the clatter of metal against the concrete. Seconds later,

Mellow lay motionless on the heap of waste.

Lights flickered on in the windows of the apartment buildings along the street. Harper felt nameless, curious eyes descend upon him, watching from behind the safety of curtains.

He froze; arms stretched out, legs spread apart, his weapon still aimed at Mellow. His chest ached with each gasp, his lungs tightened with every draw of cold, damp air he sucked in. All he could do was blink to keep the rain out of his eyes. Slowly, without letting go of his gun, he lowered his outstretched arms and ran to the suspect's side. Harper bent over the body and felt his jugular. It was motionless beneath his touch.

"He's dead, Frank." He dropped his head. "Damn it Mellow, you stupid drunk," he whispered between heaves of air. "What the hell were you thinking?"

He waited a moment. "Hey, Frank. Did you hear me? We lost him. Frank?" In the heat of the chase, he hadn't noticed his partner was not at his side. He glanced over his shoulder and rose to his feet. A cold taut current ran through him at the sight of a motionless Frank Gillies laying face up on the sidewalk a few feet away.

The gunshots drew curious patrons out of the bar. Gillies' shirt and cream-colored overcoat looked dark from the distance – dark red. Harper's immediate thought flashed to the pub's neon lights. The gawking faces – the sidewalk – Gillies – everything was red. "Frank!" he screamed and raced to his side. "Get out of the way!" he yelled. Harper pushed the others away then dropped to his knees.

"Frank, damn it." Blood seeped from the center of his partner's chest. "Hold on, Frank. Hold on." Harper firmly pressed a hand on the puncture wound while he speed dialed for dispatch and shrieked out a 10-55. "Officer down! I repeat. Officer down! Corner of Howard and Third." Blood gushed between Harper's fingers and sputtered from Gillies' lips with each cough.

"I called for an ambulance soon as I heard the shot," yelled the bartender. "I told you Mellow was no good."

Harper hadn't noticed Gillies' opened eyes weren't flinching away the raindrops, that his breathing had stopped, and that his hands rested lifelessly at his side.

"Looks dead to me," said a voice in the crowd. The others agreed.

Surreal sounds drifted around him not meant for his ears.

"Where the hell's the ambulance?" yelled Harper.

"It's no good, buddy. You did your best." The bartender placed his hand on Harper's shoulder and tried to console him. "He's gone."

Harper jerked the man's hands off and shoved him away. He caught sight of his own hands, his coat, and trousers. It wasn't the neon lights after all. Lights don't run between your fingers, creep under your nails, and smear onto everything you touch. And lights don't wash off. That's when he knew. That's when the knot rose to his throat and wedged against his windpipe.

A split second. That's all it took.

He closed his eyes and lowered his head. The drumming rain concealed his tears and flooded a nearby drain with Gillies' blood.

Distant sirens were too late.

3

Captain Lou Holloway's car screeched to a stop in front of the Roving Dog Saloon. The medical examiner's vehicle and the three squad cars parked in front of the bar had drawn a crowd in the early hours of March 3. Red, white, and blue lights pulsated across the faces of curious bystanders.

Reams of yellow florescent police banners encircled the areas along the sidewalk where Mellow and Detective Frank Gillies had died. Holloway rushed out of the car and made his way toward the homicide detective in charge at the scene.

"Any witnesses?" he asked.

"Yeah. A million of them. Same old thing. No one saw anything but they all have an opinion," the detective answered. "Two shots one right after the other is all they agree on. Folks in the bar said they ran out as soon as they heard them."

"What do we know so far?"

"Witnesses said Gillies was face up on the sidewalk over there like we found him." The detective pointed to the spot near the door of the bar. "The perp was twenty-three feet away." He thumbed toward the pile of trash that had scattered when Mellow fell. "Harper was standing over him, weapon still drawn when they came out."

"All the firearms secured?"

"Forensics has them and the two shells."

"Tell the lab geeks I want them working on this around the clock. No screw-ups, understand? No one leaves here until every inch of the scene is covered." Holloway looked around. "Anyone call Gillies' wife yet?"

"Couple of the guys are over at her house right now."

Holloway drew in a breath. He knew Gillies' wife would demand answers and just as rightfully, he didn't have much to tell her. "Where's Harper?"

The detective threw his head back and nodded toward one of the squad cars.

A few feet away, the medical examiner was placing one of the bodies in his van.

"Hold it, Doc." Holloway reached for the fastener's tab of the body bag and zipped it open. He looked down at Gillies' face and frowned. "Christ. Fifty-six years old."

"He never knew what hit him," said the ME. "Entrance wound is smack in the middle of his chest; bullet is still in him. I'll know more after I cut him open."

"And tell me what? That he's dead?" asked Holloway. "I want to know who and why. Move him to the top of your list, will you?"

"You got it. You'll have my report tomorrow."

"What about Mellow?"

"Close range shot. Harper couldn't have missed if he wanted to."

"How close?"

"From the size and shape of the entrance wound, I'd say no more than five to ten feet. Why?"

Holloway swung a glance down the length of the sidewalk to where Mellow had fallen. "Let me ask you something, Doc. If you had a trained professional standing that close to you, aiming his fully loaded Magnum at your chest, would you shoot the guy twenty-three feet away?"

Holloway didn't need him to answer. Sam Harper was the next person he wanted to see. He glanced in the direction of the squad car. The Captain had called Walt Harper, his former partner, the minute he heard of the shooting. Walt had wasted no time in joining his son. He was next to the car, leaning in, and talking to him through an open window.

"Walt," Holloway motioned for him to step away from the car. "How's he doing?"

"How do you think? What the hell was Gillies doing out here?"

Holloway shook his head. "I don't know." He darted a glance into the back seat and caught sight of Harper's profile. He was a good two inches taller than his old man, but he couldn't have looked more like him. Harper had his father's chiseled features, his narrow square-tipped nose, and his mother's blue eyes. The three-quarter inch scar above the left eye was his. Right now, he was soaked, shaken, and indifferent to the stains of Gillies' blood on his clothing.

"Goddamn it." Walt pulled Holloway aside. "Gillies was supposed to go after Owens on his own. He promised he wouldn't involve Sam in the sting. What the hell was he thinking?"

Holloway didn't know what had crossed Gillies' mind or what had prompted him to go after Mellow. He was still trying to sort through those questions when a familiar silver Jaguar XJ eased to a stop and caught his attention.

"What the hell is he doing here?" asked Walt.

The same question crossed Holloway's mind. He stretched out his arm and nudged Walt back.

"You let me handle this."

"He's already screwed with my life. I'll be damned if he's going to scre–"

"I'm warning you."

"That's my son in that car!"

"Damn it, you're out of the force. Should have never called you." Holloway looked him square in the eyes. "The press are here. Don't start anything; not a word out of line to him or I'll have you arrested." Holloway had seen what Walt was capable of doing when pushed into a corner and Commissioner Greg Flanagan had done just that on several occasions. Holloway wasn't going to let Walt's hatred explode. Not here, not now. "I mean it. Get back. For your sake as well as Sam's."

Holloway fixed his eyes on Flanagan as he swung his legs out of the Jag. Aside from his thinning white hair and his bitter glare, Flanagan had not changed since their days on patrol. Holloway could still see the brash rookie cop, impetuous, ready to fight anyone who opposed him. Disgust washed over him as he thought of Flanagan's ambition, his rise to the top, and what he did to secure it. Some things, like fingerprints, never changed.

Holloway glanced at his watch. Three in the morning, yet Flanagan in his khakis and yellow shirt could have been dressed for the golf course.

Commissioner Flanagan raised a hand to suppress a gurgled cough before he reached inside his windbreaker for another cigarette. He swept a glance at the press, feigned a smile, then turned to assess the scene.

"Commissioner," said Holloway. "Didn't expect to see you here."

"We have one dead cop and Harper's kid was the one left holding the gun. Why the hell wouldn't I be here? I'll be damned if I'll let history repeat itself." Flanagan's tone stung with the same chill that hardened his glare.

Holloway shook his head. "Let it go. It's a whole new world of forensics. Nothing's going to get lost. My men have it under control."

"Don't think this changes things on the Owens case," said Flanagan.

"We just lost a good man and you're obsessing over a two bit supplier?"

"You're damned right I am. It was your call to put Harper and Gillies on his case and they screwed up royally, didn't they?"

"You don't know what went down here tonight any more than I do," said Holloway.

"I want Owens right here." Flanagan slammed a fist into the palm of his hand. "Get Stewart Martin on it."

"Martin?" Holloway knew Flanagan well enough to know that arguing with him was pointless and it was potentially dangerous to question the incompetence of his nephew, Detective Martin. *But why him of all people?*

"You heard me. Brief Martin and get him on the case."

Aware of the newspaper reporters' presence, Holloway backed away from the dispute. Members of the press lined the street, yelling to get his attention; taking photographs of the scene from any angle they could manage. The last thing he needed was a front page spread in the morning paper of a showdown between him and

Commissioner Flanagan. "Yes ... sir." Holloway whispered through clenched teeth, indifferent to the sourness in his pitch that was well outside of anyone else's hearing. Holloway knew he was no longer in control the minute Flanagan pushed past him on his way to the squad car. He diverted his attention for only a moment when a fury of cross words erupted behind him.

"Get him out of here!" Flanagan yelled pointing at Walt.

Two officers held Walt by the arms while another detective kept Harper from leaving the car.

"I'm warning you, Flanagan!" Walt growled.

Holloway rushed in, pulled Walt away, and shoved him aside.

"I want him arrested!" Flanagan yelled the order to an officer standing nearby. "Obstruction of justice."

"Captain?" asked the officer.

"Obstruction my ass," Holloway said. "Damn it you two." He turned to Walt and frowned. "Jesus, what the hell are you doing? Didn't I tell you to –"

"I didn't start it." Walt shoved back. "Sam doesn't have to answer a damned question and you know it. Not without an attorney."

"All I know is that I told you to keep your distance."

"Not when it comes to protecting my son."

"Goddamn it! He's not your son – not now. He's a city detective involved in two fatal shootings. Sam Harper can take care of himself," said Holloway. "Go home."

"If I see the bastard pull the same shit again no one, not even you, will be able to stop me."

"I don't need this," Holloway growled knowing exactly what Walt was thinking. Walt's hatred of Flanagan went back years when the three of them were beat cops, but this was neither the time nor place for a fight. He pointed with his chin. "I'll take care of him just like I would any of my officers. I promise. Go home. Go on. Get out of here."

Walt ran his hand over his mouth, darted a glance toward his son, and walked away.

Holloway had watched Detective Sam Harper grow up. He had been there when they buried his mother, and by his side on the night a bullet had halted his father's career. But none of that mattered tonight – it couldn't. Flanagan was right about one thing. An officer was dead and protocol took precedence.

In his worse nightmare, Holloway never imagined history, as Flanagan suggested, would repeat itself. The incident was a similar shooting that had launched rumors and accusations. It had torn the department apart and the notion left him with only one question: What did that have to do with Frank Gillies' death?

4

It was six twenty-three in the morning; five hours since Gillies' shooting. His detectives had made the front-page spread of the morning paper. Holloway's thoughts lingered on what he had witnessed a few hours before. He was thinking of having to deal with the officers from Internal Affairs when the doorbell rang. The dreaded watchdogs of the police department, Internal Affairs, kept a close eye on the integrity of the force and acted in a swift and decisive manner whenever an officer fired his weapon. Holloway knew to expect them in his office this morning. It would give him no pleasure to witness their tactics over the next few days as they drilled Harper about the shooting. The whole thing was out of his hands.

The doorbell rang again.

Holloway lifted his glance from the pages in his hands and turned his wrist upward. *Six thirty.* He had been home three hours and had exactly thirty minutes before leaving for Police Headquarters. He folded the paper in fours and shifted his glance to the empty chair across the kitchen table. Five years this week since their split. His wife had never gotten used to the interruptions his job had inflicted on their marriage.

Holloway pushed back his chair and reached for the knot of his tie centered beneath a starched collar. He grabbed his jacket off the back of his chair and slipped it on, then secured his gold shield onto the breast pocket, and slipped his Glock into its holster. He assumed the visitor had more news about Gillies, but he had instructed his staff to call with new developments. No one had. The bell rang again.

"I'm coming," he yelled as he swung the door open.

"Di Napoli." Holloway leaned against the doorframe. "God, what the hell happened to you? I almost didn't recognize you. What's all this?" he asked, motioning at the trimmed beard.

"We need to talk." Di Napoli waited for a moment then asked: "Do you mind?"

"Come on in." Holloway gave his street a quick glance before shutting the door.

Tom Di Napoli was another second generation on the force. His father had served with Holloway and Walt Harper for fifteen years before he died in a car accident during a high-speed chase through Avondale. His mother and Mrs Holloway were close at one time, but the good intentions to keep in touch faded as fast as the years.

"You all right?" Holloway asked him.

"Yeah. Fine, been at it all night."

"I figured as much. What's going on?"

"Got a buyer lined up."

"Can he be trusted?" asked Holloway.

"Yeah."

"Are you sure?"

"A hundred percent? No. But he has the cash and is eager to spend it. The guy's high up in the Puerto Ricans' gang hierarchy."

"Where'd you find him?"

"You don't want to know. Not yet, anyway."

Holloway pursed his lips. "So it's set?"

"Yeah. It'll be clean. He just wants in and out. Everything will be just as we planned."

"Who else knows about it?"

"Just you and me."

"Keep it that way for now. What about Owens?"

"Owens won't be a problem. He's desperate to get rid of the stuff."

"What's his rush all of a sudden?"

"Talk is some muscle is out to get him. He's scared out of his skin. Just wants to do one last deal and get the hell out of Chandler."

"Can't let him do that." Holloway paused. "So he bit, huh?"

"Are you kidding? The deal's too sweet for him to ignore."

"Who's behind this muscle?"

"I'm working on it. Whoever it is, they're connected. Haven't found a trail or a lead."

"Stay on it. Can't afford anything to happen to Owens. Not yet anyway." Holloway glanced at his watch again.

"Who's going to work the investigation end of it?" asked Di Napoli.

"Stewart Martin." Holloway knew how he would react to the news.

"You've got to be kidding. He's an idiot."

"Can't be helped. Gillies' death put a major wrench into things. I had to reassign the case and Commissioner Flanagan didn't waste any time with the order either. He showed up at the scene last night. Hell, Gillies wasn't even cold yet when he gave the order. Not surprising, I guess. We both know Flanagan has more reason to see Owens behind bars than anyone else."

"Then why put Martin on it?" asked Di Napoli. "Think he changed his mind?"

"Why would he? He's convinced Owens is the one who hooked his kid on crack. Patrick is dead. All he can do is nail the bastard responsible. Hell, he'd approve planting evidence if he thought it would make the charges stick."

"Exactly. So why put a jerk like Martin on it?"

"Nothing we can do about it right now. Not while there's this other matter about Gillies to contend with. We can't just ramrod Owens into the station. I don't want to rouse any suspicions. He's too valuable to us. The upside, though, is that Martin's incompetence will give us the time we need to work things our way. I'll stall him if he starts asking too many questions."

"He wouldn't know what to ask. What about Harper? He'll want back on the case."

"I don't doubt it," said Holloway. "He'll be out of the picture on a three-week suspension. Even if he makes it back, he's not getting it. Last thing I need is an angry cop out for revenge."

"That's not his style. He's by the book, just like his old man."

Di Napoli shifted his weight from one foot to the other. "It's in the blood."

"I don't care," said Holloway, "I'm not willing to take the risk. We're too close to getting it done and there's too much riding on it. One wrong move and you and I can kiss our badges goodbye."

5

Bitter March winds blew between the headstones while the faint sound of bagpipes wept in the distance. Officers from across the country stood at attention in a sprawling blue mass that stretched across the manicured grounds.

Solemn faces encircled Gillies' casket.

A woman standing behind Harper whispered something about closure.

Like hell. Harper winced, still riddled with suspicion. The preacher's words turned into a distant mumbling. Death had crossed Harper's path before. His mother's passing had taught him how quickly the door could shut on second chances. How many times had he said he should have? *Should have done what?* He asked himself. *Take your pick, Harper*, he said to himself, *and fill in the blanks. It doesn't matter, time's up.* "Damn," he whispered and shut his eyes.

The flag-draped casket blurred before him. This was not what he and Gillies had planned for today. They were supposed to run down pushers and haul in some hookers. Gillies was going to call him college boy two or three more times before the end of their shift. He was going to tell him another crude joke, and pull rank on him too.

Educated on the streets of Chandler, Gillies possessed a vocabulary that smacked of her sewers. He had known every corner of the city and the scumbags whose dealings festered like a cancer in its shadows. Gillies was a son of a bitch who scoffed at political politeness. Harper had cringed with embarrassment at Gillies' outbursts, but what the man lacked in tact, he more than made up in raw, common sense. Harper caught himself nodding. Gillies was a classic asshole at times, but for all his vulgarity, he wanted to believe Gillies was a good cop, now more than ever.

Naked branches whipped in the wind as the minister's words of eternal life scattered and gently raised a hushed chorus of amens. Harper imagined his partner inside the box with his hair neatly combed, his fingernails cleaned and trimmed. Another gust tossed some of the flowers off the grave and scattered them along the ground. Harper reached for Deanna's hand. It felt as cold as the wind when she pulled away.

Why did he ask her to come? He wondered. *She didn't like Gillies, hardly knew him, she never cared to.*

Harper lifted his eyes from the flag across to the other side of the casket and looked at Gillies' widow. Flanagan sat at her side, patting her hand, and tried to console her. Harper's presence was naturally expected, but she had more than made her feelings known to him. Harper had gone to her house hours after the shooting. Her accusations continued to cut through him.

"Damn you, Harper! How could you let him die? You were his partner for Christ's sakes. You were supposed to cover him." She had sobbed, pounding her fists against his chest. "You son of a bitch! I hate you."

Nothing she had said hurt as much as his own guilt and resentment. The urge to lash back begged for permission; to let her know her husband's last thoughts were not as kind as she might imagine. That he knew her tastes exceeded Gillies' paycheck, and that Gillies told on their failed marriage. Harper had tried to console her but what the hell, he knew she wouldn't listen to anything he could have said. Harper could still hear her screams. Any attempt to reach out to her had further fueled her anger.

"No! Get away from me." She had cried, and buried her face in her brother's embrace.

"Haven't you done enough?" the man had glared at him and pulled her away.

Three days had passed since the shooting, yet Harper didn't dare approach her. His eyes stung and the lump in his throat swelled. A sudden burn of acid burst in his mouth.

"Sam, come on." Deanna pouted and clutched the scarf close around her neck. "Everyone's leaving. You're making a scene."

She was right about one thing. The grounds were nearly empty. Gillies would soon be a distant memory in the minds of most who had watched his interment. Harper took a few steps past the casket then turned. "Only difference between you and me is I'm still breathing and get to relive every damned minute of it." He wasn't sure if the words had slipped through his lips or were only vivid thoughts. He lowered his head, turned up his collar, and walked another few steps before a firm hand reached around his shoulder and made him stop.

"Son." Walt Harper had seen the exchange of darting glances between his son and the widow. He had been at Gillies' home too and had witnessed her brutal accusations. "She just lost her husband. People say twisted things when they hurt; things they normally wouldn't dream of saying. It's like a floodgate. Has a way of sneaking up on you when you're not looking."

"Yeah, Dad. She meant every word of it. What's worse, she's right."

"No. She's hysterical. Gillies' death isn't any more your fault than this damned weather." He shrugged his shoulders and braced himself against the wind.

All Harper wanted to do was go home and have a stiff drink. Maybe two, three, or however many it would take to numb him.

"Do you want to spend the night?" Walt kept his eye on his son's black Jeep Commander and the woman sitting inside primping in front of the mirror. "Why don't you stay a few days with me? I don't think you should be alone."

"I'll be fine. Promise I won't do anything stupid without your permission." His father's firm hold around his shoulders made him feel ten again and every fiber of his being begged to go home to the Harper farm.

"Don't worry," his father assured him. "Internal Affairs will clear you."

"Yeah, right. What about him?" he asked, nodding toward the casket. "Who's going to clear him?" Harper slipped his hands into his pockets and walked away.

6

The Second Precinct in the lower west end near the Avondale district of Chandler had been a recent hot spot of corruption. Months of investigations ended in one officer dead, two arrested, and several more kicked off the force.

Smoke curled its way up from the smoldering cigarette in the ashtray two desks down from homicide detective Dave Mann's station. He swept a glance around the old bullpen. The phones sitting on the rows of desks were unusually quiet this morning. Save for a couple of the guys that had not yet gone home from third shift, Mann was alone.

He had been, for a while.

Mann reached for his pencil holder and favorite coffee mug. His entire career fit neatly into the small storage box sitting on the desk in front of him with room to spare.

"Hey." A familiar voice broke the silence. Detective O'Brian, was premature grey at thirty-seven. The way he cocked his head to one side and folded his arms was indicative the short stocky guy was looking for answers. "So you're really leaving, huh?"

"That's right. Transfer came in yesterday."

O'Brian looked to one side of the room and then the other. He acted fearful the ghosts of the second precinct would hear. "Rumor has it you put in for the move. That so?" He ran a hand over the peppered growth of hair on his chin.

Mann didn't reply.

"Why would you go and do a thing like that? All the horseshit we've been through to clean the place up and you're leaving?"

"What did you expect?" Bad cops left a bad taste in Mann's

mouth. Corruption had tainted the reputation of every officer at the second precinct.

"Expect? I expect you to help finish what we started," O'Brian said through a set of clenched, smoke-stained teeth.

Mann gave him a passing glance as he grabbed the last few items off his desk.

"You know you'll end up with another shitty partner up there, or worse – a woman."

"Always a first time for everything." Mann positioned his commendation plaques into the box then closed the lid. The thought of a new partner had crossed his mind more than once. He checked the desk drawers again, gave the meddling detective a nod, and left.

He held the box under one arm and reached for the front door of the station when the witch's tune from the Wizard of Oz rang on his cell. He was tempted to let it roll to voice mail and later, if asked, he would pretend he never received the message. But there would always be the, "What if" in the back of his mind. What if someone was hurt? What if someone had died? The type of, "What if" he would later regret if he ignored it now. He gritted his teeth, and answered the call.

"David, I want you home immediately."

He cringed at the sound of his mother's voice.

"David, did you hear me?"

"Is Dad all right?" he asked her.

"Yes. Now listen to me. You need to pack your things and come home now."

"Can't."

"You have nothing more important to do than what's waiting for you here."

"What is it this time?"

"You know exactly what's wrong. How many times do I have to tell you what your responsibilities are to the family? To the business?"

The family business, Ashton Manufacturing, the largest automotive parts producer along the eastern shoreline, employed nearly all the residents of the city of Ashton. The family lineage dated back to the 1700's and a young Boston sea merchant named Daniel P. Ashton. But it was Mann's great-grandfather who had made the small town of Ashton his and the citizens dependent on the family business. In true Ashton tradition, his mother kept a tight-fisted grip on the helm.

"No. It's your family, Mother, your responsibilities," he said. "When are you going to get it through your head? I have a career. I don't need yours."

"Menial job, David. Going after the low life of this world. And what do they pay you these days? Nothing. It's embarrassing. No Ashton has ever stooped so low."

"The name is Mann," he said. "And no, asking me to run your business is more condescending. Moan and groan all you want. I have my own responsibilities. Get someone who's willing to work for you."

"Damn it, David, you're the last in a long line. My father and grandfather would turn in their graves if I were to put the factory in the hands of someone outside the family."

"You're a smart woman. How can you be so naïve to think that day won't come? Uncle Steven's son is dying to get in there. Let him run it for a while."

"He's an idiot."

"Since when? A month ago, you couldn't be yanked away from his side, hovered over his wedding plans as if the sun rose and fell on him."

"Things happen. We're not speaking at the moment."

"Told you to butt out, didn't he? Is that it? Damn it Mother! What's it going to take for you to understand you can't run everybody's life?"

"Don't raise your voice to me and don't change the subject." She paused for a moment. "No one has your smarts and you know it. Not even your father."

"Dad should have never given up his ambitions for yours. You're killing him. Your dreams are yours, not Dad's, and they have never been mine."

"What are you talking about?"

"Dad hates the business. He always has. What kind of threat

42

did you hang over his head to keep him there all these years?"

"You have a lot of ner–"

"I have to go. I'm due downtown in half an hour."

"David! Don't you dare hang up on me."

"Give my love to Dad, will you?"

"So help me David. If you're not in this house by six tonight I'm disinheriting you. I mean it this time."

Mann looked at the phone number reflected on the liquid-crystal display screen. He drew in another breath, and let it slip out as he snapped the phone shut. As far back as he could remember, Janice Ashton-Mann's tongue had cut to the core. He could sum up his privileged childhood in one word: Disappointment. Aside from his relationship with his father, he couldn't think of a good memory. The small box slipped easily onto the car seat next to him. As easily as the idea of a new beginning.

7

In the hours just before dawn, the city looked clean and innocent from the vantage point of Captain Holloway's sixth-floor office window in City Hall. He leaned hard against the sill and stared down on the amber-lit streets below. Traffic snarled near the exit ramp off I-54 leading into the downtown area. Lights in the adjacent buildings that towered above police headquarters flickered on in random succession.

Forensics proved the shooting on March 3 happened just as Harper had claimed. Internal Affairs had also cleared Harper and Gillies of wrongdoing. What more did the press want? A handful of unreturned messages from as many reporters were still on his desk. He wadded them up and tossed them into the trash.

Holloway watched as the day shift workers made their way back into the city for another shot at a living. Their workday would end at five. *How many of them*, he wondered, *would actually make it back home by nightfall?* He knew the average number of fatalities they investigated each week.

"That's what the press should be worrying about," he whispered shoving his hands into his pockets. "Crime on the streets, not some dead pusher, or these damned accusations of police brutality. Goddamned journalists."

On his desk were all the reports Holloway needed to close the three-week-old shooting incident in front of the Roving Dog Saloon. Ballistics had matched the bullet from Gillies' chest to Mellow's gun and likewise, the one from Mellow's chest to Harper's weapon. Gillies never got off a round. Drug and alcohol screenings confirmed his officers were clean. He never doubted that for a minute.

It was quarter past seven when he heard the knock on his office door.

Harper glanced at his watch knowing the Captain was waiting to see him. He hurried down the hall, turned the corner, and rushed past Stewart Martin.

Martin looked up from taking a drink at the fountain. "Holy shit. Who the hell cut you loose?" he sneered as he wiped the drip of water off his chin.

Harper didn't stop. He wasn't looking for a confrontation. Not now. Not today, certainly not with Martin. Whatever Martin was calling out to him wasn't important and not worth the time to respond. Martin's beef was with Gillies and Gillies was dead. Harper couldn't think about any of that right now. He had other more important things on his mind and the first of several was waiting for him right behind the double doors at the end of the hall.

"Think you're ready?" asked Holloway.

"You know I am." Harper waited for the Captain to pull his file from a drawer and allowed him time to thumb through its content.

"You've seen Doc Brannon five – six times," said Holloway while he scanned the pages. "How'd it go?"

"She's a pain in the ass."

"I didn't ask if she was your type."

Harper gripped the arms of the chair. "Got through it."

Holloway pushed Harper's file aside, "You've seen the headlines."

"Horseshit. All of it. We warned Mellow three times. He fired first."

"I know it and this will blow over, I promise. The problem is, it doesn't matter that Mellow shot first. This sort of thing happens every time one of our officers gets killed. People immediately suspect we're out for revenge. I don't have to tell you all eyes are on us right now. I have to ask you." Holloway leaned forward and looked him straight in the eyes. "Are you sure you're okay?"

"You know I am."

"God, you're just as bull-headed as your old man. Answer the damned question."

"What do you want to know?"

"You've been off for three weeks. Are you sure you're ready to put this whole thing behind you?"

"You ever forget the day Dad was shot?"

Holloway frowned and looked away.

"Didn't think so," said Harper. "Can't promise I'll get over this either." He paused for a moment. "Look, I took a pledge and I intend to keep it. Police work is all I know and I'm damned good at it."

"I see your confidence wasn't shattered."

"I want my life back. It's all right there in Brannon's report."

"I've read her assessment. Also read these other reports; ballistics, blood work, you name it. You know the routine." He thumbed over his shoulder at the stacks of papers on his desk. "There's no question you've been cleared, but I'm the one who's going to have to live with you. Me and everyone else in your unit. What makes you so sure this won't affect your future performance? That you won't hesitate the next time someone pulls a gun on you?"

"Because I didn't hang back the first time." The words spilled out of Harper's mouth before he could stop them. "Everything was by the book. You know it and I know it, so does Internal Affairs." Harper saw the doubt glaze over the Captain's eyes. No lab work he knew of could explain why he and Gillies were on Howard Street that night in the first place. Only Gillies had the answer to that one and he had taken it to his grave. "Would've been fine if Mellow had stopped when we told him to. He had no reason to run and pull a gun on us."

"It's what you train for. The unknown."

"The day I joined the force, Dad told me a cop has to be quick, smart, and he'd better be right. Thinking, he said is what gets you killed. It's a split-second decision – knowing when to shoot and when to hold fire. You would've had two dead cops on your hands if I hadn't shot him."

Holloway opened one of his desk drawers, pulled out Harper's Magnum and his badge. "Here," he said, sliding them across the desk.

Harper strapped on his holster and placed his weapon snugly in its rightful place. The weight of his gun resting against his side made him feel whole again.

"Thanks. Where are we on Owens? Want to brief me now?" he asked as he hung the badge onto his outer breast pocket.

Holloway paused and looked in the direction of the window again. "We need to talk. Had to make a couple of minor changes to the roster."

"Changes?" Harper wasn't sure what that meant, but he heard the apprehension in Holloway's tone. "What kind of changes?"

Holloway hesitated a second too long. "I assigned you to Homicide."

"Homicide?" Harper narrowed his eyes. "You said a minor change. Homicide's a whole different ball game."

"It's also a step up."

Harper was thinking of Owens, a drug supplier responsible for the deaths of countless kids and his partner's life, not his career. He and Gillies had suspected someone was tipping him off. *How is it when they finally caught him six months before, the evidence disappeared? No scumbag had that many lucky breaks without help*. "You know we were close. I thought you'd want me to finish what Gillies and I –"

"You're out of Narcotics. That's not where I need you right now."

"Jesus, it's one thing to reassign the case until I got back, it's another to take me out of the unit all together. I want to finish it. The guy is responsible for Gillies' death."

"I said no. You're not going to turn this into a vendetta and that's final."

"What vendetta? It was our case. I know it inside and out. Who's on it?" Harper demanded.

"How I arrive at decisions around here is none of your business," Holloway snapped.

"Right, so when's the next shoe going to drop? You said changes. What else don't I know?"

"You have a new partner. Dave Mann. Just transferred in from the Second Precinct." Holloway got up, stuck his head out his office door, and yelled for Mann.

"The Second? That's nothing but a festering hole for bad cops." Harper snapped to silence when Mann entered the room. The introduction was brief and to the point. Harper glared back at Holloway as he slowly stepped forward to shake his new partner's hand. He didn't know all the details, but he had heard of the dirty cop rumors, the killing of another officer, and the disgrace it had brought to the Second Precinct six months before. *How the hell did this guy fit into it?* Harper nodded, knowing if he spoke, his tone would deceive any attempt he might make to be polite. He also knew this wasn't the time to make waves.

"I've heard about you," said Mann. "You're Walt Harper's son, right?"

Harper nodded again and stepped back.

"I'm looking forward to working with you." When Harper didn't respond, Mann turned to Holloway. "I've had a chance to look through those old homicide cases you gave me. Couple of things jumped out at me on one of them. Now that Harper's back we can start working the clues."

"Damn it." Harper didn't care if the edge in his voice was offensive. "Cold ones? You're sticking me with the crap no one else wants?"

"Sit down." Holloway scowled. He excused Mann for the moment and waited until he left the room and shut the door. "What the hell is wrong with you?"

"Me? You should have told me about all of this days ago. Not dump it on my lap my first day back. And you sure as hell should have warned me about him," he said, pointing in the direction of the door.

"We work with partners around here or have you forgotten? We don't have prima donnas on the city's payroll."

"I'm not talking about a partnership. You could have assigned me to any of the others in homicide. I'm talking about him, his background. Who is this guy? Was he involved in all that mess at the Second Precinct?"

"That's enough."

"I have a right to know, don't I? What's his record?"

"I said, sit down! I don't know who the hell you think you are waltzing in here and questioning my authority."

"I'm not questioning –"

"And let me tell you something," Holloway snatched Harper's psychological evaluation file from his desk. He gripped it and shook it in front of Harper's face. "I don't give a damn if Brannon and every lab in the city say you're ready to come back to work. I'll decide that for myself. And until I'm a hundred percent sure you're not going to crack under pressure, I'm going to keep my eyes on you so close you'll be looking over your shoulder in the urinal. You got that?"

Harper pressed his lips and ran a hand through his hair.

"Take it or leave it. Right now I don't give a damn which." Holloway threw the file back on his desk. He growled under his breath to see its content spill onto the floor. "You say you're ready, then you damn well better prove it. Last thing I need is for you to screw up with the press sitting front row and center and the Commissioner perched on my back."

Silence fell between them. Harper knew he had breached the limits. Friendship or not, Holloway wasn't a man to be pushed. He was as bull-headed as he was fair, and right now, there was too much at stake to cross him. But the apology Harper needed to say was stuck in his craw.

"Unless you want to turn in your gun and badge again, you're going to do exactly as I tell you to do without an argument. Understand?"

A nod was all Harper could muster.

"And that includes working with whoever the hell I order you to work with."

Harper frowned, feeling like a bug pinned to the wall. "Fine – all right."

"What happened to you? Where's this attitude coming from? Gillies' death affected all of us."

Harper managed to express his regret, but persisted with his concern about Mann.

"Listen to you. Where do you get off anyway? Mann's no stranger to police work. He's a six-year Homicide veteran. Excellent recommendations and, for your information, a clean record. He's a good man. I wouldn't have taken him if he wasn't."

"Dad worked alone the last two years on the force," Harper reminded him.

"Yeah, and the damned fool nearly got himself killed in the process." Holloway curled his lip then turned and looked out his window again. The sun was now well above the horizon of the city that only moments before had been nestled in darkness. "You're a good cop, just like your old man, but you're not him. Don't let your ego get the better of you. Not today." Holloway faced him. "It's not often I can team two good men like you and Mann together. I would appreciate your cooperation, but I expect you to give him a chance. Do I make myself clear?"

"Perfectly," said Harper. Holloway's stare pierced through him. "What? I will – I promise." He started to leave when the Captain called out to him.

"You've got some case files waiting for you on your desk. Take the morning to go through them." Holloway returned to his paperwork. "That's all."

Harper was nearly out the door when the Captain called him again.

"By the way," he said, without looking up. "Good to have you back. And for God's sakes, Harper, play nice."

8

The rains put the Dryden Construction Company behind schedule. Given the chance, the workers would flatten the building at Broadway and Fifth to the ground in a matter of days. The foreman stood in the doorway of his temporary office trailer and kept a close eye on the crew, the dark clouds rolling in, and the company clock. If all cooperated, the lot would soon look as flat as the state of Kansas.

Ten minutes of break time left on the clock.

Two workers sat on newspapers draped over a wet concrete bench in front of the building.

"Harbor View. Ain't that a crack?" Burt sneered as he pointed to the faded sign above the limestone doorway. "Only water I see is these here pools of mud we gotta trudge through to get to the dump." He tipped back his Styrofoam cup and drained it.

His friend tossed the last few drops of his brew onto the ground before replacing the cap on his thermos. "Boss's watching. Look at him. Must be nice to have a warm, dry office to sit in all day while we're up to our ass in mud."

"Fifteen minutes are up," yelled the foreman. "Everybody get back to work! Not paying you to sit on your butts all day. Already behind schedule, don't need any help from you guys." He bit down on his cigar and watched from his perch on the steps of his office as each of the workers ambled back to their stations. The foreman took a final drag of his stogie, flipped the butt into a pool of muddy water, and slipped back inside.

"I was listening to the weatherman this morning on the way in. Heard him say we got eight inches of rain so far this month," said

Burt. "Can you believe it? It's some sort of record I guess. More rain on the way, too."

"Don't know about eight inches. All I know is the boss'll be a pain in the ass to live with until this job gets done. This dump should've come down on its own years ago. Well, sounds like we're ready to roll. I hear Betty's engine purring." The two men laughed at the ceremony to name the wrecking ball.

The men of the Dryden Construction Company christened her Blasting Betty during a drinking binge on the afternoon the foreman's third divorce was finalized. The men had snickered at the foreman's opinion of his ex-wife. She was ruthless, he had said, in her accusations of his infidelity and, without remorse, had left him in financial ruin.

That night, as the foreman and his friends sat on the edges of bar stools, he swore she was a heartless bitch just like the wrecking ball out in the yard; big, cold, and cruel with only one thing on her mind. To knock him down and smash him to smithereens. He promised he'd never marry again. He vowed he wouldn't get trapped a fourth time. But the foreman's affairs were predictable and although none of his men would admit it to his face, the little lady did have a valid point about his infidelity. The yard was full of equipment named after his other affairs he had sworn he wouldn't or shouldn't have had. He named the bulldozer Angelina, after wife number two, and the backhoe was Candy, after wife number one for her particular preferences.

Yes, the boss was done with women this time. After all, he made the promise in front of all his inebriated pals at the local dive. But the vow only lasted a few weeks until he met Greta Nillhale. It wasn't long before the foreman wrapped himself around the finger of wife number four. The men snickered among themselves and joked that they were running out of equipment. The boss, on the other hand, thought it might be a good omen.

The foreman's right hand man sat at Betty's controls, maneuvered the crane, and positioned Betty to release her fury. She swung hard to the left and plunged into the south side of the building with an explosion of dust and falling debris. Betty left behind a hole that was twice her size. While she continued her relentless destruction, other workers began the painstaking tasks of clearing the rubble. With bulldozers and the force of raw muscle, the workers removed the debris a piece at a time. So it continued until ten forty-five on the morning of March 22.

Burt remembered the exact time the hairs on the back of his neck pulled taut and when the immediate impulse to cross himself and say two Hail Mary's came over him.

Ten forty-five a.m.

Blasting Betty did more than weaken the building's foundation and cause the bricks along the lower level of the south wall to buckle and fall on their own.

The foreman's precious timetable was about to hit another snag.

9

Harper's first day back on the job was not shaping up the way he had expected; the way he had hoped the day would begin. Breaking in a new partner was right up there with getting a tooth pulled. A major pain in the ass. He sauntered over to Mann's desk and immediately frowned at the wet coffee mug ring on the surface, the trail of Danish crumbs, and the papers strewn across the desk. He tapped twice on the surface and waited for Mann to look up.

"Come on."

"If it's any consolation," Mann said, without looking up from his work, "I didn't ask to partner with you either."

"Right. Let's go."

"What's your problem?"

Harper fixed his sight on Holloway's office door as if expecting the Captain to step out into the hall and admit to making a mistake. "So what happened?"

"When?"

"At the Second. What's the story?"

"You don't want to know."

"The hell I don't. I may not have a choice in this, but I sure as hell deserve to know what I'm getting into." Harper could feel the crease tightening between his brows.

"No. What you want to know is if I was involved. That's what you're pissed at, isn't it?"

"Well? Were you?"

Mann rose to his feet and leaned forward to meet Harper's gaze: "No."

BODACIOUS

GRAHAM WEBB

Next Appointment:

_____

Date

_____

Time

_____

Stylist Name

Harper had not anticipated the look in Mann's eyes. They were dead serious, absolute, and telling him to back down. He decided this was Holloway's doing, and whether Mann was telling the truth or not, was the Captain's problem, not his.

"Come on. The office is on the fourth."

Mann gathered his files and belongings, brushed the crumbs onto the floor, and followed Harper to the elevators.

The fourth floor area was a wide-open space where desks belonging to technical staff and rookie detectives formed neat rows the length of the room. The homicide unit was on one side of the floor, while Narcotics occupied the other half. Harper led Mann to their private office down the hall to the right of the elevator. Gillies had earned the private space. Holloway's reason for allowing him to keep it now was irrelevant; maybe it didn't even matter.

The first person to greet him was Emma, the detective unit's secretary. She was early this morning, but then, Emma had an uncanny knack for anticipating his needs. She also knew when to keep quiet and understood when silence could tarnish the truth, traits of particular importance to him.

Harper smiled when he thought of their first encounter. A big case had gnawed on his nerves. Perhaps he had been too pushy, but Emma was quick to remind him that she had survived four police commissioners, three captains, and a string of rookie detectives who had passed through the doors of the CPD on their way to the top, and that he, Sam Harper, still had much room for improvement.

This morning she waited with an engaging smile and a hug.

"How are you?" she asked.

After a brief exchange, Emma jumped into the business of things. "You'll find a stack of case files on your desk and fresh supplies in the drawers."

"Sounds like you were expecting me."

"Are you kidding?" she asked. "I'm tired of answering your calls. I'll let you get settled in before I switch the in-coming back to your line."

"Anything going on I should know about?"

"Holloway briefed you, didn't he?"

"You might say that."

"Then, I guess there's nothing more I can add. Just let me know if you two need anything." She glanced over her shoulder and rushed down the hall when she heard her phone ring.

As Harper opened his office door, he noticed Frank Gillies' name was no longer next to his on the frosted windowpane. He knew it would happen, but it stung him to know how fast death had wiped the man from existence. Gillies had led him up to this office four years earlier after he too had lost his partner. Harper thought of the irony in his comment right before they chased Mellow down. Be careful, Gillies had said. I hate breaking in new partners.

"Should have taken your own advice, pal," Harper mumbled under his breath.

Gillies' empty desk was to the right. All his pictures were gone; his pencil holder, his clock that never kept the right time. Every personal item was gone. Only the lingering stench of a chain smoker's habit and the standard office supplies served as a testament to his existence.

"That's yours now." Harper gave the office a quick glance. In the wake of change, he was glad for the familiarities he felt here. Even the squeak of his chair was a welcoming note.

Mann placed the files down and looked around at his new surroundings. The framed quote that hung on the wall directly in front of Harper's desk caught his attention.

"Even when a case appears to be nothing more than an unfortunate accident, don't assume it's closed until all the questions are answered, all the hurdles are jumped, and facts are backed by indisputable scientific results."

Mann glanced over his shoulder. "Your motto?"

Evasive or not, *No* was all Harper could say. Holloway said to give Mann a chance; he said nothing about getting in bed with the guy. There would have been nothing wrong in telling him someone had given the quote to his dad years ago. Still, there was no cause to get too chummy too soon. Harper knew how fast things could change; how trusts could be broken. He scratched his cheek as a way of putting off the inevitable task of wading through the stack of files waiting for his attention. The last entries in the files were over five years old and he instantly knew his heart wasn't in it.

Harper had no intention of using the pencil he had grabbed from its holder other than to tap it against his desk. The Owens case was all-consuming. So were his disappointment and the mounting questions the past hour produced. He tossed the pencil and left the room.

Good, Emma was still at her desk.

"What's the scoop?" he asked her, nodding toward his office.

"On what?"

"Oh him. Mann. You see the personnel files. What do you now about him?"

Emma gave him a playful smile. "Come on, Detective. You can be more direct with me. What's on your mind?"

"The mess at the Second Precinct. Why'd he transfer?"

"Ask him yourself."

"I did. We didn't exactly hit it off."

"That's not like you. You always –"

"Don't lecture me. Not right now."

"All right. Have you ever heard of Ashton Manufacturing?"

"Yeah, big conglomerate. Family owns half the town of Ashton. So what?"

"His mother is Janice Ashton-Mann. Dave doesn't have to be here. He stands to inherit the entire family fortune."

"You're kidding, right? What's wrong with him?"

"He's stubborn like you. Thinks he can make a difference. Didn't Holloway tell you?"

"Tell me what?"

"Why he moved you into Homicide. To team you two up."

Harper looked off.

"Sam?"

"We never got that far."

"Who got assigned to the Owens' case?" he asked her.

"I can't discuss it."

"What's the big deal? It's going to come out eventually."

"Holloway left specific instructions that you are out of it."

"I know, but whether he likes it or not, I am involved. All I want to know is who's working the case."

"I can't. If he finds out I told you I'll lose my job."

Harper knew it wasn't a fair request, but if he couldn't investigate it, the least he could do was watch from the sidelines.

"Gillies died because of that scum. Indirectly, maybe, but Owens was the reason we were there in the first place."

"I know," she whispered and lowered her gaze.

"Come on, Em, who covers for you when you're running late? Do you really think I'd let it slip?"

She tapped three brightly polished nails on the desk and diverted her glance from him. "You know, supplies came in yesterday and what with the phones and all, I haven't had a chance to put them away yet. Do me a favor will you, listen for my phone. I'll be gone at least 10 – 15 minutes." She looked down one side of the hall and then the other before she fingered the blue file folder she kept in the lower in-tray and inched it into view. "Wouldn't want any missed calls." She started to walk away then stopped. "Oh, before I forget." She reached into her drawer. "This key was in Gillies' desk. I have no idea what it opens. Do you?"

Harper held it in the palm of his hand and studied it briefly. He had never seen this key with a three-quarter inch blade and rounded bow. The key with the marking SL317 imprinted on its surface was insignificant and the least of his problems. The more important matter right now was the information Emma suggested was inside the blue folder. He slipped the key into his pocket and watched as his secretary disappeared around the corner. He gave the hallway a guarded look, flipped open the file and slid his finger across the pages of assignments before coming to an abrupt stop.

"Stewart Martin. Son of a bitch." He pushed the folder back into its place. As he thundered back toward his office, he promised himself he'd get back on the Owens case one way or another. Harper drew in a breath while he tried to sort through his thoughts. Mann was examining old lab photographs when Harper returned to their office.

"Humility isn't my best card." He waited a moment wondering if Mann would even look up. "Did you hear me?"

"Yeah." Several uncomfortable seconds followed before Mann broke his silence. "What do you expect me to say?"

"Nothing." He shrugged. "Nothing, I guess. What case do you have there?"

"What exactly is grinding at you?" Mann let the pen drop out of his hand and leaned back in his chair. "Losing your partner, not wanting a new one, or just wanting to turn back the clock?"

"That's none of your business."

"It is now. No different than you accusing me of being involved in the crimes at my old precinct."

"I didn't accuse you."

"What the hell was it then? It goes two ways, partner. Either we trust each other or we don't. Officers die all the time. It affects everyone. If you want to talk about it, fine. I'll listen. Otherwise, cut the pouting and let's get to work."

Harper narrowed his eyes. He'd been called many things during his career, but spoiled wasn't one of them. Their difference in opinions was about to escalate into a full-blown argument when Emma hammered on the door.

"Holloway. Line one. Human remains found in an apartment building on Broadway and Fifth."

10

Harper studied what was left of the Harbor View Apartment building. The recent rains had saturated the soil throughout the site allowing the water to pool in potholes and tire tracks. Harper reached for the pair of rubber boots he had thrown into the trunk. As he slipped them on, he glanced up at the approaching uniformed officer. "You the first on the scene?" he asked him.

"Yeah, call came in about fifteen minutes ago. Me and my partner were two blocks away."

"What do we have?" Harper asked.

"Workers found human bones inside one of the walls."

"What about the Crime Scene Unit?"

The officer nodded toward the building.

"Is Carter Graves with them?"

"Yeah. We couldn't do anything until he got here. He and another tech are over there," he said, thumbing toward Carter Graves and his assistant. They were walking around the exterior wall near the far end of the building. "Medical examiner's on his way."

"You two start questioning the workers. See what you can find out about this place." Harper nodded at the construction worker coming toward them. "Is this the foreman?"

"No. He's back in his office. Over there," he said, pointing at a small white trailer sitting on what used to be the apartment building's parking lot.

Harper watched as the man in the navy down vest and muddied work boots and jeans waddled toward him. The man struggled to lift his leg from the suction between his feet and the mud.

Harper waited until he was within earshot. "Detectives Harper and Mann, CPD, Homicide."

The man focused his narrowed eyes on the badges. "Guess you're here about the bones too, huh? They're over there." He pointed in the direction where Harper had seen Carter seconds before.

"We need to talk to your foreman. You want to get him?"

The round-faced man turned and plodded back through the sludge leaving wide footprints in the softened clay. Mud caked the lower rims of his jeans and each step splattered another layer.

Harper snapped on a pair of latex gloves and headed toward the forensic specialists. He glanced up again at what remained of the building. Even an untrained eye could see it was unstable. He wondered if there would be any viable evidence to collect or preserve, but knew the lab team would work the scene just as if the building was new and the body was fresh.

The foreman stepped out of his trailer with a flashlight in his hand and two hard hats. "Good. You're here. Maybe now we can get on with this. Put these on." Handing the detectives the yellow domed hats, he thumbed at the rubble behind him. "The place is ready to fall. Come on, some of your people are already here. Watch your step there," he said, pointing to an obstacle course of bricks, some still held together with mortar, and large chunks of concrete. The foreman took the detectives to the lower level of the south wall and pointed to a large hole just above the concrete foundation. He pulled back the plastic sheet one of the men had tacked up to cover the cavity in the wall. "That's how we found it. If the outer wall hadn't dropped off, we probably would've never seen it. Here," he said, handing Harper the flashlight.

"How old is this building?" Harper aimed the light into the hole and leaned in for a closer look.

"Built in 1946, whatever that makes it."

"Sixty years," said Mann.

Harper could hear Carter hustling to secure the scene. Standard procedures or not, with the outer wall on the verge of collapse, it seemed futile to rope off what remained of the former apartment with the standard yellow vinyl ribbons. Besides, none of the workers were venturing anywhere near the scene.

"When did the last tenants leave?"

"As far as I know, five – six years ago. Place sat empty since then." The foreman glanced up, distracted by the activity going on around him. "Owner refused to bring it up to code. Couldn't rent it. Heard he quit paying his property taxes. Lost the dump, so here we are."

"Has anyone touched anything?" Harper stepped away and handed the flashlight to Mann.

"Yeah, well kind of. Not on intention or nothing. One of my guys was clearing out the rubble, see? Reached in and grabbed hold of a rag. You know, yanked it out. That's when he saw what it really was. Don't have to tell you, they all freaked out after that. I couldn't get any of them near the place. Bunch of wussies." The foreman looked past Harper to what Carter was doing. "Say, how long is this going to take? Damned weather already has us two weeks behind schedule."

"I'd go put on another pot of coffee and kick back if I were you," Harper told him.

The foreman grumbled something under his breath and walked away in the direction of his office.

Harper flipped open his cell and speed dialed the number for the medical examiner.

"Doc? Harper here. Are you sending someone to 429 North Broadway or not?" Harper glanced over his shoulder at the gap on the brick façade. "Put a rush on, will you. Yeah, the workers found it; it's an infant sealed up in one of the walls. That's it, the old apartment building." He paused to hear a laundry list of things the ME's staff was busy working on now. "Don't have the luxury of time, Doc. Damn the proper procedures. If the place starts to topple I'm getting them out of there myself."

Yolanda Cruz, a petite middle-aged woman, and the assistant ME were the next to arrive at the scene. She had worked side by side with Harper on many occasions. A red bow secured her jet-black hair near the nape of her neck. In one hand, she carried a forensic kit, in the other a small plastic box for the remains, while a camera swung from her neck.

"Sam Harper." She shook her head and grinned. "I should have known something was up. No wonder Doc was grumbling. When did you get back?"

"Hey Yolanda. Good to see you. Come on. It's over here."

Yolanda glanced up at Mann. She motioned her hands were full and couldn't shake his, but nodded. "And you must be the new partner. Lucky you."

"That's what they tell me."

She returned her attention to Harper. "The boss said it's a baby?"

"Hold it," yelled the foreman, handing her a hard hat. "I'd cut the yakking if I were you and get to it. We set up some supports, but this damned ground's so soft it's not going to hold long. You better get a move on it."

As they walked toward the wall, Harper gave Yolanda a run down of what he knew about the case so far.

Yolanda set her things down and looked into the cavity. A cloth covered a portion of the tiny skull and one of its hollow eye sockets. She raised the camera up to her face and took several photographs before pulling the cloth away from the darkened remains.

"Need to know how old the bones are," said Harper. "How soon will you know?"

"Can't help you there."

"Sure you can. Just give us an estimated timeline," he told her.

"I'll be able to approximate the child's age and state of health at death and, if you're lucky, the cause of death. Aside from that, forget it. No way to test it. I can tell you this much, nothing's going to happen until I get them back to the morgue. Has Carter done his bit here yet?" She asked, as she lifted the lid to the container.

"He's working on it," said Harper.

"Hurry him up, will you?" She looked at the bulge in the wall above the hole. "If the rest of this wall comes down, it'll crush the bones, not to mention what it will do to me."

After years of neglect, the building wasn't going to give up too many clues, but Carter wasn't one to give up either. He was working on the inside of the cavity and the surrounding wall area; Mann had joined the officers in questioning the workers. Harper stayed back with Yolanda as she placed the bones into the container.

With the preliminaries out of the way, Yolanda removed the child's remains.

"These never get easier, do they?" he asked.

"No sir. They sure don't. Come here, baby." She cradled the bones in her hand and handled them as if she were holding fine crystal.

"Babies are the hardest. You wait. When you have your own – then you'll know what I'm talking about." She reached into the cavity again and frowned.

"What is it?" he asked.

"I don't know." Yolanda pulled a small faded pink stuffed bear from the wall and briefly examined it. "Doesn't seem as if this baby was just tossed in there. Someone must have cared." Her saddened eyes reflected the pain only a mother would understand. "Maybe a stillbirth. Young mother didn't know what to do. I've seen this type of thing before. Carter! Here," she called out as she placed the toy inside an evidence bag for Carter to seal and log. "You'll need this."

"Some twisted sense of love," said Harper.

"Stop by first thing in the morning. I should have time between now and then to examine the remains and give you a preliminary. You understand I'm not making any promises."

"I know. Just give it your usual all."

She placed the cloth in the box on top of the remains and continued to sift through the dust and debris for the tiniest particles that might have fallen to the bottom. She kept at it until she was satisfied she had retrieved all the bones there were to gather.

While Yolanda made her way back to her van, and Carter wrapped up his evidence collecting, Harper turned his attention to the foreman. "We'll need the name of the former landlord. Do you have it?"

"I might. I'll have to check. Come on back."

Harper recalled the quote hanging in his office wall. But this didn't feel like an accident, the questions were mounting, the hurdles were unknown, and those indisputable test results seemed unlikely.

"What do you think?" he asked Mann.

"Desperate people don't act rationally. Natural death or not, what they did with the body makes it suspicious. What bothers me is that we may not be dealing with an old murder."

"What do you mean?"

"A body will decompose at a faster rate when exposed to the elements. Inside that thin outer wall, the body might as well have been out in the open. The more body mass, the faster it will decompose."

"But this was an infant."

"Doesn't matter," said Mann. "No way of knowing how long it took to decay. Killer could still be in the area."

"So where do we start?"

"We look for the unexpected. Somebody always screws up. No such thing as a perfect crime."

"Guess one of us has to be optimistic." That was a big maybe in Harper's opinion. "For every minute we spend trying to solve one of these cold ones, there are probably half a dozen new murders we could be working on with a better chance of success." He was thinking of Owens, out on the streets pushing to kids who were dying in hordes.

The whole thing was negligent. As negligent as killing an innocent child and placing him in a wall or Holloway's decision to assign Martin to the Owens case. His stomach rolled into a tight wad.

11

Holloway's warning about the Owens case continued to tumble around in Harper's head reminding him of the promise to stay away from it. His glance dropped to his desk and the stack of files he hadn't looked at since before their morning call to the Harbor View Apartments. Holloway, it seemed, was determined to see Harper make good on his promise.

He gathered his notes on Baby Doe and tucked them into a folder. He wouldn't stay late tonight. Just long enough to knock back a soft drink and gather his bearings. As he reached into his pocket for change, he fingered the key Emma had given to him. She was right, he thought. It didn't belong to any of the cabinets in his office. Its short blade and round bow seemed more like a key to a briefcase or a locked box. Neither of which he had known Gillies to have. The thought to call a locksmith crossed his mind then quickly faded after tossing the key into his top desk drawer.

He dropped the folders in the top drawer of the vertical file, slammed it shut, and pushed in the lock. It didn't catch. He pushed on the lock again and glanced down at the bottom drawer. It was ajar, refusing to close. With a vigorous pull, he yanked it open to reveal an assortment of pain relievers and other first aid items. Something near the back was keeping the drawer from shutting. Harper dropped to his hands and knees, reached in, and touched a familiar flat, smooth object. The plastic case contained a computer disk; a CD labeled in Gillies' writing.

Harper's suspicions piqued again. Gillies had refused to use computers, insisting on writing everything out. The disk made it clear Gillies had lied again. He slipped the disk into the computer and drummed his fingers. A list of files came up; he clicked on the first. His partner was keeping track of his gambling debts on the ponies. There were several entries of a hundred dollars on a horse named Great Fire. That explained why his partner had borrowed money. At least something was starting to make sense. He closed the file and went to the next one. Harper opened three more before coming to what made him narrow his eyes and pulled him in close to the monitor – diary entries – conversations Gillies had had with Owens.

"And who is, 'the man?' All right, Gillies," he whispered as he printed the pages. "What the hell were you into?" Harper yanked the pages from his printer and returned the CD to its case. He grabbed his coat, slipped the pages and CD into his pocket, and went home.

Rush hour traffic stalled bumper to bumper for miles on the eastbound lane of the turnpike. An impatient finger tapped on the steering wheel. Harper darted a glance at the Litchfield exit and then at the rearview mirror. With a final look at the endless line of cars, he quickly cut to the right and took the exit.

City lights faded and black asphalt turned into a winding country road. After a while, the city of Chandler and police headquarters were nothing more than a glow of lights on the horizon. Harper could drive the thirty minutes of road blindfolded without missing a turn and knew his father's home was just over the next crest.

The light in the kitchen was already visible from the main road. He was minutes away from trading the madness of the day for his father's reassurances.

"Dad?" Harper could see his father leaning over the stove while the aroma of meatloaf and caramelized onions rushed to greet him. He knew to expect an accompaniment of mashed potatoes, green beans, and dinner rolls. Since his mother's passing, instant potatoes and canned vegetables were the next best thing to homemade. Their discussion soon focused on his first day back to work and his new partner.

"Dave Mann. Holloway seems to think he's okay." Harper shrugged.

"What about you? You're the one working with him."

"He's not Gillies."

"Thank God for that."

"What do you mean?"

"Don't get me wrong. Gillies was an okay guy," said Walt, glancing at his son. "He was a good man in his day." He winced as he bent over to remove the loaf from the oven.

"Is it your back again?"

"Yeah, just give me a minute." Seven years before, at fifty-two, and after twenty-eight years on the force, Walt retired from the CPD with the bullet fragment lodged uncomfortably close to his spinal column.

Harper helped him to a chair. The sporadic ache that occasionally knocked his father out reminded him of the risks involved in police work. Watching Gillies die made the imminent danger more tangible.

"How much do you know about Gillies?" Harper asked as he finished bringing the food to the table.

"About as much as you, why?"

"How much?"

A frown creased Walt's face. "What's wrong?"

"Just answer the question."

"I know he cared about the work, but he got careless. No seasoned officer in his right mind would have approached an armed suspect without the proper precautions. You want to tell me what's bothering you?"

"Gillies lied to me about Mellow shooting someone. Why would he do that? Why lie about something he knew I'd check out?"

"Maybe he wanted you to figure it out. Then again, could be he was trying to protect you."

"From what?"

"Who knows? Hell, you know Gillies was an odd sort. Best way I can describe him. Half his problem was never letting anyone in on what he was up to."

"Holloway say anything to you about it?"

"No."

"You'd tell me if you knew, right?"

"You know I would." Walt reached for his beer and took a drink. "So, what about this new partner?"

"He's all right. Can't really tell in one day. All I know about him is he's rich."

"What do you mean, rich?"

"Heir to the Ashton fortune. He's also a transfer from the Second Precinct. You know what kind of a mess they had there."

"Was he involved?"

"Not according to him or Holloway. Do you suppose Holloway had any say in the transfer or was he forced into taking him?"

"Holloway isn't the forced-into-anything type. He wouldn't have anyone in his department who doesn't pull their own weight." Walt served himself and passed the platter. "Not like some of the others."

Harper knew the comment referred to Holloway's predecessor who was now the police commissioner, Greg Flanagan. "So explain to me why Stewart Martin's still around."

"Being an ass isn't grounds for dismissal but that's beside the point." A grin tugged at the corners of Walt's mouth then faded. "No one wants to be the one to fire the Commissioner's nephew."

"No, it's exactly the point. Holloway moved me into Homicide. Assigned the Owens case to Martin."

"I know."

"Since when?"

"Since the last time I talked with Lou. We always talk, you know that. Personally, I think it's a good decision; great move for you."

"I'm out of Narcotics, Dad."

"Oh come on, are you saying you're going to miss the scum you had to deal with on the streets?"

"No. It's not that. I don't like to leave things hanging."

"Like what? Owens?"

"Was the move your idea?"

"Oh for the love of Mike, what makes you think I have any

clout when it comes to Lou's decisions?"

"You two were partners; he's your closest friend. The case is too big for Martin to handle. He's a cocky son of a bitch who doesn't know anything about Narcotics."

"That's the first thing I've heard you say tonight that makes any sense." Walt grinned again and spread butter on a piece of bread.

"Found something tonight," said Harper. "Gillies was keeping personal notes on the Owens case. Several entries referred to someone he called, 'the man'." He caught a hint of interest in his father's eyes. "What is it?"

"Nothing," said Walt.

"Have any idea who it is?"

His father shook his head.

"Anyway, I'm going to read through them; see if there's anything worth investigating."

"And what?" asked Walt. "You intend to share the notes with Martin?"

"Hell, no."

Walt winced as he leaned back in chair and studied his son. "What were Lou's exact words when he took you off the case?"

Harper recognized the expression on his father's face; he had seen it often when he was growing up. It came right before one of his father's famous lectures and right after a slap on the hand. He wished he had kept his mouth shut, but it was too late now; the trap had sprung and he couldn't get out of it.

"He didn't want me turning the case into a vendetta."

"Then I suggest you heed his warning." The stern tone of a professional replaced the warmth in his father's voice. "Stay out of it."

"Whose side are you on, anyway?"

"Yours – always yours. What did you expect me say? Orders are orders and from where you're standing, you don't have much of a choice. You've got your whole career ahead of you. Don't toss it away."

His father's comment sounded remarkably similar to Holloway's suggestion that he not let his ego get the better of him.

'Not today,' Holloway had told him.

"It's a matter of principle," said Harper.

"What principle? Gillies is dead. You were out on leave for three weeks. Like it or not, the case had to be reassigned. That's standard procedure and you know it. Quit being so damned stubborn, it's going to land you in more trouble than you know."

"Gillies knew more about the Owens case than he let on. I think he was involved."

"Let it go," his father said dryly. "I'm telling you to stay out of it."

"What the hell's going on?"

"Just giving you some free advice."

"No. I can see it in your face. How much do you know about it?"

"Nothing. But if you're right, and he was doing something underhanded, it's going to come out sooner or later and you don't want to be anywhere near the damned case when that happens. Understand?"

For the first time in his life, Harper didn't believe him. They shared an inquisitive nature, so why wasn't his father pressing to understand his suspicions?

"I can tell you one thing," said Walt, pointing at his son with his fork. "Lou's giving you a chance to prove yourself on your own merit without Gillies. Potential or not, you have to do your part, and right now that means focusing in on your assignments and nothing else."

Harper laid down his fork and glared at him. Even if his father were right, it would have been nice to get some sympathy.

"Go on. Eat up," said Walt. "I want to show you my workshop after supper. What's the matter? Thought you said you were hungry."

"What workshop?" Harper asked as he forked a piece of potato.

"I've been taking a course in carpentry. Made a couple of things I want to show you. Don't look so surprised." Walt took a drink and let the words form in his mouth. "Your mother's been gone six years and all the tears in the world won't bring her back.

Thought it was time I did something besides sit around this empty house dwelling on the past."

Harper remembered the night she died. Her senseless death was devastating, but neither father nor son could have prevented it. The drunk driver who cut Catherine Harper's life short had eluded capture. His brother Paul never forgave them for not finding her killer. She had left a haunting void in their lives and it would continue to be the crux of their sorrow.

While his father cleared the table, Sam stepped into the den and raised the cover over the keys of his mother's old upright piano. The smell of polished wood washed over him. He closed his eyes and thought for a moment before touching his fingers to the ivories. As an old favorite melody sprang to life, his thoughts focused again on Gillies' CD and the answers it might contain.

12

"What's this about the kid they pulled from that dump on Broadway? Right here. Front-page headlines. Since when do I have to get my news from the goddamned newspapers?"

Holloway didn't let the Commissioner's gruffness rattle him. He held the phone away from his ear and swung his chair in the direction of the window. "Morning, Greg."

"Well?"

Holloway drew in a deep breath and gathered his thoughts. "Can't tell you much more than what's in the paper. It was an infant – that's all we know at this point."

"Why didn't you call?" The edge in Flanagan's voice cut through the line.

"It's a routine homicide," he said, puzzled by Flanagan's interest. "It's too early to throw up the red flags. Harper and Mann are on it."

"Harper? You assigned Harper to it?"

"Yes. What's this all about?" Holloway rose to his feet. "Something on your mind, Commissioner?"

Flanagan coughed and cleared the phlegm from his throat. "The city needs that medical building and the two hundred jobs it promised."

"I don't see what you're getting at."

"No, you wouldn't, would you? We can't afford this kind of publicity or the delays," said Flanagan. "Harper was on the front page of this city's two newspapers for days after Gillies' death. Can't risk another scandal. Not now. Find him a desk job until this is over."

73

"There was no scandal and you know it. He's a seasoned officer of this department. What's gotten into you anyway? We should know more in a day or two." Holloway could hear Flanagan's rattled breathing and imagined his face engulfed in a cloud of cigarette smoke. "I'll call you the minute we know something."

"Last time I heard that was the night Gillies got it in the chest."

"I told you Harper was cleared of all charges."

"Yeah you did. After I left three goddamn messages for you. Had to corner you in the can."

"What's got you on edge this time? I haven't heard you get this wound up since we fished the Beneli boss out of the bay."

"Politics. You wouldn't understand," said Flanagan. "Wait until the mayor sees the headlines. Surprised he hasn't called me already."

"I understand politics and bureaucracy. Is there something more to this you want to tell me?"

"Don't question me. Not after the way you've kept me in the dark on this case."

"Didn't think I was … questioning you."

"Remember one thing, Holloway. You're just as dispensable as the next guy."

Holloway closed his eyes and pinched the bridge of his nose. "Right. Threaten me all you want, but I've never left you out of the loop. I'll call you as soon as we know something."

"You do that, Holloway. The mayor's got his heart set on the ground-breaking ceremonies for the new building. Put a lid on this damned case."

"Old or not, it's a crime and we're going to follow proc–"

"Get it done."

13

Alvin Quinn stood in his kitchen staring up at the empty shelves above the stove. His fingers combed through the wisps of hair on top of his head. He darted a glance toward the stack of dirty dishes in the sink then shrugged his shoulders. The last of the bread was on the counter. He picked off the mold that had grown along the bottom crusts; spread each slice with peanut butter and a swipe of grape jelly.

Wiping his hands on his shirt, he shuffled toward the kitchen table. The grease stained court order, that had arrived by messenger two months before, announced the foreclosure on the Harbor View Apartments. It was right where he had left it. Its creased and crinkled surface reminded him of his fury when he read the legal jargon describing his financial failings. He had wadded the paper into a tight little ball and had thrown it against the wall before rethinking his actions.

All them years wasted, he thought. "Gonna tear the thing down anyway. Somebody else's problem now," he muttered. With a sweep of an arm, he brushed the court order aside and pushed it into the stack of old newspapers that had collected over the past several days.

He hadn't been able to put the Harbor View Apartment building or the foreclosure out of his thoughts. They had tugged at the back of his mind since he read the announcement of its demolition in the paper.

"What's a guy to do, anyway?" he asked himself. "Work hard for what? Dust. That's what. Nothin' but dust. Once the damned thing's down, it'll look like it's never been there. Won't be nothin' left for no one to see." Quinn pulled the soaked stogie from his mouth and took a bite of his lunch.

He was still chewing when the kitchen phone rang. It was the only working contraption in the house. Problem was, only the bill collectors called these days. Quinn let it ring a few more times hoping the caller would give up, but this one was persistent. He grabbed the phone on the seventh ring, swung it up to his ear, and barked: "Yeah?"

"What the hell have you done?"

The man's words stung like the swipe of a razor. Quinn's eyes darted, his hand wrapped tight around the receiver. "Who is this?"

"They found the kid. You were supposed to take care of the goddamned kid. What the hell were you thinking?"

Quinn's face squeezed into a tight frown. He slammed the phone into its cradle and tossed his sandwich aside. He could feel the pulsing movement of his heart thumping against the wall of his chest. The phone rang again making him jump. This time he swallowed hard before answering. "Look, I owned the dump, all right? But I don't know nothin' about no kid."

"Bullshit. Can they trace it?"

"Trace what? Whadya talking about?"

"Don't play games with me. Were you smart enough to keep things clean?"

Quinn couldn't speak. He didn't dare.

"Answer me! Can it be traced?"

"Who are you? Whadya want from me?" Quinn yelled again, spewing spit into the mouthpiece.

"No surprises, Quinn. I want no surprises. Understand?"

The man knew his name. How did he know his name? Quinn didn't want to hear what the man had to say, but he couldn't walk away from him either. Who was he kidding? Quinn knew exactly what the man was asking. He thought back to that night. As far as he knew, there were only two other people alive who knew the truth and the three of them had sworn each other to secrecy. The man on the phone wasn't one of them.

"Yeah, I got it. No surprises," he hollered back. "How'd ya get this number?"

"Know this, Mr Quinn. I know exactly where that dump is you call home. Bad neighborhood. High crime. People get wasted there all the time and no one thinks anything of it, least of all, when a worthless scumbag like you disappears."

"Ya don't scare me." Quinn jerked back the curtains and darted a glance out of his kitchen window.

"I don't threaten and I won't be knocking on your door either. If I come looking for you, you won't have time to worry."

But worry did crease Quinn's face. He tried to place the voice but couldn't. "Whadya want?"

"Peace of mind. That's all. No surprises."

Quinn rubbed a callused hand over his face wiping the sweat from his brow and above his lip.

"Well?" The urgency in the man's voice turned into a plea.

"Sure. Like ya said. No surprises." The connection broke off abruptly as Quinn mumbled the words. "Hello?" He frowned still holding the receiver to his ear, unable to pull himself away from the drone. "That's right. No surprises," he whispered. Quinn hung the receiver back in its place and shuffled to the kitchen window again. His mind raced as he tried to recall every detail of that night. "Wasn't my fault," he whispered, wondering if he could really be sure. After all these years, only one word came to mind.

"Shit."

14

The far end of the dimly lit hallway was barely visible from the elevator doors. Harper knew the black and brass sign above the last door to the right pointed the way into the city morgue. He also knew what to expect on the other side. The chill in the air would be as cold as the look of the stainless steel surfaces that dominated the autopsy room. It would permeate his clothing keeping them cool to the touch moments after leaving the place. White tiled walls shimmered under the bright florescent lights. The spotless floor, a large suspended scale, and three polished stainless steel tables, situated in the center of the room, were as expected as the smell of disinfectant that masked the stench of death.

Harper's glance swept in the direction of a small white cloth on the center table. He suspected the reason for his and Mann's visit was lying beneath its folds. It didn't have the mass to fill up the space and quiet the echo of their footsteps.

"Over here, guys." Yolanda pulled back the cloth to reveal the tiny human skeleton she had assembled hours before. "I sifted through as much of the debris as I could. Still, a few of the bones are missing; others hadn't formed yet. But for the most part, she's all there."

"She?" asked Harper.

Yolanda nodded. "It's my best guess. Gender-specific characteristics don't develop until after puberty, but the blanket and teddy bear we found with the remains were pink, so …"

"Very scientific, Ms Cruz." Harper rested his hands on the edge of the cold table. "Age?"

"Doesn't look like she could have been much more than a few days old," said Mann

"Judging from the suture lines on her skull she wasn't. A week at best," she told them.

"Cause of death?" Harper leaned in for a closer look at the small skull that could have easily fit in the cup of his hand.

"It's near impossible to say." She pointed to abrasions on several of the tiny bones. "See these? I thought they might have been stab injuries until I examined them closer." She paused for a moment. "They're teeth marks."

"Several here on the femur." Harper lifted the fragile right thighbone and rubbed his thumb over the markings. He studied it for a minute or two before carefully returning it to its place.

"I've been at this for twenty-two years and it still makes my skin crawl to think of it. But let's face it," said Yolanda, "those old building are infested with rats. Anyway, I didn't find any physical signs that point to the cause of death. I'll run a toxin test on the bone marrow, see if anything comes up."

"All well and good but none of it is going to get us anywhere without knowing how long she's been dead," said Harper.

"Figure somewhere between a year and the age of the building," she said. "There's no testing mechanism for what you need."

"Then there's no way of knowing where to start looking for suspects," said Mann.

"If it makes any difference, she was a full-term baby." Yolanda reached into a tray near the remains. "I did find one other thing wrapped up in the blanket. Here," she said, holding up a small medallion sealed in a plastic bag.

Harper examined it closely. "St Jude. This could be anyone's. No engraving, nothing. I've seen hundreds just like it. The priests down at St Paul's hand these out like baseball cards."

"I didn't know you were Catholic," said Yolanda.

"I'm not. Good friend is. Always has one of these around her neck."

"Patron saint of lost causes," said Mann.

"And cops." A faint grin tugged at the corners of Harper's

mouth. "Could be it just led us to our first clue."

"What's that?" asked Yolanda.

"Someone in that apartment was a Catholic. The priests at St Paul's might remember them."

Neither detective spoke on the ride from the morgue to police headquarters or to Forensics housed in the lower level of the building. The look on Mann's face told Harper he was working the case in his head. Harper's thoughts lingered on the baby's bones and caught himself wondering what she might have looked like. He had seen countless corpses before, gruesome sights that had affected him. Some he had managed to forget. Twenty-four hours ago, he had fought the idea of working homicide, now an infant tugged at him, making it near impossible to turn away.

"You have kids?" asked Mann.

"Not married. Why?" asked Harper.

"Is it hard for you to work a case when kids are involved? You know, without letting it get to you?"

Harper's thoughts flashed back to the number of children he had taken to the morgue. Eight months before, a woman had come to from a cocaine high to find her two-year-old son dead on the floor from an overdose. The face of the redheaded toddler who had swallowed a small piece of crack rushed into his mind.

"I lost count, some as young as two, cashed in on the crap their junkie parents left lying round. The ones who survive grow up to be like their folks. They lead crap lives and end up dead or wasted." Harper glanced out the car window and spotted a couple of teen boys running down the street and into an alley. "There's two of them now," he said, as he radioed dispatch. "Nine in the morning. Should be in school. Those two are looking to score if they haven't found it already." He gave the order for a uniformed unit to pick them up and signed off. "Cycle never stops. Kids having kids and killing each other off. What's easy about it?"

When the elevators doors opened onto the lower level of police headquarters, the detectives followed the well-lit hall to the lab.

Harper reached for one of the double glass doors but stopped short of pulling it open.

"Dave, it hits everyone. She was days old. Barely opened her eyes. Never had a chance at anything." He thought of the rats gnawing her flesh. "Someone tossed her away like yesterday's garbage and we're going to find whoever did it."

Harper glanced into the lab through the glass doors. Carter Grave's youthful face, blond spiked hair, and fine features deceived his expertise in forensic medicine. He was too busy studying the slide in the microscope and jotting down notes to notice them as they entered the lab.

Carter looked up from the specimen when he heard Harper's tap on the table. He frowned and glanced at his watch. His eyes were small, brown, and intense behind the thickness of his wire-rimmed lenses.

"Harper. It's early, even for you. What's up?"

Harper reached into his pocket and took out the small plastic bag containing the St Jude medallion. "Yolanda found this wrapped up with Baby Doe's remains from the Harbor View. It's probably a long shot, but check it out, will you?" He raised his hands to his hips and gave the spotless lab a quick glance. "Tell us you found something."

"In less than a day?" Carter grinned. "I'm good but not that good."

If Harper knew anything at all about Carter Graves, it was the man's tenacity for solving puzzles. "Right. We'll take whatever you have."

Carter seemed pleased with the compliment. "I did manage to find a couple of things that might help kick-start the investigation."

The men leaned in, prepared to listen as Carter reached into a box for their first clue.

"This toy." He held up the plastic evidence bag containing the faded pink teddy bear now matted with years of dirt that had settled inside the cavity. "I looked up the manufacturer, Kantar Brothers. Seems they made minor changes to the style; small variations in color, bows, color of the eyes, some had –"

"Carter," Harper motioned for him to stop the dissertation of needless details. "Cut to the chase, buddy."

"Anyway, this particular design was made between 1987 and 1990."

"Sixteen to nineteen years," said Mann as he jotted down the dates.

"Don't know if this matters or not, but Kantar Brothers sold that bear exclusively in this area to a few discount stores, but their largest buyer was Community Hospital's maternity ward." Carter carefully placed it back in the box and reached for the next item.

"Community could still have records of the births then," said Harper.

"If she was actually born there," said Mann.

"You want to see my files on the number of deaths we processed from that apartment building, Detective? Everything from gunshots to stabbings. The place had a reputation known to everyone on the force. You can bet none of the tenants bought the kid that bear. It came from the hospital."

"What about the blanket? Anything there?"

"It's your standard, hundred percent cotton baby blanket sold in most stores across the state. Actually, across the country. Except, for one thing. Found blood on it. Type *B* to be exact."

"Any chance it's the baby's blood?" asked Harper.

Carter arched his brows and answered with a decisive: "No." He carefully placed the blanket on the table and allowed the fabric to bend along the well-preserved folds. "Look at the splatter pattern of the stains. What do you see?"

Harper examined the folds, carefully lifted them with the end of his pen, and considered the stains' point of origin. "The blood is on the outside down along the lower edge," he said. "Seems it dropped in an almost perfect vertical direction."

"Right on the mark," replied Carter. "There's something else though. The blood seeped through from the outside in. There's no blood on the inside of the blanket where the baby's body would have been in contact with it. The blood belonged to whoever held her at some point around the time she died."

"How do you know that? What makes you think the stain's not pre-existing?" asked Harper.

Carter pointed to the folds of the cloth again. Dirt and the elements inside the wall cavity had made the fabric stiff. They preserved the position of the creases where the blanket wrapped around the body. He pointed a gloved finger to a drop of blood on the edge of one of the folds. "See this? The blood that fell on this side of the fold matches the bloodstain on the section of cloth beneath it. It's no accident."

"What about DNA?" asked Mann.

"The sample's too old. The chances of finding a viable DNA fingerprint are slim to none by now."

"But you're going to try, right?" Mann persisted.

"No."

"What if it's there? Are you just going to let it go?"

"I know my DNA, detective. If you're lucky, DNA finger-printing from blood might last a few years, after that it's completely unreliable. At best, we're talking about a sixteen-year-old case. DNA is not going to be there making it a waste of my time and resources."

"What's left then?" asked Harper.

"Best I could do was to get you the ABO type. Whoever was holding the baby had type *B* blood."

"All right," said Mann, "let's assume it's not the baby's blood, we can't use blood type to prove who killed her. I mean, if you have three people in the same room and all three have the same blood type –"

"Chance of that happening is nil," said Carter. "All you need is one person who –"

"Right. Why don't you whip something up in one of these test tubes and show us where to start?"

"The person with type *B* blood held her last," said Carter. "May not be the killer, but you can bet he knows who is."

"Enough already. Both of you. Stop." Harper threw Mann a glance. "We keep looking. There could be a million and one scenarios on how the baby died, but eventually, only one will fit."

Harper didn't need his new partner to point out the problems with the case. Without blood DNA, there wouldn't be any way of matching the child to the parents if they were lucky enough to find them. For now, the blood was nothing more than another piece of information.

"I do have one more thing for you. Over here." Carter led them to a large worktable on the other side of the room. He reminded them that the workers had found the remains through an opening on the outside of the building. "The interior wall section stayed intact and there it is."

The partners exchanged glances as they approached a table where Carter had assembled large sections of plaster together like a giant jigsaw puzzle.

"What are we looking at?" asked Harper.

"That's the interior portion of the wall just above where the remains were found. I suspect most building managers, especially in low-rent neighborhoods like that one, try to save money by doing their own repairs. Consequently, the jobs aren't always going to be perfect. Fortunately, you're dealing with a cheap-ass landlord who fell neatly into the category."

Harper paid attention to Carter's explanation of how one would go about fixing a hole the size of the one used to slip in a small body. Carter also elaborated on the types of materials from which one could lift fingerprints.

"But, what better than to have the clumsy ox place a hand on the wet plaster?" Carter pointed to the black smudges of dusting and the perfectly preserved handprint embedded in the plaster.

"Sweet." Harper grinned.

"Yeah, that's what I thought." A smug grin crept across Carter's boyish face. "Somebody had to seal it up. Logically, that person was either the killer or someone close enough to be trusted with a major secret."

The detectives waited for Carter to reveal the name of the print's owner. He seemed to delight in the intentional pause. He let them hang for an uncomfortable second or two longer.

"Well?" asked Harper.

"Life as we know it isn't perfect, gentlemen. I ran the print against the AFIS – came up zilch on a match."

15

It was just after five in the morning. Harper had been up since two. He couldn't remember the dream, just the jolt of his awakening. The overnight lows had caused a thin coat of frost to form along the deck that stretched across the back of his home, yet sweat glistened on his brow and soaked his undershirt. He pulled it off and used it to wipe his face. He sat back in his black leather chair and looked out through the patio door toward Chandler Bay.

He and Mann would get back on the trail of Baby Doe's killer today, but Frank Gillies had been on his mind since he opened his eyes three hours before. Harper had read every word in Gillies' notes and scanned his phone logs. The calls to and from Holloway and Commissioner Flanagan were hardly suspicious. What was it he saw in his father's eyes when he mentioned Gillies' notes?

A frown wrinkled his face when he heard a key rattling in the front door lock. He closed his eyes and drew in a breath. "Damn. Not now."

"You're up." Deanna sounded surprised as she flipped on the lights in the foyer.

He squinted, attempting to adjust his eyes to the intrusion.

"What are you doing here?" He forced himself to his feet and shuffled toward the kitchen. He threw her a quick glance as he filled the carafe with water and poured it into the coffee makers' reservoir. *Whose bed had she warmed tonight*, he wondered. It didn't matter. They were like strangers. They had been for weeks. Gillies had urged him a dozen times to break it off. For now, it was easier to ignore her infidelities than to confront them.

"I haven't heard from you in days." She rolled her eyes and

looked around the darkened living area, "I don't know how you can stand to be cooped up like this. You're no fun any more."

"You weren't exactly invited, you know. You never answered my question. What are you doing here?"

"I left my blue sweater. It has to be here someplace." She slipped off her coat and tossed it over the back of a chair.

"In the closet."

The force of her pull on the sweater flipped the hanger onto the floor. She left it where it landed and joined him in the kitchen.

"You need a haircut," she snapped. "You look like crap."

He rubbed his eyes. His initial infatuation with her had vanished in measured segments of time with every insensitive act and word that had spewed from her mouth. Gillies was right. He had let this go too long. He had been unwilling to face the truth about their relationship, just as he had been unwilling to face Gillies' betrayal.

"You got what you came for and I have to be at work in another two hours. You need to leave."

"What's wrong with you?"

"Do you really have to ask?" He scooped out a measure of coffee and turned the pot on to brew. Did he need to explain to her that Gillies was his best friend and partner for the past four years? Worse, that now he suspected Gillies of being a dirty cop. Would she understand anything that didn't involve her?

"It's time to get on with your life. Our life," she said.

"That's rich. Who the hell do you think you're fooling?" He raised his hand to the back of his neck and rubbed at the tightness that ran down his arm. He rolled a shoulder in a circular motion. Still, the knot wouldn't ease. "Tell you what, you go on ahead. I'll get on with life when I'm good and ready."

"And what am I supposed to do in the meantime?"

"You're going to do whatever you want to do, with or without me."

"And just what does that mean?"

"It means I know about you and Tom, and the other guy you went away with for the weekend. Jesus, Deanna, you were with someone else the night I needed you most."

"Tom and I are just friends and you knew the weekend thing was a group outing. You could have gone."

"I was busy, remember? A little matter of my partner's death. And what about the trip to New York right after that? The one I had to hear about from your friend, the stockbroker. I suppose you'd like me to forget about your pregnancy scare. Who is he?"

"What are you implying?"

"I'm not implying a damned thing. It's a straight forward question."

"No one." She turned her back.

"Why the hell do you insist there's anything left between us?"

"Quit being suspicious. You're the only one I've bee–"

"What kind of an idiot do you take me for? I've been depressed, not stupid!"

She stared at him in stunned silence.

"Ah, forget it." He waved it off. "I don't care what you do."

"Harper, you are one self-absorbed guy. Your job, your family, your partner – there's no room for anything else in your life."

"No room for this crap, that's for sure." The towel in his hand slammed onto the counter top. He clenched his teeth. "You knew going into this how it would be. You want someone on your time, when it's convenient. It's not going to be me. The job comes first."

"That's what I'm talking about." She pointed an accusing finger at him. "When was the last time you came home at a decent hour?"

"What the hell did I ever have to come home to? You? You lost interest right after our engagement." The words fell from his lips before he could stop them. Gillies' numerous warnings about women came back to him. His late partner was crass, but right. He could still hear his voice. A woman like Deanna, he had said, ya date her, take her home, have an affair, but ya never commit your life to her.

"I stood by your side for six months waiting for you to solve each of your blasted cases." She tossed her hair back away from her face. "But there's no damn end to it, is there? There's always another case waiting for you."

"By my side? Again, where were you the night Gillies died?"

"Don't get on me because I'm not sitting around the house waiting on you while you're out playing cops and robbers," she shouted.

"My point exactly. If you're not supportive of me now," he yelled back, "what delusion should I have you'll be there for me after we're married?" Her silence told him all he needed to know. "You don't get it, do you? I'm not going to change and there will always be another case waiting for me."

"I can't accept that," she said.

"I wouldn't expect you to. You'll always be indifferent to other people's needs." Harper squeezed his eyes shut and raised his hands to his temples. He slammed his fists on the counter top as the persistent throbbing in his head peaked. "You don't have an ounce of compassion for anyone but yourself."

"Compassion? I have compassion. I wasted an entire afternoon at his funeral, didn't I? His widow didn't even want you there. Treated you like crap, and you took it. Like a wimp!"

"Stop it, Deanna. Stop it! You don't know a damned thing about it." His brows pinched again as his thoughts went back to Gillies' bulletproof vest. Given the chance, he wished he could scream at Gillies just one more time. He knew if he didn't follow regulations and wear the damned vest, he'd lose his pension. No wonder your widow's pissed, he'd tell him. You left her penniless, you stupid ass.

"No, I won't," she continued. "Face it, your job has been the root of our problems all along. We wouldn't have any arguments if you had a normal job."

"We're done!"

"A nine to five; you're smart, there are other jobs besides police work, you know." She continued to shout over his voice.

"I took an oath."

"Oh, please," she said with a roll of her eyes.

"When's the last time you took an interest in what my days are like? I make more life and death decisions before nine o'clock on any given morning than you'll ever make in a lifetime. This is who I am. Not some idiot who shuffles papers around until five then goes home to sit in front of the television because that's all life has to offer him." Harper pressed both hands against the counter, leaned in, and hung his head as if praying for her to leave. He took the kitchen hand towel to his face. Deanna had said something about him being tired and they could work things out later. "Get it through your head. There's nothing to work out. We don't even like each other any more. The sun's barely up and we're in the middle of a goddamn screaming match. There's no way I'm living the rest of my life like this."

"And what about me?"

"You've managed to satisfy your urges without any help from me," he said, unwilling to raise his eyes to look at her. He had expected her to storm out before now, to yell at him again. Instead, she remained motionless.

"We're done." He loathed his anger as much as her arrogance. "Just go."

Deanna slipped off her engagement ring and tossed it onto the table, letting it land with a clink. Harper didn't look up until he heard the door slam behind her.

The three people he cared about most had betrayed his trust. Gillies wasn't around to give answers and Deanna would never admit to her faults. Yet Harper was sure he could easily put them both out of his mind if he had to. Not so with the unsettling angst brought on by his father's lie. He hadn't imagined the shift he caught in his father's eyes or the misgivings he felt in his presence. There was a sinking feeling in his chest. How far was he willing to push for the truth and what would he do when he found it? He picked up her ring, bounced it once in the palm of his hand, and threw it against the wall.

16

The aroma of freshly brewed coffee filled the small kitchen of the modest brick home on Pigeon Road. Roxanne Lewis cringed as she pulled the lapels of her pink robe close to her chest and glanced at the clock on the wall. It was the same clock her husband had dubbed a practical timepiece when he hammered the nail into the stud for it above the sink. It hung there for eleven years as a daily reminder of how insignificant and mundane her life had become.

"Are you coming down?" She exaggerated her southern drawl. Her voice was still groggy with sleep. "It's nearly seven-fifteen; your coffee's ready." She drummed her fingers on her slender hips and waited for a reply. If he responded, she didn't hear him. "Rude snob," she said under her breath knowing no one would hear or pay attention to her if they had. She dropped two pieces of bread in the toaster and settled down with the morning newspaper.

Her first cup of coffee was inches away from her lips when a headline caught her attention. The third district councilman argued a case to increase property taxes again. She rolled her eyes and wondered what her husband would add to the list of things they couldn't afford if the city hiked the taxes again. There was scarcely a thing left to cut from their modest existence.

"Getting rid of a magazine subscription or two won't hardly make a damn bit of difference," she mumbled into the page. All she had left were her plants. "It'll be a cold day in hell when I give up the greenhouse," she huffed.

Her eyes swept across the page to the next headline. A two-inch article noted the attempts to rid city hall of the pigeons that roosted atop the statues and lights in front of the building. This one produced a smirk. She had no use for either the birds or the cops. As far as she was concerned, they could eliminate both without any sense of loss.

"What's the smile for? It's out of character for you, isn't it?" he asked.

She didn't hear him come in, didn't reply to his crass remark, nor did she have to look up to know he scooped one and a half teaspoons of sugar into his coffee and stirred it three times before taking a gulp.

"Bird poop."

"Excuse me?" he asked.

"Must be a slow news day," she said, without lifting her eyes and turned the page. "Your toast is up."

"Will you get my shirts today?"

Yes, she told him.

"Don't forget to call the plumber about the toilet. An ounce –"

"Of prevention. I know. You told me last night. I'm not stupid, you know."

His eyes bored into her as he chewed his toast then washed it down with black sweetened coffee.

"Don't forget. I'll be late tonight again."

"It's tax season. Since the day we married, you've been late every night of the week during tax season. Why in the world would today be any different? Can you just answer that for me?"

He glared at her then buttered his second piece of toast.

"So, any plans for today?" he asked, ignoring her questions.

"Can't think of any. Probably do the same thing today I did yesterday and the day before that." Again, she mumbled her words into the fold of the paper.

"What about dinner?"

"Oh, stop it for goodness sakes. I'm not done with my first cup yet and here you are going on and on about your dinner. It's getting late. Don't forget your lunch. It's in the ice box." Diverting his attention to the time was all it took to get him out of the house. Was it too much to ask to drink her coffee in peace? To read the paper without the same drill and twenty questions?

He raised his napkin to his mouth and tossed it in the trash.

Roxanne lifted her eyes off the page and watched as he put his cup in the sink and squeezed a neat little crease onto the fold of the brown paper lunch bag. She frowned at the sight of him nudging his glasses up the bridge of his nose. His predictability made her skin crawl. Next, he would check his watch. Today, its hour hand was off by a minute according to his precious timepiece hanging on the kitchen wall. He made the adjustment, gave her the usual peck on the forehead, and left.

Roxanne pretended to read. Her eyes swept off the page when she heard the front door shut behind him and waited for the familiar scraping of his car's tailpipe against the curb. Another smirk pulled at the corner of her mouth.

"Thank God."

She turned to page three, lifted her cup to her lips again, and then stopped. The one hundred or so words of print rendered her motionless. Her hand froze inches away from her lips as she read the short article on the lower left hand side of the page. An investor planned to sue the City of Chandler. The construction of his five story medical complex at the corner of Broadway and Fifth would have to wait pending a murder investigation.

She almost missed the piece. Had she stared at the text for a minute or was it five? Either way, she felt numb and had to remind herself to breathe.

17

For Harper, driving into the Avondale area of Chandler brought back the image of Gillies lying on the sidewalk with Mellow's bullet planted in his chest. He briefly flashed back to that night. Mann asked him a question. He was fine Harper told him as he kept watch for 1088 Sixth Street, the address of Alvin Quinn, the former owner of the Harbor View Apartments and their first call of the day.

Five more cross streets would land them on Howard and four blocks to the east was Third. The Roving Dog Saloon was there, only a few blocks away.

Rows of ramshackle homes with boarded up windows and abandoned buildings were familiar sights in this section of the city. Nearly all of his and Gillies' drug busts had happened along these streets and in the narrow stretches between the buildings where broken bottles and sharp-edged objects became their nightly obstacle course. He had no recollection of the homes that now blurred together as he and Mann drove past. Harper remembered only the pursuits, a few of the faces, and the eventual arrests. The evening's shadows had masked the condition of the homes.

Quinn's home was a modest brownstone one-story structure with an abandoned clothes washer the owner had left rusting at one end of the open porch. Time and the elements had exposed random areas of bare wood beneath layers of paint on the windows and doorframe, but the wrought iron security storm door seemed brand spanking new.

A short, stout man in his late sixties answered the door on the second knock. He ran a hand from his brow back through the sparse clump of hair at the crown of his head. His thin T-shirt bore a surprising splash of color – the single brownish-red stain immediately below his chin.

"Alvin Quinn?" Harper removed his sunglasses and peered through the grates on the door.

"Yeah?" A cigar stub dangled from Quinn's mouth as he spoke. "Who wants to know?"

"Detectives Harper and Mann, CPD," he said, displaying his badge. "We need to talk about a situation at your former building on 429 Broadway."

"What situation? That's all been settled. Everything done nice'n legal like. Got them papers right here, somewhere."

"We need to talk."

"Can't help I'm broke, ya know," Quinn insisted. "The judge was supposed to take care of all that."

"May we come in?" After a sleepless night and his fight with Deanna, Harper was in no mood for games. "Would you rather go downtown?"

"Ah." Quinn rolled his eyes. He curled his lips in disgust and shook his head. "Suit yourself." He pulled up his pants that had fallen below his abdomen and shuffled away from the door.

Heavy curtains darkened the front room of the home and mimicked the tattered appearance of its occupant. Harper waited a moment for his eyes to adjust before starting his line of questions. "The workers at the site found human remains entombed in one of the walls of the Harbor View." Both sets of eyes locked on Quinn and waited for a hint of acknowledgment.

"Remains, huh? That's news to me." A frown swept cross Quinn's face as his eyes darted beneath a set of bushy eyebrows.

"That's right. In what used to be apartment 1C," said Mann. "You wouldn't know anything about that, would you?"

"I didn't harbor no killer if that's what ya're wantin' to hear. Besides, I'm not the first guy to own the place, ya know."

"But you did own it between 1987 and 1990, right? In fact you were the legal owner until you lost it eight months ago." Harper didn't need Quinn to respond. He had all the facts he needed about

Alvin Quinn and his failed business practices in a file on his desk. "You look like the type of guy who knows his business. Imagine you also remember every one of your tenants."

"Could be," Quinn replied.

"We understand you still have the records," said Mann.

"Yeah, yeah, I got 'em in the back room. Judge told me I had to keep 'em a while. Wouldn't want to do nothin' illegal or nothin'." Perspiration began to bead on his forehead.

"Good." Harper handed him a warrant. "We need them."

"Why? I can tell ya anything ya want to know."

"Now, Mr Quinn." Harper motioned for him to move.

Quinn bit down on his stogie and narrowed his eyes. "It'll take me a while to sort through 'em. I had people movin' in and outta the place all the time. Maybe ya oughta come back later. Ya know, give me time to put 'em in order."

"Just hand them over – now," Mann ordered. "Let's go."

Quinn led them into a small bedroom near the back of the home.

"If I'd known youse was comin'," he said, shoving a stack of old phone books out of the way, "I woulda cleaned the place up." He kicked a couple of pairs of old shoes aside then swept a pile of rags and papers off the floor in the center of the room into his arms. Papers flew out of his grasp. He let out a huff as he grabbed them again and tossed the pile into chair. "Stuff kinda gets dumped in here, ya know?" he mumbled. "What ya want is over there, in them boxes by the dresser."

The men stepped over more clothing before reaching the seven boxes stacked one on top of the other along the opposite wall. They started to pick them up to take them out to their car.

"Ya didn't say nothin' 'bout takin' them outta here." He frowned and bit down on his cigar again and veered it to the other side of his mouth.

"We have a warrant for them," said Mann.

Quinn said nothing.

"Something you want to tell us, Mr Quinn?" asked Harper.

"No, now wait. Don't go gettin' in a huff or nothin'. Go on, take 'em. Knock yourself out. But I didn't do nothin' wrong. Ya can't prove nothin' neither. Damn people and their kids. Nothin' but trouble." Quinn mumbled and curled his lip. He looked at them for a moment before pulling the stub from his mouth and throwing it into a chipped glass ashtray on the edge of the dresser. "Yeah, that's right. There, take 'em. But the judge said I need 'em back, hear?"

"We'll see to it ourselves," Mann assured him, then gave Harper a guarded look after Quinn shuffled out of the room. "Catch that?"

"You'd have to be deaf to miss it."

"I say we take him in," Mann whispered.

"No, I want to see for myself why he's so insistent on sorting through these first. Besides, he's not going anywhere. We'll just leave the noose out and see who he drags in with him."

It was half past noon before they loaded the boxes into the car and finished with Quinn. The third day on the case had produced little more than the possible sex and age of the baby, a four-year range in which she might have died, and a property owner who knew more than he was willing to say.

The usual noon crowd packed into the Pig and Whistle Pub located in the middle of the business district. A group of customers had gathered near the front door. As Harper and Mann took their seats, Harper caught sight of Stewart Martin sitting in a booth at the other side of the room. "Crap."

"What's the matter?

"Stewart Martin. Have you met him?"

"No. Should I have?"

"Not if you can help it."

"Who is he?" asked Mann, turning around in his chair.

"An ass. He's also Commissioner Flanagan's nephew."

"And that makes him an ass?" asked Mann.

"No. He manages it on his own. He and Gillies used to get into it all the time."

"What about?"

"Not sure what started it. Must have been a territory thing. Martin always complains Holloway gives him crap assignments, but even the easy cases eventually landed on someone else's desk. He goes through the motions but doesn't work them. Not the way they should be."

"Nephew or not, guys like that usually have something hanging over someone's head," said Mann.

"He's not smart enough to figure an angle."

"So if he was Gillies' problem, why let him bug you?"

"Holloway assigned him to the Owens case."

"You're obsessed with this Owens guy, aren't you?"

"He represents a loose end, that's all."

"What exactly makes him so special? He's a dealer, right?"

"We've never been able to catch him with anything," said Harper. "We suspected someone was tipping him off. Makes more sense than to think he's smart." He wondered if Gillies had gotten in over his head. "Something must have happened with the case while I was gone. Holloway won't even talk to me about it."

"It's his problem. We're going to have our hands full with Baby Doe and the other cases on our desks," said Mann.

"Holloway dogged us about him all the time to get him. It doesn't make sense for him to change his mind and assign it to Martin."

"Get over it. Seriously. You're out of Narcotics," said Mann. "It's only going to get you sidetracked."

Funny Mann's words would echo his father's warning. Harper glanced across the room again. "Stay away from him. He'll stab you in the back first chance he gets."

"I'll keep it in mind. Why do you think I put in for a transfer to headquarters? To get away from jerks like him."

Harper wondered when Mann was going to get around to the incident at the Second Precinct.

"It'll take some time to go through Quinn's records," said Mann. "He's hiding something. I can feel it."

Harper agreed, disappointed Mann had changed the subject.

"I've been thinking about the finger prints Carter found on the plaster board. We have seven boxes in the car full of papers covered with his prints."

Harper nodded and agreed again; the lab would be their next stop.

"We should've taken Quinn in," said Mann.

"On what charges? Even if he knows something, we're not ready to question him. Let him stew a while. I have a feeling he'll try to squirm out of it, get confused and when he trips over a few lies, we'll nab him."

Harper wondered how many tenants were included in the seven boxes other than those who had lived in apartment 1C. "Someone has to remember something." He was about to say something else when he felt a gentle touch of a small hand on his shoulder.

"Hey handsome."

"Abby." He jumped to his feet and gave her a hug. Abby, the only brunette in Harper's life – at least the only brunette he cared about, had the same mischievous spark in her eyes she had as a child. Her short curly hair mussed softly around her face made him think of a summer day when she had caught her first fish in the pond near his parents' home.

"I'm sorry about Gillies. Are you okay?"

"I'm fine."

"Are you back to work yet?" she asked.

"First week back. Want to sit down?"

"I'd love to, but I can't. I need to get back to the office."

Abby was his best friend and the only woman he could talk to without fear of rejection or ridicule. But he had seen the way she could pull a man in and hold him steady with her smile. She was doing it now to Mann. Harper looked over his shoulder at him. With the introductions out of the way, they tried to convince her to join them.

"You sure you can't stay?" asked Mann.

"I'm sure. Some other time, maybe." She smiled and squeezed Harper's hand. She glanced at her watch. "I have to run. I'll call you later. Okay?" She said her goodbyes, slipped Harper a kiss, and left.

Mann turned in his seat to watch her. "What's your story with her?" he asked. "Were you two – you know."

"No. We grew up together. She's the kid sister I never had," said Harper. "Always looked out for each other."

"What does she do?"

"Works for an architectural firm." Harper glanced up. Abby was near the door when he noticed Martin. He was waiting to pay and had made it a point to tilt his head and glanced down at her legs as she walked past him. Martin snatched the change from the cashier's hand a little too fast for Harper's liking. He rushed to his feet and out the door after him. "Let her go," he yelled.

"Sam," Abby tried to pull away from Martin's hold.

"Let her go!" Harper screamed the order to Martin as he pulled them apart and stood between them. "You want to press charges?" he asked her hoping she would.

"No. I'm fine – really."

"What's the matter Harper?" Martin sneered. "Am I crashing in on something else of yours? First your case now your girl?"

Abby stopped and looked back. "Sam?"

"Everything's fine. Go on. I'll call you later."

"Now that's sweet," Martin continued to sneer as he adjusted the knot on his tie.

"What the hell is your problem?" Harper growled.

"Only problem I see is you. We were just talking."

"Like hell you were."

"You're just like Gillies, always butting into what doesn't concern you."

"Enough with this bullshit. Gillies is dead. Drop it," said Harper.

"It'll never be over. Gillies went against the code. He was a snitch. Just like your old man."

Harper lunged toward him, clenched Martin's lapels in his fists, and threw him against the brick façade of the building. The blunt force hitting his back and head stunned him for a moment; long enough for Harper to reconsider a right jab to the ribs.

Martin slumped forward, reached for the back of his head, and felt a trickle of blood. "Son of a bitch. Keep an eye over your shoulder, Harper. It's not over between us."

18

It was forty-nine degrees under the noon sun. The cops who just left Alvin Quinn's home had their coats on, yet here he stood, in his dingy thin undershirt, hiding behind a pair of dirty curtains, sweating like a pig. Quinn pulled the kitchen curtain aside and scanned his street. He wanted the cops out of sight before he called down to the Roving Dog Saloon.

"It's me," said Quinn.

"What the hell are you doing calling me here?"

"I need your help."

"What do you want now? I'm not a damned bank, you know."

"It's not like that. Ya gotta help me." Quinn could hear the chime of the cash register in the background and the customers' voices rising above the hiss of the grill.

"I've got a noon crowd waiting for their lunch and the damned cook didn't show. I can't talk."

"But ya gotta." A tightness pressed against Quinn's chest "Now, Charlie. It's important!"

"Everything's a damned emergency to you. Who's after you this time?"

"The cops."

"I don't have time for this."

"They found the kid."

Chuck Toomey made no comment.

"Charlie? Ya there, Charlie? Did ya hear what I said?"

"Jesus," Chuck said, above a whisper. "I heard you. When? How?"

"They're tearin' the damned buildin' down. Didn't ya read the headlines? Two cops just left my house. They didn't come out and say it was the kid. But damn, how many bodies could there be in the dump?" Quinn shuffled his feet and paced as far as the cord would allow.

"What'd you tell them?"

"Nothin'. They just came lookin' for my records, ya know the contracts and receipts."

Another whispered curse came from the other end.

"What the hell am I suppose to do? They had a warrant and everythin'. I had to." Quinn paused. He waited a minute longer. "Holy Jesus, say somethin'! They're gonna come back. I know they're gonna." He glanced at the small square clock hanging cockeyed above the sink. "We're screwed, Charlie. Jesus, we're really screwed now."

"When did they show?"

"Ten minutes ago, tops." Quinn continued to pace back and forth. He stopped, wiped the sweat from his brow, and then paced some more. "Ya know what this means, don't ya? If they figured out who I am, they're going to put the rest of the thing together and fry our asses right off."

"First of all, you're going to quit your damned babbling. You show any kind of panic and it's as good as wearing a guilty sign around your stupid neck. All you have to do is remember they can't trace anything back to us. Anyone could have put the kid in there. Besides, a pile of old bones won't tell them a damned thing. Their investigation is dead before it gets started."

"They talked about specific dates though. How the hell would they know that? Huh? They know, Charlie. I'm tellin' ya, they know somethin'."

"Why the hell you put the kid in there is beyond me. Damn it Quinn, the bay was five miles away. If you would have tossed it in, we wouldn't be having this conversation."

"Shit! How the hell was I supposed to know? I never thought –"

"Damned right you never thought. I ought to go over there right now and wring your fat, worthless neck."

"And there's another thing. Some guy called here about it too."

"Who?"

"I don't know. Wouldn't say. But he knew too much," said Quinn. "Who could it be, Charlie? I thought it was just the three of us."

"Never mind."

"Never mind? I'm the one the cops came after. What the hell am I supposed to do now?"

"Shut up and let me think."

Quinn mindlessly obeyed. He could still hear the muffled voices of customers in the background. "Charlie?"

"Listen, just because you owned the place doesn't give the cops any reason to pin this on you. You got that?"

Quinn paused for a minute. "Yeah. I guess you're right. But what if –"

"The worst thing that can happen is they'll probably call you in for questioning."

"What the hell for? I gave them all they asked for. They had a warrant, Charlie. A goddamned warrant for the shit."

"Damn it, pay attention. No way they can put this one together, but they gotta start some place and you're all they have. My guess, they'll want to talk to you about the tenants. You ran the place. They'll ask you stuff like who lived there and when. You just stick to the facts. You got that?"

"Yeah, sure I get it."

"You show them your records and tell them anything you remember about the crackheads who rented the place. That's all. Hell, half of them are probably dead by now. While the cops are busy chasing them down, we can rethink this mess."

"And if it's not all?" asked Quinn. "What then?"

"They can't prove a damned thing."

"I don't know. Ain't never been good at lyin'."

"If you don't play this cool, I'm going to kill you myself. That's not a threat, Quinn. Do I make myself clear?"

Quinn wiped his brow again with a fleshy hand then ran his palm over his upper lip and listened.

"If they haul you into the station and pressure you, you tell them what happened."

"But –"

"Shut up and listen," said Chuck. "If they start fishing around about the kid, you tell them what happened; exactly the way it went down, but leave me out of it. Understand? I wasn't there and had nothing to do with it."

"But I ain't takin' the heat for it."

"Like I said, you just tell them what happened. J O took the kid, remember?"

"Nah, Charlie. That's not how it went."

"Damn it Quinn you can't remember anything straight any more. Who you gonna trust? Your old pal Charlie or that head of yours?"

Quinn frowned. He was so sure he knew what had happened. He remembered the kid and the kid's mother. But the pictures in his head were like dim flashes. They were in and out as fast as a firefly lights the June night. They didn't stay lit in his head very long either. Charlie was right. Charlie was always right. His mind hadn't worked right since he took that last blow to the head. Damned near killed him that time. "You Charlie. I trust ya. But J O? What if they don't believe me? What then?"

"They'll believe you. The cops can't wait to get their hands on him. In fact, they'll probably buy you a beer for the information."

"What if they ask for his real name?"

"You don't know it."

"I know," said Quinn. "That's what I mean. Won't they want the guy's real name?"

"You fucked up idiot," he whispered. "Of course they'll want it, they'll have to get off their dead asses and work for it. I have to go. You just … well, just make them think you're cooperating. That's all. Now stay away from me. Don't come near my place and don't call me again."

Quinn held the receiver to his ear listening to the monotone sound coming out of it. He scratched his scalp and hung the receiver back in its cradle. He shuffled across the worn kitchen linoleum and brushed back the curtain above the sink again. It had been a while since he felt this panicked. Not since he fought with that hooker over the rent. *Stupid broad made the rent every night on her back. Besides, he barely touched her. Hell, wasn't his fault the whore tripped over her feet and flew down the stairs. Never knew a neck could bend like that; messy too.* But this was different. It had followed him home and it was ready to take a bite.

19

Day three. One clue and no leads. Finding the person responsible for the baby's death after more than a decade seemed nearly improbable. That's what Harper was thinking as he and Mann separated the rental contracts into piles and searched for possible suspects. *One name – all they needed was one name*, he thought. Someone who lived in 1C with an infant some time during the four years in question. It was the single most crucial piece of information they needed to take the investigation to the next level.

He and Mann should have gone home hours ago, but the hope of finding a lead or the smallest clue in Quinn's records seized them. Hours passed, the list narrowed, but his calculated guess was a third of these former tenants were probably dead.

"So far, I found three possible leads," said Mann.

"I've got four. That works out to about a new tenant every six months. No wonder Quinn went broke. They probably moved out as soon as he remembered to collect the rent."

Mann laughed as he thumbed through the contracts. After a moment, he stopped, frowned, and flipped back through the stack. "There's a huge gap in these dates," he said, motioning for Harper to see for himself. "Look, Quinn had someone moving in one right after the other until this Roxanne Ewing left on June 3, 1990. No one moved into 1C again until the following January." A smug grin slipped across his lips. "1990. That's sixteen years ago and fits right in there with how old Carter said the toy bear is. And look." He pointed to the answer the tenant gave to question number five. "She had a kid. I think we got ourselves our first lead."

"It has to be." Harper tapped his finger on the desk.

"What are you thinking?" asked Mann.

"The smell of that little decaying body kept him from renting the place out." Harper returned to his desk and sat down. "It'll be interesting to see how Quinn explains himself out of this one. According to these," he said, thumping at the documents on his desk. "Ewing moved out on June 3. Need to work back from there."

They exchanged their knowledge of decomposition; how quickly it starts after death and at what point the gases would start to let off odor.

"If she died around the time Ewing moved out, the trapped heat inside the wall would have been twice the outdoor temperature and it would have accelerated the process." Harper's thoughts rushed back to the rats. He was about to throw out another comment when he heard the knock on their door.

"Detective?" Alvin Quinn stood in the doorway holding his faded red and green plaid cap in his hand.

"Mr Quinn." Harper exchanged glances with Mann. "We were just talking about you."

"Ya were?"

"Have a seat." Harper stepped out around to the front of his desk and leaned back against it as he pointed to one of the extra chairs in the room. He waited for Quinn to settle in and hoped he'd spill another bit about the tenants in 1C. "Yes, we've been going through your records."

"Any problem, Detective?"

Harper crossed his arms. "Not yet. Looks like you've kept track of everything that went on in the building. I mean, you were on top of things, right?"

"Yeah. Ya know, I tried. Just couldn't afford it no more."

"I bet you knew every one of your tenants too, huh?"

"Yeah, sure. Most of 'em. What're ya gettin' at?"

"We need you to fill us in on something."

"Oh?"

"Kind of strange, actually," Mann interjected.

"What is it?" Quinn asked, leaning forward in his chair.

"From the looks of things, you kept the apartments rented constantly. One in, one out, another in," said Harper.

"Yeah, I never had no problem keepin' 'em rented."

"Exactly." Harper narrowed his eyes and stared at the little man fidgeting in the wooden straight back chair. "So why did apartment 1C sit vacant from June through the end of December in 1990? That's seven months without a tenant or rent money."

"Seven months, huh?" Quinn raised his brows and pouted as if surprised. "Could have been anythin'. We was always havin' pipes break, that kind of stuff."

"Pipes?" Harper frowned and ran his hand across his mouth. "Seven months of repairs, though. Must have been a heck of a lot of damage; probably cost you a pretty penny, right?"

"Oh, yeah. Maintenance ain't cheap, ya know." Quinn rolled up his cap and squeezed it.

"So you'd remember something that extensive – that costly."

"Well, I –"

"We didn't find any receipts for repairs. Care to be more specific?"

Quinn was pokerfaced. He blinked and remained silent.

It was almost undetectable; the way Quinn's eyes grew slightly bigger when Harper asked the question. It wasn't much, but enough to tell Harper Quinn was trying to think of a way to weasel out of answering his question.

"Nah. I can't. Not off the top of my head." He looked away. "People was breakin' stuff all the time. Can't expect me to remember every little repair."

"Doesn't sound like a little repair to me," Mann played along, "but you know what, Mr Quinn. We don't really care about the pipes. Just the body."

"Hey, I already told youse, I don't know nothin' about no body."

Harper didn't believe for a minute that broken water pipes had anything to do with the gap in time. Still, they didn't have any reason to hold him, but he was curious to know why Quinn had stopped by the station. He studied how this little man's eyes darted from one side to the other then asked: "What's on your mind, Mr Quinn?"

"I ah … was thinkin' about things and … ya know."

"What things?"

"People. Ya know."

"What people?"

Apprehension flashed across Quinn's face like a man who had reached a dead end.

"What people?"

"Well, I … no one I guess. This whole thing with the buildin' and all gets a guy thinkin' is all."

"Whatever it was, it must be important. Police headquarters isn't exactly on your way home."

Harper glanced at his watch. It was seven forty-five in the evening. *Who did Quinn think he was fooling, anyway?*

"Nah, I was comin' back from some place. Didn't make no special trip or nothin'. Guess I was curious to know if ya found what ya was needin'." Quinn eyed the stacks of papers on the desks with a stretch of his neck for a better look.

"As a matter of fact, we did. What do you remember about Roxanne Ewing?"

"Roxanne?" Quinn squinted and looked around the room. "Ah, ya know, my memory … it ain't what it used to be. Boxin' took care of it. Used to be pretty good in the ring. Them were the days when ya could still find a good fight and a broad to follow ya home when ya won. Know what I'm sayin'?" He smiled displaying a discolored front tooth.

"Roxanne Ewing. Come on, Quinn. She was the last person to live in 1C before the pipes broke. Remember?" asked Harper.

"Couldn't say without lookin' at my notes there. Ya mind?" Quinn pointed to the neatly stacked rows of papers on one of the desks.

"Here. Is this what you need?" asked Harper.

Quinn took the contract and slid his finger across the page as he read. "Yeah, I remember her now. Roxanne Ewin'. Like it says here, moved in on March 10, 1990. Only got the first month's rent out of her. She was ready to pop a kid out when she moved in.

Neighbors complained about the kid's cryin', later on, I mean. The broad was always high on somethin'."

Harper took back the contract from Quinn. "Did you evict her?"

"Nah, left before I had a chance to do anythin' about her."

"She owed you for two months. Most landlords wouldn't be that patient."

Quinn shrugged his shoulders. "Guess I was just soft on account of her condition 'n all. Kept thinkin' she'd pay up. But not her. Caused nothin' but grief, that one."

"She lived alone?" asked Mann.

"No exactly. Always had company if you get my meanin'. I mean, somebody had to knock her up, ya know what I mean?"

"What did she have?" asked Mann.

"Have? Whadya mean, have?"

"The baby. You said she was pregnant when she moved in. Did she have a boy or a girl?" He asked again.

"What do I look like? Some nurse maid?" asked Quinn. "A kid, how should I know? Never paid attention to stuff like that."

"Could have taken her to court," said Harper.

"Wouldn't of done no good."

"Why not?" asked Mann.

"She left in the middle of the night. Stood me up on what she owed. Knowin' her, she probably got what was comin' to her. Never saw her again."

"What do you think was coming to her, Mr Quinn?" asked Harper.

"Whoa, not that I wished her no harm. The broad ran around with a rough bunch, is all. Know what I'm sayin'? She was always drunk."

"Do you remember anything else about her? Did she work anywhere?"

"Not a thing. Some people ya're better off forgettin', if ya get my drift."

It was later than Harper had intended to stay. Quinn wasn't talking and the real reason for his visit was still a mystery. "All right Quinn, thanks for coming in, but we need to get back to work. We'll let you know if we need anything else."

Quinn stared at Harper and squeezed his cap.

"Something else on your mind, Mr Quinn?"

"Ya gotta know, I got nothin' to hide." Quinn lowered his gazed and started to leave.

Harper waited until Quinn reached the door. "Oh, one more thing, I suggest you find the receipts for those seven months of repairs."

Quinn frowned, lowered his gaze again, and sauntered out of their office.

Mann leaned against the doorframe watching their visitor disappear into the elevator. "Sleazy little cuss, isn't he? I bet he doesn't have anything to hide. Memory isn't that bad either." He stretched his arms up and cradled his head in the cup of his hands. "What do you suppose that was all about?"

"He's covering his tracks. He can sweat it out while we locate this Ewing woman."

Harper stepped out into the main office area and glanced across the rows of desks in the homicide section of the floor. At eight p.m., only a skeletal crew of technical staff was at their desks.

"Hey, Troy," he called out to one of the men. "Do me a favor. Need a current address for a Roxanne Ewing, last known address is 429 North Broadway, Apartment 1C." He looked over Troy's shoulder in hopes of a quick result. After a few minutes, the computer screen flickered through files, and then stopped.

"Nothing," said Troy.

"Hold on." Harper left and returned with an armful of rental contacts. "Do a search on these. Need a current on as many as you can find. I'll be in my office."

"Maybe Quinn has it right this time," said Mann. "Maybe the mother is dead. What's the plan then?"

"We keep looking for the one neighbor who remembers her; knows what happened and isn't afraid to get involved." Someone had to know what happened sixteen years ago to silence a baby's cry.

Their first stop the following morning was at Ben Franklin Junior

High to talk with Gene Stone, the seventh grade history teacher.

"Sorry," said Stone. "I only lived there a month. Not long enough to get to know anyone. Not that I would have wanted to, mind you." He crossed his arms, seeming indifferent to the plight of his former neighbors.

"Why's that?" asked Mann.

"Are you kidding? The place was a dump. And those people – nothing but low lives. Whatever happened to them, they had it coming."

That was the second time Harper heard that comment in as many days. "You lived there. How bad could it have been?"

"Don't remind me. I didn't have a choice."

"And the others did?" asked Mann.

"Look, I'd like to help, but I kept to myself on purpose. Those people breed into that lifestyle. I wasn't like them."

"Those people? You want to enlighten us, professor?" Harper knew the Gene Stone types. He'd dealt with professors just like him in college. The intellectual snobs who started life bare butt like everyone else. Somewhere along the way, they turn into a puffed-up version of themselves. Stone's attitude made Harper think about Gillies. His arrogance was as ignorant as Gillies' low opinion of a college education and just as dangerous.

"You know what I'm talking about." Stone said just above a whisper. He looked around to make sure none of his students were within earshot before he continued. "Drug addicts, whores. The only reason I stayed as long as I did was the price. I was in college for Christ's sakes; it was all I could afford. But price or not, I got out of there after the first time I came home and found a rat the size of a small possum sitting on my kitchen counter."

Mann swept a glance toward his partner as he turned the ignition. "Warm kinda guy, huh? Just the type I'd want teaching my kids someday."

"Haven't you heard? 'Love thy neighbor' doesn't count when they're crackheads."

"Where to now?" asked Mann.

The next four people on their list gave similar stories, and then they caught up with Mary Kemp, a social worker at the Gateway Community Center.

"Sure, I remember them," she said.

"Them?" asked Harper.

"Yes, Roxie and that creep who stayed with her. My apartment was right next door; walls were paper-thin. Sixteen years old and pregnant."

"Sixteen?" Harper frowned. "Do you remember this *creep's* name?"

"Joe. That's all I ever caught."

"What are we talking about? A couple of teens playing house or what?" asked Mann.

"Oh no." She shook her head without taking her eyes from Mann. "Older. Probably in his twenties at the time. Granted, she looked a lot older. I didn't know her real age until later or I would have reported it."

"What can you tell us about him?"

"Not much. Medium height, bushy light brown hair, scrawny, had a nasal tone and always seemed nervous about something. Chain smoker, that one."

"What was her relationship to him?"

"Beats me. They weren't married or anything. I do know the jerk wasn't the baby's father."

"How do you know? Is that what she told you?"

"No. She wouldn't tell me. Said she couldn't. Call it a woman's intuition. I knew." Mary turned to punch the keys on her keyboard and pulled up the name of Roxanne Lewis.

"You sure we're talking about the same woman?" asked Harper.

"Oh yeah. Positive. I was just getting started in my career so I was impressionable at the time. You know, wanted to save the world." She rolled her eyes gesturing a look of disgust at the incompetence of the system. "I don't think I would have forgotten her even if I wasn't a social worker."

"Why's that?"

"She had the thickest southern drawl I ever heard and pretty long, red hair. But aside from that, the poor girl was scared to death of Joe."

"Did you ever see or hear him threaten either her or the baby?"

"Detective, guys like him never threatened. They pounce without warning. She was his punching bag. The poor girl was always walking around with bruises – big bruises. I tried to call the police a couple of times, but she wouldn't press charges."

"And your conscience didn't bother you? Why didn't you get her out of there?" asked Mann.

"I was young myself." Her helpful tone turned curt. "She couldn't find her way out of a paper sack, let alone out of that relationship. I see that type of thing all the time. Look who I'm talking to, as if you two don't see the same. Yeah, I could have taken her out of there and she would have fallen right back into the same trap with him or someone else. Anyway, I tried to talk with her the few times I caught her sober. I never could get through to her."

"When's the last time you saw her?" asked Harper.

Mary looked at her screen again. "February 18, 1993. She had kept my business card and actually stayed in touch for a while." Mary toggled to another screen and searched for additional information. "She went through detox in the fall of 1990. Married a man by the name of Ned Lewis a couple of years later. Quit calling here after she got married. Most of them do once they find a way out. Guess I can't blame her for wanting to leave the baggage behind."

"Did she ever say what happened to Joe?" asked Mann.

"No. All I know is she got away from him, thank God."

"According to the former landlord, Roxanne moved out without giving notice. Did she ever talk to you about her plans to leave or what happened in the days before?" asked Harper.

"Afraid not. I didn't know she had left."

"Were you in the building on that day?" asked Mann.

"No. I had gone to my parents' home in Boston. I was there for a couple of weeks. Roxie was gone by the time I got back. I was worried about her. Wondered how she would manage on her own."

"Anyone else in the building hear anything?"

"No. I checked around in different shelters. No one seemed to remember her. Anyone with half a brain would have remembered her. That baby of hers cried constantly. I offered to help her with it."

"And did you?"

"No. She wouldn't even let me see it. I was just glad our paths crossed again." Mary jotted down something on a piece of paper. "Here. That's the last address I have for her. Say, do you archive your 911 calls?"

"Yeah, we can go back a few years. Why?" asked Harper.

"I don't know if this matters or not, but she told me she made a 911 call a few days after she moved out. Maybe you can get something from the tape."

"Did she say why she made the call?" asked Mann.

"Something about her baby. But it didn't make sense."

"Why not?" asked Harper.

"Because when I asked her if the baby was all right, she said, she wasn't sure, but she didn't seem all that concerned." Mary sat back in her chair and crossed her arms. "She wouldn't talk about it after that. Strange too."

"What is?"

"Whether they love them or not, mothers always talk about their kids. They'll either brag or complain. I never did see the baby and Roxie never mentioned her again."

20

"911 Essex County. What's your emergency?" asked the dispatcher on the sixteen-year-old police tape recording.

"Someone took my baby."

"State your name please."

"Roxanne Ewing."

"Speak up, please." The counter measured a seven-second pause. "Ma'am? Are you there? State your name please."

"Roxanne Ewing."

"What address are you calling from?"

"I don't ... I'm at a phone booth."

"Can you give me the street names of the nearest intersection?"

There was another pause on the tape.

"Ma'am? Are you there?"

"Yes. I'm ... I'm here."

"What's the nearest intersection?"

"I don't know." The tape had captured her panicked breathing. "Hoyt. I'm on Hoyt Street."

"Did you say, Hoyt Street?"

"Yes."

"You're the child's mother?"

A four-second silence.

"Ma'am? Hello. Are you still there?"

"Yes, I ..."

The recording picked up the sound of a scuffle and the click of a broken connection. The 911 call made at seven thirty-five on the evening of June 5, 1990, lasted exactly thirty-two seconds. Harper listened to the tape several times, honing in on the whispered, anxious, young voice of the girl on the phone. Hers was the only distinctive voice on the tape. There was no way to determine if someone was with her or had interrupted the call. *Two years later*, he thought, *and the 911 enhanced system would have told the operator exactly where Roxanne was.*

"I don't get it," said Mann. "The baby died, the mother or the creep she lived with placed her inside the wall, and they left. Why report her missing two days later? It doesn't make any sense."

"We don't know that's what happened. We can't even say for sure the girl on the tape is the same Roxanne the social worker told us about." Harper grabbed a copy of her renter's contract and slipped it inside his breast pocket. "Right now, all we have are a lot of assumptions and the word of a social worker with a sketchy story. We can't assume anything at this point. What we need is proof."

Their best lead so far was Mary Kemp, and she knew nothing of the night in question. Still, if the information she gave them about Roxanne was correct, they now had a better chance of finding her. DNA would confirm if she was the baby's mother, but the results were still days away.

"Let's hope this address isn't a dead end." Harper glanced at his watch. It was a quarter past six. "Come on. We're not going to know anything sitting around here. You drive." He threw Mann the car keys and followed him out.

The Lewis home on Pigeon Road was a typical 1950's ranch style structure situated in a quiet, well-maintained middle class subdivision. Soft lights from the living room windows and a black sedan parked in the driveway told the detectives someone was home.

"This ought to be interesting," Mann said, out of a corner of his mouth as he rang the doorbell. "Can't wait to see her face when we tell her we found her baby and need her DNA to prove she's a killer."

"Let's just see what she has to say."

The porch light flashed on. A woman in her early thirties answered the door. Her modest, well-groomed appearance belied her former lifestyle, but based on Mary's description of Roxanne, there was no doubt in Harper's mind they had found her. Her southern accent hung on every word.

"Yes?" she asked, without unlocking the screen door.

"Detective Harper, Chandler PD Homicide, ma'am. This is my partner, Detective Mann. Is this the Lewis household?"

"Homicide?" she gasped. Her green eyes darted quickly between the two men. "What's wrong? What's happened?"

"Are you Roxanne Lewis?"

"Yes," she answered.

"Was your former name Ewing?" asked Harper.

The sweetness in her southern smile faded from her lips. The crease between her brows deepened and her eyes again darted from one man to the other then back again.

"What's this all about?" she whispered.

"Are you the Roxanne Ewing who resided in apartment 1C of the Harbor View Apartment building between March and June of 1990?" asked Harper.

"That was a long time ago, Detective."

"Yes or no."

"Yes. I don't understand."

"We have reason to believe a homicide was committed in the building around the time you lived there. Just need to ask you a few questions."

"The one I read about in the paper this week?" She crossed her arms. "I don't know anything about that."

"We understand you placed a 911 call on June 5, 1990, regarding your daughter. Our records show you reported her missing." Harper had no idea how she would react to the question. Would she slam the door in their faces and run out the back or would she crumble and tell them about the events that led up to the baby's death?

"My daughter? 1990! What does she have to do with your investigation?" She closed her eyes and sighed. "Goodness, you gave me a fright." She opened the door and stepped aside. A teenage girl sat on the couch, curled up in an afghan, watching television and unaware of their visit. "As you can see, Caitlin is just fine. A bit under the weather at the moment. Nothing more than a cold, but I promise, she is just perfect. I don't know what you gentlemen thought you'd find here, but I believe you are mistaken."

A swarm of questions rushed through Harper's mind as he stared into the home's front room. "I see." He was unable to take his eyes from the girl.

"My goodness, but you men look like you've seen a ghost." She smiled, seemingly amused by the looks on their faces. "It's a mistake. That's all," she said, and started to shut the door.

"May we come in?" he asked.

"No." She raised her hands to her hips. "You may not. I've answered your questions. What else is there?"

"You reported your daughter missing. Is she your daughter?" asked Harper, pointing at the teen.

"Why of course she is! What kind of question is that?" She glanced back over her right shoulder again, stepped out, and shut the front door behind her. "Well, after all these years. I'm certainly glad it wasn't a life or death situation," she sneered. "My daughter is fine. That's a fact and as plain as a set of footsteps on fresh fallen snow."

Yes, Harper could see Caitlin for himself. What he couldn't see was the logic. Where had they made a wrong turn? The identity of Baby Doe suddenly slipped farther from their reach. Without a warrant, he couldn't even ask to see a birth certificate. Still, he wasn't ready to walk away. Not yet. "You lived at 429 North Broadway for three months. Is that correct?" he asked.

She frowned. "I've already answered that."

"Answer the question."

"Yes."

"Is this your signature?" Harper asked showing her a copy of the rental contract.

"Yes."

"Who was Joe?" he asked.

"Joe?" She feigned a smile. "Now how in the world do you know about Joe?"

"His last name," said Harper. "What was it?"

"I don't know. I just knew him as Joe. Nothing more than acquaintances."

"But he stayed with you often, right? According to a former neighbor, he practically lived with you."

"What neighbor?" She frowned and slowly shook her head. "Detective, I find your questions a tad too personal. You came asking about my daughter, and as you can see, she's alive and doing well. You have no right –"

"Ma'am. I guarantee we have every right. We can do this here or downtown. Either way, you need to answer the question."

"Joe isn't her father if that's what you're thinking." She drew in a breath and glared at him. "He was a shameless son of a bitch who took advantage of me at the lowest point in my life."

"Who is her father?" asked Harper.

She studied their faces. "What difference could it possibly make? Now I think you've gone far enough."

"I'll tell you when we've gone far enough. Now answer the question."

"I don't know."

"Do you remember Mary Kemp? The social worker you went to see some time after you moved out of the apartment?" asked Harper.

"Yes."

"You wouldn't tell her the name of the father either. Why?"

"I don't know who he was, but I hope he's dead. Not a day goes by that I wouldn't love to rip the bastard's heart out. I told Caitlin her daddy is dead. I intend to keep it that way, if you don't mind."

He frowned. She was right, of course. They came to inquire about her daughter and there she was, in the flesh, popping her gum in front of the television. The look on Mann's face reflected his own misgivings. Unless they could prove she was lying, they would have to stop this line of questioning. They would need more information before they could ask for a sample of her DNA. Instead, Harper asked her for Caitlin's date of birth. Just for their records, he assured her.

"May 31, 1990."

He nodded, made a note of it, and started back toward the car when Mann turned on his heels and shot her another question.

"Excuse me?" she asked.

"Caitlin, you reported her missing. Where did you find her? Just curious."

Her eyes darted again. "I … I don't remember." She raised her fingertips to her forehead and shook her head. "I guess Joe had her. That was so long ago. Obviously, she wasn't missing."

The tightness at the corners of her mouth gave Harper added cause for suspicion.

"We apologize for the intrusion ma'am." He lied. She had taken too long to answer and her eyes couldn't fake her uneasiness. "Sorry to bother you." He handed her his business card. "Just in case you think of something."

She forced a smile and returned to the safety of her home.

"Oh, Mrs Lewis," he said. "One more thing. Do you have other children?"

"No. Caitlin is our only child." She lowered her gaze, closed the door, and flipped the lock.

Mann shoved his hands into his pockets and followed his partner back to their car.

"You know, when I was in high school, we had a black lab. Buddy was five years old when he ran away. Loved that dog. Posted notices all over the place trying to find him; flyers, ads in the paper, called the animal shelter two-three times a week every week for two months."

"What's your point?"

"It was a dog, Sam. A big beautiful lab, but he was just a dog. I can tell you exactly everything I did and who I talked to in trying to find him. How is it she can't remember who had Caitlin?"

As they walked toward the car, Harper glanced over his shoulder at the Lewis' home and caught Roxanne watching them from behind the living room curtains. The speed with which she shut the drapes was one more reason to give her a closer look.

"Let's pay a visit to records in the morning; look up Caitlin's birth certificate."

"How's her record going to help identify our victim?" asked Mann.

"I don't know, but now I'm curious." Harper loosened the knot on his tie and leaned his head against the headrest. "So, did you ever find your dog?"

"No. I knew I wouldn't after the first couple of weeks, but it didn't keep me from looking."

21

A towel draped around Abby's slender body. Her hair was still wet; beads of water trickled down her back as she pulled down the covers on the bed. She allowed the towel to drop to the floor as she slipped the nightshirt over her head. On her way back to the bathroom, the snapshot in the white frame sitting on top of her dresser made her stop.

The picture was of a steaming July day in the summer of her twelfth year. The heat of the noon sun and the smell of freshly mowed grass were vivid memories. Her braids had started to come undone and smudges of Massachusetts soil had covered her flamingo pink top. Mr Harper had just finished the yard work. Abby could still see him wiping his brow and the back of his neck with a towel and chugging back a cold glass of water. She also remembered why she had needed that cast on her arm.

Abby returned the towel to the hook behind the bathroom door, lay down on the bed, and studied the picture again. The scrawny blond kid with the goofy grin sitting next to her on the front porch steps made her smile. They had leaned their heads together just before his mother took the picture. Sam Harper had always been her best friend.

As she studied the picture again, the sounds of that July morning came back to life.

"… eight, nine, ten. Here I come ready or not!" Sam had yelled.

From her spot behind the old maple tree at the far end of the yard, she heard Sam call and scamper around as he tried to find her. The game never lasted long once Abby faked a sprint then let him catch her. That Saturday morning had been no different from any other Saturday at the Harper farmhouse. She and Sam were going to play until lunch, and then Mr Harper was going to take them for ice cream. That had been the plan until Sam tackled her to the ground and caused her to fall awkwardly on her arm.

The pain rippled up to her shoulder on the way to the hospital. She'd never forget it or Sam's guilt-ridden face. Later in the day, they were resting on the front porch steps when he gave her a kiss on the cheek. Her injury hadn't been his fault. They were kids doing the things kids do on a hot summer day. Injuries were nothing new to Abby. She was a tomboy. Everyone knew it. That wasn't the first time she was rushed to the emergency room; it wasn't the last time either. But by the end of summer, something had changed between them. Hide and go seek became a child's game they never played again.

They grew up that summer, but she never forgot the innocence of his kiss.

"Damn it." She cursed at herself.

She should have gone to him when Gillies died. The hell if Deanna didn't like her. Sam had always been there for her. Even today when that jerk got fresh with her, she thought. *He had gone to her rescue. Where was she when he needed a friend? She had failed him, but she'd make it up to him somehow.* "I promise," she whispered as she placed the picture down on her nightstand and turned off the light.

22

The day wasn't a complete washout. Quinn's records and Mary Kemp's statement had led them to Roxanne Lewis. Even if it turned out she wasn't the victim's mother, her reactions to their questions were enough to spark suspicion. Her path had crossed with Quinn's at the Harbor View Apartments and they were both staying quiet about something.

Harper slid behind the wheel of his car and tossed a glance at Gillies' CD. It was still on the passenger's seat where he had left it. He promised his father he'd leave it alone, but the Owens case wasn't entirely out of his mind. Abby and the incident with Stewart Martin earlier in the day were also pressing concerns. Harper pulled into traffic, reached for his cell, and dialed her number.

"Are you all right?" he asked her. "He didn't hurt you, did he?"

"Sam." She paused. "Who was that guy?"

"No one. He won't bother you again. I promise. Just make sure you keep your doors locked."

"We haven't talked in a long time."

Harper glanced at his watch. "I know. It's been crazy. What was your rush today?"

"Had to get to the subway terminal. It's a long story."

"I'm listening."

"My boss keeps a locker there. He forgot something he needed for a meeting." She paused for a moment. "Sam? Are you there?"

"Yeah, I'm here." But the mention of the subway terminal reminded him of the many recent times Gillies had gone there; two or three stops a week without reason. Not a day went by without an argument in recent weeks or a need for his partner to borrow money. A twenty here, a ten there. After a while, Harper quit keeping track. He wasn't sure what had sparked the memory, maybe it was the gambling debts listed in Gillies' disk.

Abby's voice suddenly pulled him back into the conversation.

"… didn't want to bother you either. Sam? Are you all right?"

"Sorry. Have a lot on my mind right now. What'd you say?"

"I said I called and left you a message when your partner died. Did you get it?"

Yes, he heard her messages, but that was as far as he took it. "Should've called you back."

"I almost stopped by once, but … Deanna. I didn't want to cause any problems."

"I broke it off, Abby." He glanced up at the streetlight waiting for it to change.

"I've missed you," she said.

Their conversations always led back to some comical event in their childhood. This time was no different then it veered to the subject of Dave Mann. She seemed pleased to know his partner had asked about her and made him promise to give him her number. Now he had one more reason to pay close attention to Detective Mann.

It was late again, as usual, when Harper gathered the mail and the evening newspaper before nosing the car into the garage. Gillies was still on his mind as he walked into the kitchen and tossed the car keys into a basket he kept on the counter. With the newspaper tucked beneath one arm, he shuffled through the day's mail then tossed it aside.

Harper's thoughts were on his late partner's racehorse, Great Fire. What was so special about it for Gillies to bet on him five times in a row? He switched on his computer and let it boot.

While he waited for the connection, he returned to the kitchen and stared into a near empty refrigerator. There was nothing to eat beside whatever sat wrapped in foil near the back of the fridge, the package of cheese, and a stick of butter. He didn't know why he bothered and pushed the door shut. It was after nine, the pains of hunger quit nagging hours ago.

The familiar sound of his computer flickering to life drew his attention. Harper typed in a search for Great Fire. A moment later, several results came up for the great fires in history; Chicago, London, Rome. He narrowed his search to racehorses. There was no horse past or present by that name nor could he find any races to match the dates Gillies had listed. He stared into the monitor as he rubbed the tightness that had settled around his neck. Finding no pattern to the entries or clues to their meaning, he shut it down. The only thing that made sense to him now was a hot shower.

Steam curled up around him. The strain of the day seemed to dissolve with every pulsing jet of water that pressed against him. He had just started to relax when the hammering sound of water against his head made him flash back to the rain then zoomed in on Gillies' face. Harper pushed back, away from the water's flow and wiped off his face. The rapid, shallowness of his breathing was unexpected. How long would it take before the simplest things would stop reminding him of their last angry words? The uneasiness he had felt about the bartender had surfaced again along with a fierce craving for a Scotch and soda.

Howard Street was quiet tonight. Similar to the night Harper and Gillies waited for Mellow. He eased into the same spot across the street from the Roving Dog Saloon and killed the engine. With one hand pressed over his mouth, he waited and gathered his thoughts. The plan was easy enough; talk with the bartender, see what else he knew about Owens.

The rains had washed away the evidence of his partner's death from the sidewalk. Inside, the Dog had the trappings of *déjà vu*. Casing a room was second nature to him like looking both ways before crossing a street. Chuck was standing at his usual place behind the bar talking with one of his customers. With the exception of the late Mr Mellow, an identical assortment of patrons dotted the establishment. Lifeless eyes glanced up at him when he walked in then quickly lost interest. The look of discontent on their faces told him this dive was the best life had to offer. He didn't know what empty desires brought them here every night or why they stayed for the final call. It didn't matter; he hadn't come to console them. He had his own problems and reasons for being here. Even if the bartender wouldn't talk, at least the Scotch would let him forget his miserable life until he opened his eyes in the morning.

Chuck tossed him a nod.

"Scotch and soda," said Harper.

"Say, you're that cop, aren't you? The one who was here a few weeks ago. Gillies' partner."

Good. Harper wouldn't have to remind him of their last conversation. Now all he had to do was find a way to get him to talk about Owens.

While Harper waited for his drink, he caught a glimpse of his pale features in the mirror behind the bar. His face was drawn and the circles under his eyes told of a string of sleepless nights. Gillies, his father, Deanna. Each one had drained his spirit with the sting of betrayal. He turned away and switched his attention to the picture gallery next to the mirror along the back wall.

"Chuck. That's your name, right?" Harper asked the bartender as he nodded toward the photographs. "Navy days?"

Chuck rolled up his sleeve to expose his anchor tattoo. "Got this in '62. Vietnam, Pacific Fleet. Some of the roughest and best times I ever had." He straightened the two photographs that were hanging askew then reached for the third. "This one's always falling down." He took the third photograph and slipped it beneath the counter.

Harper let him talk about the war, his return home, and life as a barkeeper. They talked about Gillies too. Chuck claimed he didn't know him very well. Just a regular guy who stopped by once in a while for a drink and a little inside information on some of the street scum.

"Gillies ever talk to you about betting on the ponies?" asked Harper.

"Him? Are you kidding? Biggest tightwad I've ever seen. He never paid for anything. Not around here anyway," he said, giving the towel a toss over his shoulder. "Didn't strike me as the betting type."

Two drinks into a conversation and Harper had nothing to show for it. Bartenders chat, but they don't tell. He was as tight-lipped as a priest in confession – the poor man's shrink. What had he really expected to gain from it besides a couple of stiff drinks that were going down a little too well? His glass was half-full when he started a tab and ordered a third. Decidedly, the only way to find out about Owens was to bring him up himself.

"Yeah, Owens used to come in here all the time," said Chuck, "but he made himself scarce after you blew Mellow away."

"That night, did you see Owens the night we were here?"

"Yeah, couple of hours or so before you showed up."

"Like Mellow. You were supposed to call us next time Owens showed. Why didn't you hold him?"

Chuck pulled down the towel from his shoulder and wiped the clean surface in front of him. "Look I'm not a cop, all right? Owens got into a scrape down by the docks. Whoever he pissed off beat the crap out of him. He tried to come in here looking for another fight."

"With who?"

"Anybody. The guy's a thug. Hell, I made him leave. Didn't need any more problems with Mellow sitting in the back booth. Those two hated each other." Chuck lowered his glance, tossed the towel under the counter, and nodded toward the men sitting at the other end of the bar. "I've got other customers. Whistle when you need a refill."

Chuck walked away a little too fast and Harper had to wonder what it was about Owens that made Chuck squirm and dodge the question. He gave his glass a gentle shake and watched the ice twirl around through his drink. Chuck was wrong about Gillies never making a bet. Maybe Gillies' gambling habit was none of his business but Owens was, or at least he had been, until Gillies decided to take a chance with his life and lost.

23

His contact would show up any minute Owens assured himself. He inhaled the earthy smell of more rain and heard the rumbling of a distant roll of thunder. The sidewalks were still wet from the last downpour an hour before. He paced in and out from the shadow of the nightclub doorway and glance down at an empty street. He stopped, cupped his hand around his lighter, touched the flame to his cigarette, and squinted the smoke from his eyes.

"This deal," he muttered to himself, "is it, Jimmy boy. If ya don't do it now, won't ever happen. That's for damned sure."

He crossed his arms and pressed them close to his chest to keep from shaking. He was getting too old for the game. He promised himself after this deal was done he'd head south. He wouldn't pack and he wouldn't look back. None of the bastards who wanted a piece of him would ever get it. The incident on the highway four nights before didn't register at first. *Why should it? People were always speeding around that curve.* The driver who lost control and rammed into the side of Owens' car sent him careening off onto the shoulder and against the metal railing. *So what?* He'd seen it happen a million times, but when the same car eased down his street later that evening, then showed up again two nights later parked outside the his favorite pool hall, he knew what was up. The guy with the seven-inch blade waiting for him behind the hall confirmed his suspicions. Someone wanted him dead and he wasn't going to stop and ask who or why.

Owens reminded himself he could have whipped the young punk with the blade if he had wanted to. Twenty years ago, he would have without hesitation. The little ass was lucky all he wanted was out.

He thought of the warmest place he had ever known. "Alabama." It was home to everything he had known before moving to Avondale in his early teens. "Always wanted to go back down to A-la-ba-ma." The words dodged past his chattering teeth.

Three in the morning brought a lull to the night's street activities. Except for the two cars that raced through the nearby intersection and bottomed out on the lower section of road, Zucker Street was deserted. Even the whores had abandoned their posts by the curb in exchange for a warm, dry bed. Leaning against the chilled limestone façade of the Kitten Klub, he cowered away from the wind. He took another drag from his cigarette and exhaled in short, shallow puffs. Owens allowed the curls of smoke to hit his face while he stomped circulation back into his feet. After a minute, he continued to pace. Three steps in one direction. He stopped – turned. Three steps back.

"Where the hell is he?" He clenched his teeth. "Ten after. If ya don't show …" He flipped the butt onto the sidewalk. Raw nerves triggered the obligatory look over his shoulders. It wasn't the heat sparking his fear. He was used to looking out for cops; he had done it all his life. Living in the slums of Avondale did that to kids. Hustling and breaking the law was a way of life. By his late teens, every cop on the beat knew him.

No, he thought, *this was a hell of a lot more than a bunch of cops lookin' to make their quotas*. The tightness in his chest was thanks to the thugs who were waiting for the minute he let down his guard.

"Mellow knockin' off that damned cop, nothin' but a stupid-ass move. Heat's everywhere now." He rammed his hands into his pockets as he muttered to himself. "Hell, wasn't even near the goddamned dive," he said, above a whisper. Owens was taking a risk coming out into the open, but the deal Di Napoli offered was too good to be true. "Maybe too damned good."

He had no choice. He'd have to chill for a while, take his cut, and get the hell out of town before anyone noticed. Owens glanced up one side of the street and then the other when he heard the low rumbling of a broken muffler.

The fenders of the 1988 black Camero had rusted beyond repair. Two holes remained on the driver's side door from the bullets intended for Di Napoli. They were a constant reminder for him to keep his guard up. He gripped his Ruger and leaned across the front seat to open the passenger door. Getting the door handle fixed was one of those things he didn't have to time to do.

Owens stomped his feet twice and turned his back to the wind again before getting in.

"'Bout damned time, motherfucker," Owens mumbled, then after a pause snapped. "Where the hell ya been? I've been standing out here freezing my ass off for damned near an hour. Damn, didn't think ya'd ever show up. Ya're lucky I waited for you."

Di Napoli turned his head. The streetlights cast a shimmering reflection on the wet asphalt making this part of town look cleaner than it was beneath the surface. "Like it makes any difference to me. You want the information or not?"

"Yeah. Yeah. Come on. Move this damned piece of shit."

De Napoli pointed to the empty stretch of road ahead. "It's the middle of the night, not a soul in sight, and this fine heap of metal ain't goin' nowhere until you cough up your end of the bargain." He aimed his Ruger at Owens' chest. He frisked him for the feel of a weapon.

"I'm clean, man."

"I've heard that one before. All right. Let's have it." He focused on Owens' hand as he slipped it inside his jacket. *Just how fast could he return fire*, he wondered, *if Owens surprised him with the barrel of a gun instead of the money?* "Easy. Just do it nice and easy."

"I'm just gettin' your dough." Owens pulled out a thick brown envelope. "Here, man. It's all there, tens and twenties just like ya wanted. Count it if ya want."

There was no need to count it. He had Owens' fingerprints on the envelope; that's all he wanted. "I'll take your word for it. Open the glove compartment," said Di Napoli. "That's it, drop it in."

"All right, ya got what ya want, let's go already." Owens growled as he glanced over his shoulder again and tapped a finger on his knee. "What are ya waitin' for? Drive!"

Di Napoli pressed his lips. His movements were slow and deliberate as he kicked the car into gear. "You know the warehouse on Plum Street?"

"Yeah, yeah. Right there on the docks, man. Next to the water tower."

"That's it. A week from tonight, dock thirty-two at the south west corner of the building."

"Next week? What the hell?" Owens demanded. "I can't wait a week. I need the dough, man! I told ya I gotta have it now!"

Di Napoli had driven six blocks when he gripped the steering wheel and slammed his foot on the brakes. The forced tossed loose objects onto the floorboards.

"I ain't playing games," he hissed. "Get out."

"Nah, come on. Don't do this, man. Hell, ya got the last of my bread and everythin'."

"You're nothing around here – a has-been." Di Napoli pointed an accusing finger at Owens' face. "You've got one last chance and this is it. Word is you're marked. You're dead and don't know it."

"Who told ya that?"

"What'd you do? Skim the top off a deal? Who'd you piss off?"

"Nobody. Whadya know about it?" Owens demanded.

"Someone wants to see you dead. So who is it?"

"Beats the shit out of me." Owens frowned and looked away.

"They probably will and me along with you if they catch us together. You don't have a say in any of this, *capicce*? I'm taking all the risks, so you keep your eyes and ears open and your mouth shut."

"It's just a bunch of punks. No one's going to mess with me." Owens rolled his eyes.

"That so? Tell you what, let's test your theory. How 'bout if I throw you out as bait and see who grabs you first." Di Napoli met his glare.

"Be cool, man. Jesus, be cool." Owens yanked at his collar.

"Well? What's it going to be?"

"I'm in, man. I'm in. Would ya just get movin'?"

Rain had collected along the uneven surfaces of the road and swished under the weight of the car. Owens was still fidgeting, looking over his shoulder out the back window when they arrived at the abandoned church where he lived.

"Two in the morning," said Di Napoli. "Dock thirty-two. You're a minute late, you're out of the game. Got it?"

Owens nodded

"Go on, get out."

"Wait a minute. Who's the contact?"

"I'll be in touch," said Di Napoli.

"This better not be a set up." Owens grabbed Di Napoli's coat sleeve in a fist.

"Hey! Get your filthy mitt off me!" He pushed him away. "You think I'm crazy or something? I'm a businessman, just like you. Now get the hell out of my car before someone spots us."

Owens had barely gotten out of the car and slammed the door shut when Di Napoli raced away. As Owens gradually grew smaller in his rear view mirror, Di Napoli reached for his cell. "Captain? It's set. Yeah, have it right here."

24

Aside from a pounding headache, a parched throat, and the sour taste of booze in his mouth, Harper woke up with Roxanne's face etched on his mind and the swift way in which she had drawn the curtains. A mental note of the day ahead formed while he ripped the dry cleaner's bag from one of his shirts and finished dressing.

Was it fear or shock that registered in her eyes at the mention of her former name? Whichever it was, his question triggered a reaction. Why? Her daughter was alive. He and Mann both saw the girl. She could fake a smile, but not her composure. Until Baby Doe's DNA results came in and they had more facts, he could only assume she was guilty of something.

In Narcotics, Harper never had to sift through someone's past to get to the truth, just their garbage and dirty laundry. Piecing together a case without trace would take weeks, maybe months. Harper swept a glance at the red numbers glowing on his alarm clock and immediately thought of the stack of cold cases waiting back at the office. If he left now, he would have a good hour to himself.

Harper waited for his partner to hang up his coat, get his coffee, and lumber back into the office. "Quarter past eight. You're late."

Mann tapped his watch. "Nah, I'm good."

"Here."

"What's this?" Mann asked, taking the slip of paper from Harper's hand.

"Abby's phone number. She asked me to give it to you."

A grin tugged across his partner's face. He stared at the note then looked up. "What's the matter?"

Harper leaned forward and watched Mann slip the note inside his wallet and return it to his back pocket. "Abby's a grown woman with a mind of her own, but she's like family to me. Do you understand what I'm saying?"

Without saying a word, Mann cleared his desk of the previous day's mess; the empty pop cans, candy wrappers, and wadded pieces of paper before meeting Harper's gaze. "Yeah. She's like a sister. I remember. What's it going to take to get you to trust me?"

The first order of the day was to locate the girl's birth certificate and then talk with Quinn, but the Records Office wouldn't open for another hour.

"You know," said Mann. "I've been in Homicide going on six years and I can't remember the last time I was so sure of something that turned out to be this wrong. Every bit of information we have led right to Roxanne's doorstep."

"Don't kid yourself." Harper took a drink of his coffee. "She knows more than she's letting on. We're not taking her off our list until the DNA tells us we're wrong."

"But you saw the girl. Wasn't that the point of going to see her?"

"Yeah, initially, but I'm curious about the 911. Roxanne may not have anything to do with the remains, but all we have is her word that Caitlin is her daughter."

A worn path on the black and white tiled floor leading into the Records Office and its cheap wood paneling projected a cool reception for those needing service. The counter in the tiny lobby ran the width of the room, steps away from the main entrance. By design, it ensured visitors stayed in their proper place. A lean, straight-faced clerk immediately greeted the detectives. The clump of peppered hair she wore tightly pulled back and pinned near the crown of her head appeared as unremitting as the permanent crease between her eyes.

"Yes?" she asked, through a pair of thin lips. Her mouth barely moved, then quickly snapped shut and dipped down into tight little pockets at either corner. She seemed indifferent as she reached for the slip of paper from Harper's hand with Roxanne's name and Caitlin's birth date. It was obvious she was neither impressed nor intimidated by their badges; a clear message of how little clout the detectives had when it came to the documents kept in this office. Several minutes later, she came back with two slips of paper in her hand.

"Here you go, Detective. Caitlin and Britni Ewing born, May 31, 1990, to Roxanne Ewing – no father mentioned." The woman's tone reflected her disapproval.

"What did you say? Caitlin *and* Britni?"

"Yes, apparently they're twins."

Mann rolled his eyes and sneered under his breath. "Surprise, surprise. She lied. Imagine that."

"Are you sure?" Harper questioned the clerk.

She pressed her lips into tight rims again and narrowed her eyes. "Detective, our records are impeccable."

"I certainly hope so. I'll need a copy of those." Harper pushed the documents back across the counter to her as he flipped open his cell phone and dialed the Captain.

"We just got our first break. The Lewis woman had twin girls. Birth date matches Baby Doe's approximate age. We'll have her in interrogation within the hour. Get Carter to meet us there with his kit."

The visit to Alvin Quinn would have to wait.

25

The camera inside Interrogation Room 1 captured Roxanne Lewis's face. Her feet were flat on the floor, hands folded in front of her on top of the metal table in the center of an otherwise barren room. Her shoulders were slightly slumped forward, a pensive gaze stared down at the table, concern shadowed her face. Slender fingers gingerly dabbed at her eyes. She returned a pair of tightly folded hands to the table surface and continued to wait.

Harper, Mann, Captain Holloway, and Kay Terrill, the assistant prosecuting attorney, studied Roxanne from the other side of the two-way mirror.

Harper observed the shake of her hand and the way she raised it to the necklace she wore around her neck. She held on to whatever was dangling from it. "That social worker we talked to is convinced Roxanne was a victim of circumstances."

"Based on what?" asked Mann. "A one-sided account of a sixteen-year-old run away?"

The Kemp woman had admitted she had been an impressionable young social worker eager to save the world. Maybe that's all it was, an impression of innocence. But was it innocence or guilt that kept Roxanne from accepting Kemp's offer to help? Then again, why hadn't the social worker pushed to know the fate of the baby? Sixteen years after the fact, Lewis' omission of the truth painted a different scenario. At this point, any thoughts she might be innocent were premature.

"What do you think?" Holloway asked Terrill.

"They all look trapped at this point," she said. "Let's see what she has to offer."

"This ought to shock the truth out of her." Harper looked at the Captain and waved the file folder he had in his hand before he pushed open the interrogation room door.

Roxanne bolted straight up in the chair and quickly slipped her hands onto her lap.

"Why am I here?" she asked. Her gaze followed them into the room.

Harper motioned for her to wait. He draped his jacket across the back of a chair, rolled up his sleeves, and took a seat. He switched on the tape recorder. "April 1, 2006, ten fifty-two a.m., Chandler Police Headquarters, Interrogation Room 1. Cross-examination of Roxanne Lewis. Present are Detective Sam Harper, Detective Dave Mann, and Roxanne Lewis. Case number J1480." He looked straight into her eyes. "For the record, state your full name, address, and age."

"Roxanne Gail Lewis, 1203 Pigeon Road, Chandler, Massachusetts. I'm thirty-two years old."

Mann walked across the room and leaned against the wall next to a small grated window. "Can I get you anything to drink?" he asked her. "Water, soft drink, coffee?"

"No. No thank you." Her voice strained for composure. "Why am I here?" she asked again.

"You weren't completely honest with us, were you?" asked Harper.

"I beg your pardon?"

"We know."

"You know what? I answered your questions. I don't understand why I'm even here."

"You're here to tell us about your daughter."

"Caitlin? You said you were investigating a murder," she said.

Harper removed the copies of the birth certificates from a folder and placed them in front of her.

Her eyes didn't open wide with surprise as Harper had expected, nor did they seem frightened or anxious. A frown wrinkled her brow. She looked more confused than afraid at the sight of her daughters' birth certificates.

"Why didn't you tell us?"

"Tell you what?"

"You had twins."

"I ..." Her mouth was agape. "I didn't think it mattered. I thought you were looking for Caitlin."

"You lied when I asked you about other children."

"Caitlin is my only child," she insisted. "Britni was adopted a few days after she was born. She hasn't been mine for years."

"The girls are twins, right?" asked Harper.

"Yes, but –"

"Caitlin and Britni."

"Yes." She lowered her gaze. "I just don't see what Britni has to do with anything."

"She's the focus of our investigation. I suggest you rethink your answers from here on out."

Tears quickly welled in her eyes. "Britni? I didn't lie. Just didn't know what you wanted, I still don't. Britni was days old the last time I saw her. What's happened? Why are you investigating her?"

Harper drew in a breath. Her questions were logical and to the point, but her next reaction would say more to him than anything she could vocalize. "We don't think Britni ever made it out of your apartment. We found the remains of an infant entombed in one of the walls of 1C. Your apartment, correct?"

Her eyes grew wide, her breathing became shallow, and her glance darted for answers. "What are you saying?"

Harper removed the ME's photograph of the tiny bones from the file. "We have every reason to believe these are the remains of your daughter."

"It – it can't be. You're lying."

"Your DNA will decide it one way or another."

Mann looked past them at the two-way mirror and motioned to those standing behind it. "Tell Carter we're ready for him."

"Oh my God." She brought a hand up to her mouth to stifle a cry. "How?" she asked above a whisper.

Harper returned his attention to the file and pulled out another picture for her to look at. "Does this mean anything to you?"

This time she looked confused as she studied the enlarged

picture carefully. "My medallion," she said, letting the photograph slip from her grip. She immediately reached for the necklace around her neck. "I lost it years ago. I replaced it with this one," she said, pulling the necklace out for Harper to see. "Where did you find it?"

Carter walked in with his kit and stood in front of her. "Open please." He swabbed the inner lining of her cheek, slipped the swab into a protective case, and motioned to Harper. "I'll let you know as soon as it's ready."

"You lived at the Harbor View Apartments between March and June, 1990," Harper continued. "Is that correct?"

She nodded.

"State your answer for the record."

"Yes, that's right."

"And you moved out after three months on June third. What happened in the days leading up to June third?"

"I don't know what you want from me. I was drunk most of the time. That part of my life is a blur," she cried.

"Maybe this will clear up your memory. Murder carries a death sentence in Massachusetts. There is no statute of limitation on murder and right now you're our primary suspect." Harper paused hoping the fact would settle in. "Did you kill Britni?"

"No!"

The firmness in her voice was as unwavering as it was unexpected.

"I couldn't! How could you even think it?"

"What happened?" he asked. "We know the neighbors complained about the babies' crying. What'd you do? Smother her with her blanket?"

"No!" Tears welled as she shook her head nervously.

"Is that how it happened?" Harper rose to his feet and leaned toward her. "We found the blanket. Is that what you did? You were drunk and couldn't stand her any more. That's it, isn't it?"

"Yes – no!"

"Couldn't take the constant crying. Got on your nerves, right? It would me. Who could blame you? Listening to her infernal crying all day long."

"No! Stop it!" she yelled.

"First you smothered her, then you wrapped her up in her own blanket. Am I close?"

"No. Why are you doing this?" she screamed.

"Come on Roxanne, admit it," said Harper. "You had more reason to get rid of her than anyone else. The last thing you wanted was a baby to look after."

"I didn't do it," she wailed.

"Then who did?"

"I don't know!"

A deafening silence swallowed them.

She bit down on her lip, shook her head again, and whispered: "All these years I thought she was alive! How could you think I would hurt her?"

"How did Britni die? Roxanne, answer the question. What happened on the last day you saw your daughter alive?"

"I don't know," she cried.

"The death penalty is looking you right between the eyes." Harper pressed on. "Better to go down for your own crime than someone else's. Is that what you're doing? Covering up for someone else?"

Her eyes burned with hatred. She leaned forward and pounded her fists onto the medical examiner's photograph. "No. I want you to find whoever did this!"

"We will." Harper stepped back. "When you tell us what you know. We can treat you like our only witness or a suspect. What's it going to be?"

She remained silent.

"Either way, you start talking now."

"I can't tell you what I don't know."

"Oh, you know," he said. "You just don't realize it. From the beginning. Let's start with you and Joe. How did you two meet?"

She threw her head back and closed her eyes briefly before letting her gaze fall back onto him. They seemed inert, stripped of the spark Harper had seen in them seconds before.

"I was sixteen," she began, "living on the streets when he found me. I should have never gone with him. Would have been better off dead."

"You said he wasn't the father of your girls. Who was it then? A high school sweetheart? Who?"

"Hardly." She looked away from him. "What difference does it make now?"

"Every difference in the world if he had anything to do with Britni's death. A baby died. *Your* baby and someone covered up her death in the lowest, most heinous way imaginable. You want to be part of that cover up?"

"I'm not."

"Then who is the father?"

A tear trickled down her cheek when she closed her eyes; she swallowed hard. "I was raped," she whispered.

Harper swept a glance at Mann's then back to her. "Who was it? Did you report it?"

"No."

"Why not?"

"Joe would have killed me. I couldn't," she said, still unwilling to look at him. She stifled her cry with the back of her hand.

"You were a minor, Roxanne. Where was your family? Why didn't you go to the pol–"

"He was a cop! All right?" She scowled through clenched teeth. Her hands slammed open onto the table. The anger in her voice rose above his. "He was a goddamned cop. That's all I know! One of yours, Detective."

"Is that what he told you?"

"No."

"Then how do you know?"

"I just do."

"Prove it."

"I can't."

"I don't believe you."

"Yeah, right. Like that shocks me. He was a friend of Joe's. You find Joe and make him tell you. The bastard pimped me out to him and never bothered to let me in on their little secret – even after I was pregnant. The son of a bitch liked little girls. Who the hell was going to believe me, a runaway? You answer that one and we'll both know!"

The weight of silence settled over them again.

She turned away and Harper backed off. Mann mumbled something under his breath, crossed his arms, and turned his sight out through the dirty glass panes of the grated window.

Her allegation ripped through the speakers behind the two-way mirror. "Son of a bitch," Holloway muttered under his breath and shook his head. "If this gets out." His eyes focused on Roxanne's face. Her anger was too convincing. There was nothing about her to imply she was lying.

"Lou, listen," said Terrill, "rape is hard enough to substantiate in a recent case. She can't prove she was raped and you know it."

"She won't have to."

"Not after all these years," Terrill assured him. "If she didn't report it, there's no proof or evidence it ever happened. She certainly can't prove the man was a police officer."

"Jesus, don't you get it? She won't need evidence. I can see the headlines now: A sixteen-year-old has Chandler cop's child." He choked back on the rage and the urge to ram his fist through the two-way mirror. "God damn it."

"Obviously she had intercourse, but rape?" Terrill crossed her arms and studied Roxanne's image on the monitor. "That's going to be a tough one to prove at this stage."

"Rape or not, she was underage!" he growled. "You know as well as I do how the game is played. Just yell dirty cop. The minute the press gets a taste of this, they'll set up the guillotine and pull the goddamned lever. No questions asked. They'll start at the top and go straight down. By the time they're done, there won't be a man left on the force."

26

"Last call." Chuck switched off the red neon lights outside the Roving Dog Saloon. He gave the place a quick glance as he slipped behind the counter and finished rinsing the glasses he had been washing. No one budged or made a move for the door. He stacked the glasses in rows of threes before glancing up again.

"Hey!" he yelled. "I'm closing in twenty minutes."

One man looked at his watch, drained the last of his beer, and shuffled toward the door. The couple sitting in the back booth ignored his announcement. The old man slumped forward on the bar holding his head up with the heel of his hand had a half beer to go.

"Hey, pops." Chuck rapped hard on the bar. "Better call it a night. You all right?"

The old man nodded.

"Need a cab?"

"You payin' for it?" the old man slurred his words and waved him away. "I'll be fine." He tipped the long neck back and emptied it. "See ya."

"Yeah. See you." Chuck tossed the towel over his shoulder and followed him to the entrance. He watched the old timer stagger out and then locked the door behind him. The couple in back continued to nurse their drinks.

"Hey!" he yelled again. "Ten more minutes you two." He gathered the open bottles of whiskey and bourbon and returned them to the mirrored shelf. The old photograph hanging askew on the wall behind the bar caught his attention. A careful nudge straightened it for a moment before it tipped into a slant again. He

144

wiped the glass clean and briefly studied it. It was the one of him and his buddies on the S.S. Wisconsin.

The Navy had promised a chance to travel, but his tour had consisted of countless months on a ship cramped in close quarters with fifteen hundred men with nowhere to go except into battle. He was nineteen, impressionable, and a million miles from home. He had no dreams before going to Nam and fewer hopes when he returned. Depression had taken its toll. At twenty-four, he was back in the States; a drunk, a killer, and sitting in prison for a crime he hadn't intended.

He never saw the man step off the curb. It was a hit and run from something he couldn't remember. He didn't belong in a place where a wrong word or an unintentional glance was reason for any number of untold atrocities. Where men doled out trust to a worthy few and friendships were bartered for like cigarettes. It was a glitch in his past that was always one step ahead of his future. "Damned hypocrites," he muttered.

Chuck could never go back to who he was before Vietnam. The unusual became the normal and the normal was bizarre by any standard. He sealed his fate by accepting the abnormality of his life and used it to his advantage. Chandler, he had learned, was full of cons looking for new connections and the Dog was the perfect front for easy money.

"All right!" Chuck hollered. "The place is closed, you two," he shouted again to the couple making out near the back. "Go find yourselves a room." He waited by the door for them, then locked up again, dimmed the lights, and poured himself a shot of bourbon.

He had just given his thumb a lick before counting a stack of dollar bills from the cash box when a noise in the storage room made him cut a look in that direction. Slowly, he reached for his gun in the drawer. Edging closer toward the storage room door, he pressed his body against the wall, and waited. He quietly cocked the gun and allowed the intruder to step into the bar. "Hold it right there."

"Holy shit! It's me, man." Shock flashed across Owens' face. He hadn't expected to feel the hard barrel of the handgun press against his right kidney. Instinctively his arms went up in the air. "What the hell is wrong with ya? Ya old fool. Put that damned thing down before ya hurt someone."

"That's the point, isn't it?" asked Chuck. "I couldn't have asked for a more perfect situation. I shoot an intruder in self-defense. The city will hail me as a hero for ridding it of another piece of shit."

"Quit screwin' around. Put the piece down, will ya?"

"What the hell are you doing in here?" Chuck pressed the gun harder against Owens' back while he frisked him.

"Had to see you about somethin'."

"Is that right? What's with the sneaking around?"

"Shit, your back door was unlocked. How the hell did I know ya'd try to shoot me?" He glanced over his shoulder then inched closer to the bar. "Put that damned thing away. I'm clean."

"You're either the bravest son of a bitch I've ever known or the dumbest. Sneaking in here like that. You're full of smart moves these days, aren't you?"

"Sure as hell didn't think ya'd go crazy. Guess if I have to die, it might as well be here. At least it's dry," he said rubbing warmth onto his arms. "Better than the gutter out back."

"Must be your lucky night at that," Chuck sneered. "Only thing keeping me from blowing your head off is not wanting to clean your fucking brains off my floor. That, and the fact that I'm tired and want to go home. Get out of here."

"No, need to talk. We got problems."

"*We* don't got problems and you and me got nothing to talk about. The cops are after you and I don't want to be anywhere close when they take you down."

"See. That's what I always liked about ya." Owens stepped up to the bar and took a seat. "Ya're so damned … what's the word?" Owens narrowed his eyes. He took a cigarette from the pack, placed it between his lips, and raised his lighter to it as he searched for the right definition. "Perceptive. That's it." He tilted his head back and blew out the smoke. "Perceptive. Yeah, ya're still damn sharp for an old geezer. Only one problem. Story I hear on the street is the cops are lookin' for a baby killer. Know any?"

"Nasty business."

"What are we goin' to do about it?" Owens placed his money on the bar. "Give me a long neck, will ya?" He took another drag. "They say Harper's the one in charge of it."

"Yeah, I know, and he's one anxious pup eager to please the brass. Get his credibility back after Mellow wasted his partner. You know, Harper blames you for that cop's death. He's been asking about you."

"I wasn't anywhere near the bastard when Mellow blew him away."

"No one was supposed to be."

"What are ya sayin'?" Owens narrowed his eyes. "Ya put a contract on that cop? Ya stupid ass."

"You really think it matters to Harper who blew him away or why? He wants you so bad he can taste it." Chuck smirked. "All he needs to know is when and where he can find you."

"I had nothin' to do with the cop or the kid. Only reason he'd come after me is if someone ratted on me. That wouldn't have crossed your mind, would it?"

"Harper doesn't need any help from me. When he puts two and two together, you'll be as good as dead."

Owens placed his elbows on the bar and leaned in. "The hell he will. Like to see him make it stick. You and me both know what went down that night with the kid. What I want to know is just why the cops think I did it?"

"Harper's gotten to Quinn, you moron. Just how long do you think it'll be before a smart kid like Harper figures things out?"

"Not if we get him first."

"Where do you get this 'we'? *We* ain't doing nothing together. Least of all kill another cop."

Owens took a swig of his beer. Chuck didn't have to tell him about Harper's determination. The dick had been a prickly thorn in his side at every turn waiting for him to screw up. He had managed to stay out of sight until Mellow got stupid.

"I wouldn't be surprised if they haul Quinn in for questioning," said Chuck. "He's probably over there right now spilling his guts about the whole damned thing. And if I know him, his version is going to place you smack in the middle of it."

"He can talk all he wants. Cops'll have to prove it."

"My money's on Harper. He'll want to believe Quinn's story. He'll look at this thing from every angle to make sure you're guilty. Proof is, he's not even in Narcotics any more and he's still after your sorry ass, isn't he?"

Owens didn't respond.

"Hell you never know. It's not like the old days when fingerprint and blood type was all they could work with. They're solving old cases all the time."

"They got nothing on me."

"The cops have everything down to the size of your shorts on record. Anything you left behind can place you at the scene and convict you. The way you flip your cigarette butts around, you can bet they're gonna find one."

"No way."

"Who's to say Quinn didn't let one slip inside that wall? Hell you lived there. Your hair was all over the kid and hair don't go away. DNA, Owens, all your shit's on record."

Owens looked at the cigarette smoldering in his hand and half believed he might have done just that – left a butt behind. "Doesn't prove I did it."

"You really stupid enough to think Harper needs more?" Chuck smirk. "He's gonna to press your sorry ass and iron out your wrinkles."

"Give me another one." Owens shoved the long neck away. His mind raced. The incident happened sixteen years ago. Things didn't seem so clear any more. "I never touched the kid and ya know it."

"And who's gonna believe you? You got a rap sheet as long as the Massachusetts Turnpike. Harper will be one happy prick when he sends you down for murder."

"Nah, the man won't let it come to that. He's got more to lose than anyone." *The man*, as Owens called their silent partner, had protected Chuck and Owens in return for their silence.

"Like hell. He's royally pissed. Ask Quinn. He got a call from the man when they found the kid's bones. You think he's going to lift a finger to help you after your stupid threat?"

"He knows I didn't mean it. Pissed me off, that's all. He broke his promise. Said he'd keep the heat off me. Damned near landed me in jail."

"You're such a fuck up. The man's not one to be questioned."

"Shit, I wouldn't have ratted on him. I was just pissed. I told him so."

"Well, you're screwed now. The deal's off. Now you've got Harper on your ass again and no one to protect you from Homicide." A wry grin pulled at a corner of Chuck's mouth. "Wouldn't want to be you."

"What makes ya so damned sure about any of this?" asked Owens.

"You may not have pulled the trigger, but your name was on Harper's mind when the cop went down and that's all he remembers. Are you stupid enough to think he's going to stop to ask any questions? Jesus. He's going to come after you with everything he's got and nail your ass to the wall."

Owens gulped his beer. Chuck was right about his record and he was right about the cops wanting him on drug charges, but killing babies wasn't in him. He was uneasy about Chuck's arrogant grin, but things were starting to fall into place; the hit and run, the thug at the pool hall with the seven-inch blade. "It's you, isn't it?"

"Me what?"

"Ya hired a thug to kill me, didn't ya?"

"Hell I wouldn't waste my money. I'd shoot you myself."

Images flooded Owens' mind. Of course, Chuck would do anything to protect the man. Owens gripped the bottle by its neck and slammed it against the bar shattering the bottom off and exposing sharp jagged edges of glass. "The car, your friend with the knife, ya knew where I'd be. Ya couldn't kill me, so now ya're gonna frame me for the kid's murder."

"Hey! You were there and in on the deal like the rest of us. Can I help how it comes out?"

"Ya son of a bitch. Ya're not goin' to get away with it," said Owens. "This is your mess. Ya killed the kid and left it up to that idiot Quinn to get rid of the body. He's the one who fucked up and he's gonna pay for it."

"Who do you think Quinn's more afraid of, you or me?"

Owens had to think about Chuck's implication. Quinn had no sense of his own. "He's not smart enough to plan his day. What kind of bullshit did ya feed him?"

"The kind that will plant you six feet under and get you out of my sight."

Owens rushed to his feet. The stool shot back and slid across the floor. "Ya son of a bitch. I'm gonna –"

Chuck cocked his gun and shoved it hard into Owens' face. "You're gonna do what?"

27

Harper leaned against the wall, fingered the change in his pocket, and kept an eye on Roxanne. She was still sitting at the table in the middle of the room trying to collect her composure. It was time to continue; he took a step forward. His thoughts lingered on her accusation. The alleged rape by a cop had added an unexpected twist to the baby's murder case. A cop, sixteen years ago. The current force was made up mostly of men and women around his age or younger. That fact alone would eliminate a third of the active men as suspects.

"Who was it, Roxanne?"

She looked up and scowled. "I told you all ready. I don't know."

"Color of hair, eyes, height. You have to remember something."

"Why don't you ask me what he did to me? I still have the scars." Her face contorted with anger.

Had she pushed the memory out of her mind like the constant Gillies flashbacks he wished he could stop?

"Give us something to work with – anything," he told her.

"What difference does it make now?"

Harper raised a hand to his brow to soothe the tightness that had rippled across it. There was no bending the laws, especially not by a cop. "You were a minor, Roxanne. Wrong any way you cut it."

She closed her eyes and took a deep breath as if trying to cleanse herself of the burden. "He was careful to not let me see his face. All I remember is his car. Got a glimpse of it on the first night. White Mustang – still smelled new."

"What about him? Start with his age."

"I don't know, more than twenty less than fifty."

"Great," he said, unable to disguise the annoyance in his tone.

She lowered her gaze.

"Just focus on the facts, all right? Think back to that single moment and tell me what you see."

"A moment?" She huffed and shook her head. "He raped me three times." She paused. "I was four months pregnant the last time he called for me."

"What do you mean … called for you? Were you prostituting yourself?"

"No!"

"Then what do you mean he called for you?"

"Joe. He made Joe take me to him and blindfolded me before … The guy had something on him. I was the pay back. Guess the idea of his child growing in me finally turned him off; the bastard. He quit after that."

"Then he knew."

"Of course he knew. He had to. I was starting to show."

"Did he ever suspect that you knew who he was?"

"No. Why?"

"If he thought you'd rat him out, it would have given him motive and opportunity to kill the girls. You're lucky he didn't go after you too." Harper turned and looked in the direction of the two-way mirror. He wondered what Holloway was thinking. This wasn't a random act of violence. It was a perverted, heinous, crime against an innocent young girl. How many more girls had fallen prey to the predator who hid behind the same shield Harper had sworn by to serve and protect?

Harper allowed her to tell her story; her reasons for running away from home, and how she met Joe. It had been Joe's idea, she told him, to get rid of the girls; sell them to the highest bidder.

"Who did the bidding?" he asked her.

"Joe never said. All he wanted was the money and to save his own neck." She darted another glance at him. "Don't look at me that way."

Harper didn't know how he was looking at Roxanne Lewis, but caught himself wanting to believe Mary Kemp, the social worker, was right about her. The woman sitting before him was thirty-two, his age, but what they were talking about was a series of violent crimes against an underage girl. He thought of his own careless, innocent existence at sixteen. The rapist brutally took hers not once but three times. Maybe she would let something slip if he redirected his questions. "Let's go back to the last time you saw Britni alive. Where were you?"

"My apartment."

"Tell me about those last hours. Who was in the apartment with you?"

"It was late, probably around eleven when the front door flew open. Joe was expecting him, the short, stocky man, the building manager, I think," she said, pressing the heels of her hands against her forehead. "Whoever he was, he said everything was ready."

Harper looked across the room at Mann and nodded toward the door.

"Quinn," said Mann.

"Take a back-up unit and bring him in. Charge him with obstruction of justice for starters. I'll keep working on her." Mann started to leave when Harper called out to him. "Have his mug shot brought up with the usual assortment as soon as they get it done."

"I heard your 911 tape," said Harper. "Why didn't you report the rape?"

"Go to the police? You think I could ever trust another cop?" Roxanne asked him. "Which one of you would have given a damn about us?"

"You're wrong about that."

"I doubt it. Have you ever lived in fear for your life, Detective? I wouldn't think so. Joe would have killed me – like that," she said, snapping her fingers at him. "There's no question in my mind about it." She lowered her head and wiped her nose. "Look, I don't need you or anyone else to point out what I was. I made my choices, and I paid for them. Nothing to be proud about, but I did what I had to do to survive."

Roxanne survived all right. She was one of the lucky ones. Harper grabbed hold of the back of his chair, raised a foot to one of the rungs, and asked about the landlord.

"What's to tell? I had just changed Britni and had wrapped her in a blanket when he barged in. He grabbed her from me. Didn't say a word – just took her. That must be when I lost my St Jude medallion."

"And?"

"And nothing. We fought because he wouldn't give her back to me, but he didn't do anything other than hold her."

"He didn't try to leave?"

"No, he stood there as if he was waiting for something and then …"

"Then what?" he asked after a few edgy seconds.

"I don't know. It all happened so fast."

"What happened? Come on Roxanne. You're not telling me anything."

"Look, all I wanted to do was grab the babies and leave."

"Why didn't you?"

"It was too late."

"Too late for what?"

"Joe owed his supplier a lot of money; said if we didn't go through with it, we were all as good as dead. I begged him not to do it. They weren't his children, you know. It wasn't his decision to make. I never understood why he got involved in any of it."

"What then?"

"Caitlin was in her crib. When I tried to take Britni away from the manager, Joe slapped me. Knocked me into one of the walls. He was getting ready to come at me again when another man walked through the door."

"Now we're up to three. How many more people were in on this?"

"I don't know. I never saw him before. He's the person who took Britni. He's the last person I saw holding her."

"Anyone mention his name?"

She shrugged her shoulders. "No. I assumed it was Joe's supplier. They seemed to know each other well."

"Describe him."

"I can't. I only saw him for a few minutes. All I have is an impression."

"Try."

"I've spent the last sixteen years trying to forget."

Harper knew exactly what she was saying. Hadn't he done the same thing with Gillies? He raised a hand to the back of his neck. The muscles seemed tighter than usual. "All right. Look. What was the first thing that crossed your mind when you saw him?"

"I wanted to know who he was. And then … wait. He had a tattoo on his arm, right here," she said, pointing just above her left elbow. "Maybe two or three inches long."

"What kind of tattoo?"

"Are you kidding me?" She shook her head. "You're lucky I remember he had one."

Harper shoved the chair into the table making her jump. "Who are you trying to protect?"

"What?"

"We've been at this for three hours. You claim a man raped you three times and you can't tell me anything about him."

"What do you mean, *claimed*? How can you stand there and –"

"And you certainly aren't giving up any details about the guy you claim took Britni. Just tell me one thing you do know. Just one," he yelled, shoving a pointed finger close to her face.

"I'm not lying to you."

"Then think!" he yelled again. "Did the man with the tattoo live in the building?"

"I wasn't much more than a baby myself."

"Answer the question!"

"What do you want from me? What is it with you? I'm telling you all I know!" she yelled back. "I don't remember."

Harper had tried everything from shock to sympathy. If the answers weren't coming from her, they would have to come from the stack of rental contracts sitting on his desk. They would check each one of those tenants if that's what it would take to find him.

Harper looked at his watch. Eleven fifty-five a.m. He'd give her a break while he retreated into the next room and dialed Emma's number. They'd need an arrest record, a drug conviction, a traffic ticket, anything traceable to a possible suspect, he told her. When he returned to Interrogation Room 1, Roxanne was leaning back in her chair with her hands limp on her lap; she had her sight fixed on the table immediately in front of her.

Harper combed his fingers back through his hair, pulled out the chair, and sat down. "Was Britni dead when you left?"

"No. I already told you. She was alive," she replied. "I can still hear her crying. I really hoped someone had given her a home." She raised a fingertip to the corner of her eye.

"What did you do next?"

"I couldn't fight three men and I couldn't save both of the girls. I had to assume Britni would be given a home, so I grabbed Caitlin from her crib and we snuck out. They were in the middle of a shouting match and never saw me leave."

"Where did you go?"

"Caitlin and I went to a shelter that night, the first of many. I swear it never entered my mind Britni might be dead."

She had given them Quinn, and now it would be up to Quinn to debunk her statement. "What about your 911 call?"

"What about it?"

"If you had Caitlin and you thought Britni had been adopted, why make the 911 call?"

"Because, I thought if I reported Britni missing the police would find her and make sure she was taken care of. But I never heard any more about her until you showed up at our doorstep," she said, dabbing a tissue to her nose. "I didn't know what to think. After all these years, I couldn't have a teenager dropped on our laps. Not now. My husband is a frugal man. He was willing to adopt Caitlin. How could I explain Britni?"

Harper said nothing.

"What?"

"We had to tell your husband."

She stared at him in silence then lowered her gaze.

"He agreed to let us take a sample of Caitlin's DNA."

"What now?" Harper asked Holloway, as an officer escorted Roxanne out of the room. "She gave us Quinn, but we've got a whole lot of nothing to charge her with murder."

Holloway looked at the assistant PA for answers.

"He's right, Holloway. You don't," said Terrill. "She has no priors or convictions. All she has admitted to was a promiscuous lifestyle, dependency on alcohol, drug use, and child neglect. A typical teenage mother's story from where I stand. No judge will ever grant a murder hearing on that."

Harper cut a glance at her. "Just what in all of this do you consider normal behavior for a sixteen-year-old, counselor?" An expression in her eyes caught him by surprise. He hadn't noticed before how much she resembled Deanna.

"Sam." Holloway motioned for his silence.

"You're twisting my words," she retorted.

"What's to twist?" he hissed back. "The part where she was blindfolded and raped? You want to take a look at her scars yourself?"

"We'll have her examined," she argued.

"Yeah, that's a pretty normal thing for a sixteen-year-old, right?" asked Harper.

"Sam." Holloway gave him another warning.

"For all I know she's lying about it, but that's beside the point." Terrill raised her voice above his. "What I'm saying is that based on her statement, we don't have the slightest bit of evidence to charge her with murder. Don't ask me to make a case out of this, Harper. Unless forensics comes up with something to tie her to the crime, we have nothing. Hold her for forty-eight hours. Get the DNA results and match them. Better yet, find someone to contradict her story, gentlemen, or cut her loose."

"All right, you two. There are other issues at stake here," said Holloway.

Terrill turned her glare away from Harper and crossed her arms. "Exactly. If I were you, Captain, I'd be looking in the dirty corners of the CPD for the rapist."

"I thought you said she couldn't prove it?"

"I did," she replied.

"I can't believe any of my men would be involved."

"Holloway," she said. "We're talking about something that happened sixteen years ago. He may have moved on. Doesn't mean he's not still forcing himself on kids. Roxanne Lewis whipped out a wild card we didn't count on. Are you going to ignore it?"

"Jesus, you know me better than that," he scowled.

"Clean it up, Captain. Like you said, before the press gets wind of it." Her glance cut back to Harper. "I'll be in my office. Let me know when the next one is ready." She left, allowing the door to slam behind her. What little air remained in the room held in icy silence.

Harper and the Captain stood shoulder to shoulder peering through the two-way mirror into an empty interrogation room.

"Nothing like getting side-swiped," said Harper.

Holloway stood still. His eyes locked on the metal table where Roxanne Lewis had been sitting.

"Did you know about a rapist on the force?" Harper asked.

No was Holloway's emphatic answer. He frowned and lowered his head, slipped his hands in his pockets, and remained silent a moment longer. "Alan Jones was chief then. I thought he ran a tight ship. Dismissal would have been swift."

"As much as I hate to admit it, Terrill could be right," said Harper. "There's always a chance Roxanne is lying."

"I'm not willing to take that chance," said Holloway. "I want this handled quietly. You and Mann. Last thing we need is a scandal before we get all the facts."

"What are the facts? Where do we start? Anybody ever act suspicious before?"

"We've had our problems over the years; you know that. Thefts, improper use of force, nothing like this though. Most we've been able to handle internally."

"What happens when we find him?" asked Harper.

The two men looked at each other.

"What do you think? We'll nail him to the goddamned public wall."

"What about Flanagan? He's going to blow a piston," said Harper.

"Flanagan will know the minute I have something to tell him. I want you personally in charge of it. You and Mann dig until you find the bastard. I don't care if he's active or not. Understand?"

Ribbons of cigarette smoke floated across the room when Harper entered the lounge. "Christ," he muttered, crushing out a forgotten cigarette butt someone had left smoldering in the small, tin ashtray on the middle of the table. He waved the plume away, dropped his coins into the pop machine, and gulped down the soda.

Roxanne's accusation kept running through his mind. He thought about his suspicions of Gillies and the incident at the second precinct. Cases of dirty cops seemed to be in an upswing. He wanted to kick himself for losing his temper with Kay. She was right. They were talking about two different things: finding evidence to convict Roxanne of murder, and finding her rapist. "Roxanne hadn't asked for either of those things to happen." He crushed the can and tossed it into the trash.

Mann's questioning of Quinn was well underway in Interrogation Room 3 when Harper entered the room.

28

Owens looked up. The clouds slowly parted to reveal a scattering of stars against the moonless backdrop of the April night. Behind him stretched a row of dumpsters shoved against the wall of the savings and loan. A sour stench rose from them and mingled with the pungent odor of piss from whoever had christened the alley wall.

Owens pressed himself into the shadows of the narrow passage. He focused his sight on the building across the street; police headquarters and its double glass doors. Tonight the building was lit up like a whore luring fools to her bed. She gets what she wants, snatches their money, and shoves them back out before smoothing the sheets for another. Cops. They promise protection instead, sweeten the pot with a sense of integrity, then knuckleball a man's words into an erratic spin of lies, and label it justice.

Chuck's threats tumbled around in his head; he couldn't erase the old man's odious sneer from his mind. Dwelling on Chuck's betrayal only fueled Owens' anger. He'd put a stop to him and his back-stabbing scheme, starting with Quinn who was probably sitting in some foul, mind-numbing room. The dicks, aiming a blaring light from a single lamp directly into Quinn's eyes, would force him to point an accusing finger in Owens' direction.

"Wasn't even near the fuckin' kid," Owens reached for the half-smoked cigarette pressed between his lips. He took a long drag and narrowed his eyes, clenched his teeth, and blew out the smoke. He tugged at his collar, yanked it up around his neck. His habitual pacing began again; back and forth, stomped his feet, took another drag, stomped, and paced again. Owens ran a hand over his mouth and frowned as he thought of the man, his protector. *Where was he in all of this?*

"His damned kids. Whole fuckin' thing was his fault and now what? He disappears? Sure as hell not takin' the rap for this shit," he mumbled again.

He wondered about Quinn and the lies he was feeding the cops. "The ass won't live to testify." He'd get rid of Chuck too. They'd both disappear like chunks of ice on the Fourth of July and no one would miss them. But the man. That was a different story. He had the power to make things difficult. The man could make *him* disappear, and the cops would never question it.

Owens remembered that night and the kid; the frenzy and confusion after the bitch left the room, and then after Quinn decided to take care of things. "Take care of things my ass," he sneered, thinking of how for the past sixteen years the four of them had promised to keep quiet.

Owens didn't have a plan, he'd think of something while he waited, hoping that Quinn would walk out of the station. Maybe he'd just run him down. He grinned at the thought. He'd let Quinn get a few blocks away, sneak up on him, and wipe him out when he least expected it.

A number of cigarette butts lay scattered in a circle on the pavement around him. Owens leaned against the cold brick wall of the savings and loan and glanced at his watch. He'd stay as long as it took. "Shit. The guy doesn't know that many words." He shoved another cigarette between his lips and raised the flame of his lighter to it. He wondered what kind of bullshit Quinn was feeding the dicks. Owens took his next drag and narrowed his sight on the redhead walking down the police station's front steps. She was older now. Much older.

"Where in the hell did they find her?" he mumbled. Owens watched as she slid behind the wheel of a black sedan and drove away. He ran his hand over his lips feeling the grin that pulled at either corner. He flipped the cigarette into a puddle near his feet, hustled toward his car, and stroked the picture that was starting to form in his head. He'd have to think about this unexpected new option.

29

"Believe you?" Mann scowled at Alvin Quinn's evasiveness. "Why should we? You've done nothing but lie from the very beginning. You lied about knowing Roxanne, Britni's death, next you're going to try to stick to your story about the broken pipes. Admit it. You just couldn't get anyone to stand the smell of her little body rotting inside that wall. That's why you didn't rent the apartment out for seven whole months. Isn't it?"

Quinn curled his lips, looked down at the table, and tapped it with his thumb.

"Answer the question!"

"Yeah! All right already," Quinn scowled back. "Yeah, the place stunk like shit! Reeked all over the place. Everyone was complainin'. It was months before it cleared out."

"How many more lies are you going to try on us? Do you really expect us to believe someone else killed her? I think you did it and so will the jury."

"I didn't do it! I'm tellin' the truth!"

"You should've done that the first time we questioned you."

"I figured ya'd try to pin this one on me and I was right. Ya're doin' it now."

"Then get your story straight." Mann gave Quinn a steely glare, leaned in, palms down on the table. His face was inches away from the suspect's. "What were you doing in apartment 1C on the evening of June 3, 1990?"

"I already told ya. I was supposed to grab the kids and take them somewhere."

"Who set you up to take them?"

"Some guy."

"Who?"

"I don't know. The guy called on the phone. That's how we did things. Never knew his name."

"You never asked?"

"Nah. He wouldn't say."

"Where were you taking them?"

"I can't remember. Never went."

"Your life's on the line. What's it going to take for you to see that?" Mann waited a moment for Quinn's reaction. "How did you two connect?"

Quinn stared down at the table top and remained silent.

"Come on, Quinn. Who set it up?"

"I'm tellin' ya I don't know."

Mann shook his head. "All right. Who else, besides you and Roxanne Ewing, was in Apartment 1C on the evening of June third?" He paused again. "Tell you what. We're not even going to discuss the charges piling up against you; obstruction of justice, attempted kidnapping, extortion. Those are nothing. A walk in the park. We're talking murder here. A one way ticket to meet your maker."

"I didn't do nothin'!" Panic washed over Quinn's face as he gripped the edge of the table and angled for a way out.

"Then talk," Mann hollered. "You think whoever you're protecting would do the same for you?"

Quinn shrugged his shoulders.

"Well? Do you?"

"I ain't protectin' no one." He shook his head. "No one."

"Don't look now but they're leaving you to hang, buddy. What happened on the evening of June third? The night you went to pick up the Ewing infants from apartment 1C?" Mann drew in a breath and raised his hands to his hips. "Tell you what, Quinn. I'll make it easy on you. Here's what we already have and you fill in the gaps, all right? We know about the twins, the fight that made the hole in the wall. We even know you were the last person to hold Britni Ewing while she was alive. And guess what else? Your fingerprints match the set we found on the plaster you used to seal

163

up the hole in the wall. We have you on that one. What happened between the time you held the baby and the time she died?" He watched, waiting for a response. "How – did Britni – die?"

Quinn wiped the beads of perspiration that formed on his lip then scratched his head. "That's not true."

"What's not true?"

"The kid. I wasn't holdin' the kid."

"We have a witness who says you were."

"They're lyin' then."

"Only lies we've heard so far are yours. You were there, Quinn. Cut the act." Mann rolled up his sleeves and glanced at his watch. "It's late, half past eight. I'm missing the college basketball finals because of you." He had looked forward to the game and a Bruins' win. Irritated, he loosened the knot on his tie and jerked it down. "I don't have a wife or kids to go home to. No dog, cat, not even a dumb gold fish waiting on me. So you and me," he pointed to Quinn and then to himself, "we could sit here the rest of the night if we have to. However long it takes for you to start talking." He paced back and forth without taking his eyes from Quinn. "I could, if, I had any indication you were innocent. I'd give you that much time to prove yourself."

Nothing he said stirred Quinn to talk.

"You ever see anyone on death row, Quinn?" Mann stopped, leaned in close to Quinn's face, and forced him to look straight into his eyes. "It's a slow death. Starts the minute the doors slams shut." Mann walloped the table with his open palm and made Quinn jump. "You can see it in their eyes," he whispered then pulled back and walked away. "The life gets sucked right out of a man. Knowing the day – the minute he's going to die can't be a good feeling, can it? I'd hate to think of anyone going there who doesn't deserve it. No way out once the wheels get set into motion." Mann cocked his head and frowned. "Quinn, you getting any of this?"

"Yeah," Quinn muttered under his breath. "But I didn't kill the kid."

"Then give me proof."

"Like what?"

"A name! Who else was in the room at the time of Britni's death? "

Quinn squirmed in his chair. His eyes darted; the perspiration on his brow was visible from across the room.

"Damn it, Quinn, why won't you help yourself out of this?" Mann gave Harper a nod that signaled a different approach. "I'm trying to help you, but the Captain has a different theory. He won't waste his time with liars like you. He thinks we have enough on you right now to toss you in prison for life, if you're lucky. What do you think, Harper?"

"It's only been a few hours. Give him a chance."

"See, Quinn," he said. "Harper here doesn't agree with the Captain either. Guess it's up to you to show us who's right."

"What's the point? How many times do I gotta tells ya? I didn't do nothin' to that kid."

"And we want to believe you, but if you didn't kill her, who did?"

"Maybe the other witness is wrong," said Harper. "It happens."

"What witness?" Quinn looked as if an invisible hand had wrapped around his neck.

"Like Quinn said. It was a long time ago." Harper leaned back in his chair and rested his head in the cup of his hands. "Things get fuzzy. Maybe Quinn was alone like he says."

"You know the witness is credible," said Mann, playing along.

"Ain't no witness to nothin'. You twos just playin' me."

"But let's just say it's possible Mr Quinn here doesn't remember anyone else in the room. Maybe the witness was confused or even lying. I think we should give Quinn the benefit of the doubt," Harper insisted.

"Could be, but if that's the case, it means no one else could have killed the baby but him."

"No!" yelled Quinn.

"After all, we both heard Mrs Lewis' statement," said Mann, ignoring Quinn's plea. "You know she spilled her guts about him – how Quinn here grabbed the baby."

"Who the hell is this Lewis broad?" Quinn darted his glance from one detective to another.

"She swore to us he killed the baby." Mann pointed a finger at Quinn's face. "God I hate it when women cry. I don't think she'd lie about a thing like that. Do you?"

"I said I don't know no Lewis broad," Quinn raised his voice above Mann's.

"But you do," said Mann. "The baby's mother – Roxanne. Did we forget to mention she's in the next room?"

Quinn narrowed his small brown eyes. "Why that … I didn't hurt the kid. No way! How the hell would she know anyway? She was half stinkin' drunk that night." The look in his eyes was as intense as a smoldering flame. "If she'd listened to the rest of us, none of this woulda happened."

"The rest of us? Thought you said you didn't remember. You lying again, Quinn?" asked Harper. "Who else was in the room?"

"Forget it, Harper. His time's up." Mann shoved the chair hard against the table. "But someone's going to pay for Britni Ewing's death, and as far as I'm concerned, it might as well be him." He grabbed his jacket off the back of a chair and started toward the door. "Let's book him."

"No. Wait," Quinn shouted. He held out a hand. "Just … hold on."

Mann stopped and glanced over his shoulder. "What?"

Quinn drew in a breath. "Just let me think."

"Think? What's there to think about? You either did it, or you give us the name of the person who did." Mann shook his head and draped his jacket back over the chair. "One more time. We know you were holding Britni moments before she died." He arched his back and raised his hand to the back of his neck. "That's a fact, Quinn. We also know there was someone else in the room, besides you, Roxanne, and a man named Joe."

"Joe?" asked Quinn. "No one there named Joe. Dumb broad couldn't even get that right. The guy's name was J O. He was there all right. Another crackhead. Brought her to live in the buildin'."

Mann frowned. They were searching for the wrong name. He swept a glance in Harper's direction, but his partner had already slipped out of the room.

"What's J O's real name?"

"I dunno. Never got it."

"The hell you didn't."

"I didn't! Look, one mornin', I goes out to my mailbox and find an envelope with a hundred dollar bill in it and a note. Said this couple needed a place to stay, mentioned J O and the Ewin' dame, didn't want no questions asked. Got the same amount every week until the night she left."

"How'd the envelope get there? Someone drop it off?"

"Nah. It came in the mail."

"And you weren't curious to know who was sending the money or who this J O was?"

"I was never one to spit on a blessin'. He was a pusher. That's all I know. Didn't bother me none."

"What about the man with the tattoo? Who was he?"

"There weren't none. No one I know had a tattoo."

"Quinn, anyone ever tell you you're a bore? On your feet. Come on." Mann reached for the handcuffs. "Maybe you'll think a little clearer in the morning."

Quinn ran a shaky hand through his thin strands of hair and glanced away. "Wait a minute."

"We're done waiting. It's a simple question. Just needs a simple answer but you can't seem to come up with one." Mann grabbed him by the arm and pulled him to his feet. "You're under arrest for the murder of Brit–"

"All right!" Quinn yelled. "All right. I'll tell ya what I know. There were others there that night all right. Plenty of 'em." He frowned and turned his head. "Damned hell hole. That's what it was. I ain't takin' the rap for this shit," he muttered under his breath.

Lies were as easy to spot as a bright red hat at a wake. Mann could read the signs; the play with the hands, how a man sits, and the glint of hope in his eyes, the look of a predator struggling to catch a meal without detection. Mann caught that murky shadow swimming around in Quinn's eyes just before he turned away – seconds before fear washed over the little man's face.

"All they had to do," said Quinn, "was to hand the kids over and everythin' would have been all right. But no, all of a sudden she becomes a saint. 'No,' she starts screamin'. 'You can't have my babies.' Yeah, like she woulda made the perfect mother. Hell it's her fault the kid died. Kid woulda been all right if she woulda just kept her mouth shut. She's the one ya oughta go after," he sneered and voiced his assumption that Roxanne was dead. "How the hell was I supposed to know ya'd find her?"

"Screwed up your plans, did she?" asked Mann "Were you hoping Roxanne was dead so she couldn't finger you?"

"Nah, I mean …" He gave Mann a quick glance before shrugging his shoulders. "Her bein' here don't change nothin'. It was her kid and her fault everythin' went crazy."

"It's your word against hers, and she's more convincing," said Mann. "You better come up with a hell of a lot more."

Quinn shrugged his shoulders again. "Yeah, right. So she's yellin' at me not to take them kids then J O gets into the act. Next thing I knows, he pulls her off me, and they go at it again. Bam! J O hits her up the side of the head and she goes flyin' across the damned room. Then he throws her a punch, lands right in the damned wall. Busted a hole right in it." He rolled his eyes.

"And you, being the big man you are, stood there and let it happen," said Mann.

"Hey, I don't get in the middle of other people's problems. But the wall," he said, pointing a pudgy finger, "now that pissed me off."

"She was sixteen-years-old. A minor living in your apartment building with an adult male. He was pimping her out at sixteen goddamned years old. Her children were the result of a rape!"

"I never knew that. Hell, she was pregnant when she moved in. I swear I didn't know," he yelled back. "You can't hold that against me."

Mann choked on his rage as he rammed a fist onto the table. "Watch me. You were an accomplice, as guilty as the pimp and her rapist." Mann saw the panic radiate from Quinn's eyes. It was time to hone in on it. "Quit playing games, Quinn. We know about a third man with a tattoo. Who was he?"

"What third? There weren't no one else. Just J O and the broad," he insisted.

"You don't get it, do you? We're going to figure out who you're protecting so you might as well come clean with it."

Quinn raised a plump, callused hand and ran it across his mouth. "Ah, holy Jesus! I already gave ya the guy's name, J O. I told ya he did it."

"So where is he? Where do we find him?"

"Haven't seen him in years. Look it up. Ya got all them gadgets now. If he's alive ya'll find the little shit."

"How'd you get mixed up in all of this anyway?"

Quinn shook his head again.

"Come on! I'm the only one standing between you and the death sentence."

"All right. Look, me and J O, we had a deal goin'. I was up to my eyeballs in debt and was gettin' ready to lose the damned buildin'. J O spotted me a wad of money."

"And what was he getting in return?"

"I told you."

"Again, Quinn, what did he want in return?"

"The buildin'. He wanted to use the damned buildin' for his dealin's; drugs, women, ya know, dealin's."

"Kids? What about kids?" asked Mann. "Did J O take kids into the building?"

"Nah. What the hell would he want with kids?"

"Porn?" asked Mann. "What about porn?"

"What about it? What normal guy don't look at porn?"

"Kiddy porn. Did he ever do kiddy porn?"

"Oh hell, no. Jesus, what are ya sick or somethin'?" Quinn threw him a look of disgust. "No nothin' like that, just drugs and whores. I didn't see no other way out 'cept to let him have the place. 'Cept the use of the buildin' wasn't enough for him. He wanted favors done for him all the time."

"What kind of favors?"

"Favors." He shrugged his shoulders. "One day he tells me he owed this friend of his a wad of dough; Skipper owed someone else, and well, ya know how that goes. Said gettin' rid of the little brats would make things right."

"Who's Skipper?" asked Mann. Quinn claimed he didn't know.

Just one of J O's contacts, he told him. "Was Skipper there? Was he in on the deal to sell the girls?"

"I ain't sayin' it again. No. It was just me and J O and them kids weren't gonna be sold. Jesus, that's against the law ain't it? I was supposed to get them out of the way, is all."

"That's not the way Roxanne tells it."

"Then she's a liar. What the hell does she know?"

Quinn's stubbornness began to grate at Mann's nerves. Mann swept a glance up as Harper walked back into the room then resumed his questioning of Quinn. "You're in the apartment. Roxanne has the girls. Where's J O?"

"Right there in the room with us. Came in and jerked the kid right out of my arms. Next thing I knows the kid's real quiet like."

"Just like that?"

"Yeah."

"Why? Why's the baby quiet?"

"I don't know!"

"Where's Roxanne at the time?"

"Next to him. Drunk and pissed. The broad picked up a pan, got in a lucky punch. Busted his lip wide open."

"Say it again?" asked Mann.

"The damned broad hit J O on the mouth. Shit, he was a mess, bleedin' all over the place."

Mann met his partner's glance. "You're telling us when we find this J O guy, his blood will match the blood on this, right?" Mann placed a photograph of the plastic evidence bag containing the bloodstained blanket in front of him.

Quinn frowned and stared at the brown spots covering the frayed, yellowed cloth.

"You remember it?"

"Should I?"

"That's blood Quinn; the baby's remains were wrapped in this blanket," he said, jabbing an index on the photograph. "You placed the baby inside the wall. Do you remember the blanket?"

"Yeah, I guess."

"Whoever matches this blood is guilty of murder. Is that what you're saying? Are you willing to testify under oath J O killed her?"

"Yeah, sure. Why not. He shook her good and handed her back to me. Everythin' went to hell after that. J O took off on account the broad left with the other kid and left me there holdin' the dead one; told me to get rid of it. 'Get rid of it?' I says back. What the hell was I supposed to do with it? But I never lifted a finger to hurt them kids."

"No, of course you didn't. Except you weren't about to stop anyone else from doing it. That makes you as guilty as the guy who shook Britni and scrambled her little brains like a couple of eggs in a bowl. A scumbag like you doesn't do anything without a payback. How much were you going to make from that little exchange?" asked Mann.

"I don't remember."

"The hell you don't. How much?" he yelled.

"Fifteen grand." Quinn rolled his eyes.

"That makes you a hired killer."

"No. I didn't hurt her. All I was supposed to do was get them kids out of the buildin'. Someone was supposed to be waitin' outside. But everythin' changed when the kid croaked; I got screwed. That's what I got. They left me with a dead kid and a hole in the wall the size of Texas. That was never part of the deal," he yelled. "I never saw any of the money. Never!"

"Yeah, I feel for you. Tell it to the judge."

While Quinn's interrogation continued, another detective was searching the database for known drug pushers by the name of J O. Harper didn't know what to expect, but the answer was finally knocking at the interrogation room door. He rushed to open it, grabbed the page of photographs from the officer's hands. He stared at the picture for several seconds before jerking his head in the direction of the two-way mirror.

"Anyone look familiar, Quinn?" Harper cut into Mann's line of questions and slapped the page of photographs in front of him.

Quinn picked up the sheet, brought it close to his face, and looked at each picture with the scrutiny of a sleuth. "Yeah, this ugly guy here. He was a young punk back then." He pointed to the photograph on the upper right-hand corner of the page.

"Are you sure?" Harper demanded. "Take your time."

"Yeah, yeah. That's him. Head full of grey hair now, but I'd never forget his face. Uglier now than before."

Harper shoved a pen into Quinn's hand. "Circle it." As quickly as Quinn could get it done, Harper ripped the page off the table and rushed toward the two-way mirror. He deliberately glared into the glass where he imagined Holloway was standing on the other side. He clutched the photographs in his hand and slapped it against the mirror.

"Holy Mother of God!" Holloway muttered.

"What is it?" asked Terrill. Her glance darted from Holloway's stunned expression to the pictures, and back to Holloway.

30

It was after six p.m. when Holloway returned to his office. Mann and Quinn were still battling it out in Interrogation Room 3. Quinn was probably doling out bits of information as he saw fit. He had given them Owens; pointed him out of the photo lineup without any qualms. Holloway had witnessed and conducted enough interrogations over the years to know Quinn wasn't playing it straight. *Who else was he protecting?*

Holloway opened the mini blinds to allow the last rays of sun to slip into the room from between the vinyl slats. Letting the weight of his bulk drop into his chair, he leaned his head back and pressed the meaty heels of his hands firmly against his eyes. The Baby Doe case had revealed Owens' involvement as the child's alleged killer. That was significant, but a more pressing concern to him was Roxanne's claim about her rape. Terrill was right, of course. Roxanne couldn't prove it, but the fury he had seen in the woman's eyes was as intense and as real as any Holloway had ever seen. Rape or not, she was under age at the time of her attacks and besides, she couldn't have made up the part about the white Mustang.

"Holloway." Commissioner Flanagan stood in the doorway. He raised his cigarette to his mouth, took a final drag, and blew it out to one side.

Holloway swiveled his chair around and stared blankly at the silhouette standing before him. "Greg, didn't hear you come in." He reached and turned on his desk lamp. "What's on your mind?"

"What do you think? The kid."

"They're still questioning the suspects. I told you I'd call."

Flanagan pinched his smoldering butt between thumb and middle finger. He darted a glance at Holloway's desk and then to the end table on the opposite side of the room.

"Goddamn it, just because you quit doesn't mean everyone else has to. Where's a damned ashtray?"

"In the break room. Threw mine out. Better quit while you can. Those things will kill you."

"Don't give me that crap. Get enough of that from the old lady and all the damned health freaks and their assigned smoking rooms."

Holloway frowned. "Just stick it in the plant over there."

"Well?" Flanagan stood tall, shoulders back and erect as he crushed the butt into the moist soil.

"Well what?" asked Holloway. "It's late. Not a good time to play games with me."

"Who the hell's playing?" Flanagan reached for a chair. "I assume you're keeping Harper in line. Haven't seen his face in the paper."

"Yes. Why?"

Flanagan's steel blue eyes briefly glared at him then looked away. "Just checking. Is he over Gillies' death?"

"He's fine."

"Not still trying to figure that one out is he?"

"Whether you like it or not, he's a good cop." Holloway recognized the look in Flanagan's eyes; the way he avoided making eye contact. Holloway had seen it before, the day after he had caught Flanagan with another woman a few years ago. Flanagan had come around then too, fishing to see how much Holloway had seen or heard.

Holloway watched the way Flanagan slumped in the chair across from him; the way he leaned back, his posture; elbows resting on the arms of the chair, his legs stretched out in front of him.

"I really don't have time for this."

"I'm your commissioner. You'll make time."

"Come off it. After all these years, do you really think you can intimidate me?" asked Holloway.

"All I ever asked from you was a little respect."

"I've always respected you in public. Right now, you're wasting my time. What's your interest in this case anyway?"

"Everywhere I go I get asked about the kid. Three days later and every goddamned newspaper is still carrying the story on their front page," said Flanagan.

"It's an old case. Can't say how long it's going to take to solve or if we'll be able to."

"Heard Harper had a woman in number one earlier today. Who was she?"

"The child's mother." As Holloway spoke the words, he again fixed his attention on Flanagan's silent expressions. There was a subtle flinch in Flanagan's eyes, a rapid movement as if something unexpected had been tossed into them. He froze briefly before his gaze dropped to his lap. Bringing his feet together, he shifted in his seat.

"How'd he find her?" asked Flanagan.

"He's one of our best, you know that."

"What'd she have to say?"

"Seems she was under the impression the child had been adopted. Unfortunately, she couldn't tell us anything of any value," Holloway told him knowing the Commissioner could request the tapes from her interrogation. *What was he fishing for this time?*

"That so?" Flanagan crossed his arms. "You're sure she's the mother?"

"DNA will confirm it."

"And the father? What do you know about him?"

"Nothing yet."

Flanagan was silent for a moment then asked, "Who else are they talking to?"

"Alvin Quinn. Former building owner. Sounds like another dead end," said Holloway. "You ever hear of him?"

"Why should I?"

"He claims Owens is the one who shook the baby – killed her," said Holloway. "You don't seem too surprised."

"Nothing surprises me any more. You have a warrant for Owens yet?"

"No. We're still piecing the case together."

"What's to piece? If Quinn fingered him, it's good enough for me."

"Quinn isn't the most dependable witness I've ever heard. He can't remember what he ate at his last meal. I don't trust him, not after sixteen years. Besides, we don't have enough evidence to charge anyone with her murder yet."

"Get the damned evidence then."

"Are you asking me to manipulate the facts? Manufacture evidence just so you can have Owens?"

"Oh hell no. Not you, but now that we have him, I expect you to keep him. The Mayor wants to see an arrest – the public demands it. It's all about public opinion and the next election. Have to show we're doing all we can."

"We always do our best and you know it. You also know damn well there are no guarantees of solving a case when it's as cold as this one is. Maybe we'll get lucky this time. Only thing I know for certain is that the best we can do is give the child a proper burial."

Flanagan sat quietly for a moment before he glanced at his watch. He rose and turned to leave. As he reached the door, he stopped and glanced over his shoulder. "Pick Owens up and make the damned charges stick. Understand?"

Holloway didn't reply. Instead, he shifted his attention to the papers on his desk.

"Go ahead, Holloway. Pretend to ignore me. Just don't get too comfortable in your position. Everyone's dispensable. Even you."

Holloway didn't look up until he heard him leave. He couldn't get Roxanne's statement about her rape out of his mind. As far as he was concerned, any officer on duty in 1990 was a suspect – even Commissioner Flanagan. Holloway waited several minutes before he got up. He carefully lifted Flanagan's cigarette butt out of the potted dirt with a tissue and set it aside. Dispensable or not, he intended to clean house.

Flanagan had accused Owens of giving his son the fatal dose of crack that led to his death. No one blamed him for wanting Owens dead, but not at the hand of a fellow officer. Gillies had told Holloway about his conversations with the Commissioner days before his death. *How could Flanagan have asked Gillies to do the unthinkable?* He glanced at Owens' thick folder on the edge of his desk with disdain. He angled his desk lamp closer to the pages and began to read every line of text again, from the beginning. *Would it be there?* That overlooked, insignificant fact. The one he had dismissed as unrelated to the drug charges and tossed aside? Maybe the information would jump out at him now. He'd be happy if only it would reveal itself like a shoreline after the fog lifts in the light of day.

Holloway knew the Owens case by memory. It was all there. Every arrest since juvenile court. The dates were consistent with other records; no discrepancies that he knew of. Owens was a creature of habit, predictable, a behavior as obvious as a pattern on a quilt. He studied the pages again, but his mind kept going back to what Roxanne had said about the new white Mustang. He didn't trust his suspicions; his instincts were pointing toward a delicate situation. He reached for the phone and dialed the number of the only person he knew he could trust.

"Harper?" he paused. "No, Sam's fine. Listen, we need to talk."

Sam Harper couldn't shake off Quinn's indifference to the child's death. It was wearing on his nerves and shaking his patience to listen to his cold account.

"Like I said, they left me alone with the kid." Quinn leaned into the table and buried his face. "I took the blanket and wrapped her up again, grabbed a toy to make it look like the broad had come back and taken the kid with her. I put her in the wall, sealed it up and that was that." A smirk creased his lips as he drummed his fingers on the table. "I figured she'd rest in peace as much there as she would in the cemetery. No harm done."

Harper had heard enough. Maybe it was the image of Britni's little body being thrashed around until the veins in her head ruptured from the blow that made him ill or the knowledge Owens had been involved. Either way, Quinn's callousness had to end.

"Yeah, until the rats made a meal of her! You son of a bitch," yelled Harper.

"Ah, come on. Don't say that!" Quinn wailed with disgust.

"That makes you sick? *You're* sick!" Harper shouted again and lunged toward him.

Mann shoved himself between them. "Harper, no!"

"It wasn't my fault!" Quinn pleaded, raising his hands to protect his face. "What was I supposed to do?"

"Report it! Why didn't you report it?"

"Harper!" Mann shouted. "Harper!" Mann held his partner firmly by the shoulders. Two uniformed officers ran into the room. "It's all right, guys. We're okay. Everything's under control." Mann returned his attention to his partner. "Right? Come on buddy," he whispered, "he's not worth it! Think of what you're doing. All right?"

"Yeah." Harper sneered through clenched teeth and pulled himself free from Mann's grip.

"You sure you're okay?"

"I said I'm all right," Harper snarled then nodded, gasping. "I'm fine." Waving Mann off, he backed up to the door and stepped out into the hall. He yanked down the knot on his tie and jerked it from side to side. Bending over, clutching his knees, he tried to breathe and ease the tightness building up in the pit of his stomach then rushed down the hall.

The sound of the restroom door clattering as it swung back into the wall reverberated throughout the faded green facility. The cramping in his stomach didn't ease and he prayed no one would walk in. Harper wiped his mouth then leaned into the sink to rinse out the taste. The cold water on his face wasn't enough to cool the rage that had raced through his veins. It was all coming back in quick succession; Mellow, Gillies, and now, Britni. She was more than a few scattered bones. He knew her name, she would have grown up to look like Caitlin, and now that he understood the brutality of her death, he became ill again.

31

Spring winds howled outside the Lewis home on Pigeon Road. Roxanne could hear it whip through the branches of the birch tree in the front yard and rattle her kitchen window. The tiny room closed in tighter around her with each thought she had of Britni and the night she had left her behind.

The familiar faint sound of a tailpipe scraping against the curb announced Ned's arrival. A numb, hollow feeling swept through her. She froze, not with fear but with the knowledge of what lay ahead. Two days of silence.

How many more, she wondered.

Compassion wasn't her husband's strongest trait. He was a proud, pompous man. The kind she unwittingly seemed to have attracted all her life. He was also tightfisted, willing to support her and Caitlin but not one of his own. Of course, she had wanted to tell him about Britni. How many times had she started to do just that? Yet the words had eluded her and the perfect moment to tell him of her past addiction, the rape, or Caitlin's twin never presented itself. Maybe she should have brought it up on their first date, or six months into their courtship. Sure, she sneered, he would have understood. It had been difficult enough to find a man willing to date a woman with a child. Ned was better than most, but even he would have thrown her out on her tush, had she been honest.

"Damn it. Why can't he see me for who I am now?" Their marriage wasn't the best, but didn't their years together count for something? She turned on the living room lights and waited. He'd be in the house within seconds of slamming the car door. He would first place his briefcase down on the chair by the closet, hang up his coat, check the day's mail, and then head upstairs to his office.

He came in as predicted, but he didn't keep to his standard routine.

"Ned." She followed him down the hall. "You're late tonight. Bet you're tired."

He stopped. His hands hung at his side then clenched into a fist the moment she spoke.

"We have to talk," she said.

"Too late. Should have done it a long time ago."

"I know. I'm sorry." She studied him for a moment. "I kept your dinner warm."

He turned with a glare, quickly sweeping his sight up and down the length of her.

"Ned, I know you're upset. How many times do I have to apologize? I was young." She followed him up the stairs with her eyes. Roxanne had never seen him this angry. "I was Caitlin's age when it happened for Christ's sakes. I was raped, damn it."

"I can't believe you've kept this from me. How could you?"

"I was afraid. Afraid you wouldn't understand, just like you're not getting it now."

"That's brilliant, Roxanne. You're right. I don't understand – any of it. How could you not trust me? I feel as if I've been living with a stranger." He stopped halfway without turning. "I went to see an attorney today. I suggest you do likewise."

"An attorney? You want a divorce? On what grounds?"

"Lies. What else have you kept from me?"

She almost answered but it wasn't quite a question. His next statement negated any hope for a solution.

"It's over." He drew in a breath and hung his head. "I don't want any problems. You know what we have. I'll be fair, but I want you out of my life." He paused again and lowered his voice to nearly a whisper. "Where's Caitlin?"

"Overnight at a friend's."

He nodded. "Of course, I'll want joint custody."

"I understand." Unexpected relief rushed in. At least he was willing to care for her. "Thank you." She should cry, or scream, or do something dramatic like throw the nearest vase at his head. Instead, an amazing peace settled in. Peace, that's all she had ever wanted.

Ned earned a good living but aside from being a good father and provider, he was a callous, self-centered soul who thought he had done enough to marry her. She thought of the times he had humiliated her with his careless comments and superior sense of self-worth. She started back toward the kitchen when a chilling thought crossed her mind. *What if he fought her for full custody? He could; he adopted her*. The calm she had gladly accepted moments before gave way to panic. Roxanne glanced over her shoulder toward the stairs intent on confronting him again when the kitchen phone rang.

"Hello?"

"Roxie? Ya old Georgia Peach. Damn, woman ya looked good today."

A frown wrinkled her brow. Her shoulders pulled back while her mind tried to sort through the man's salutation. No one had called her Roxie in years. "Who is this?" She demanded to know who dared to be so familiar with her.

"A friend."

"I don't have any. How did you get this number?"

"Wasn't hard. So, Roxie girl, how much did ya tell the cops?"

A wave of goose bumps rippled up her arms like a rush of prickly needles that warned of foreboding evils. "How did you …" Only one person had ever called her Roxie girl – Joe. She stopped her instinct to slam the phone down when she heard his next comment.

"What did you say?" she asked.

"I said I know who killed your kid."

Tears welled in her eyes. Cupping her hand around the mouthpiece, she lowered her voice. "Is this some cruel, twisted joke?"

"Might be cruel, but it ain't no joke. Just think it's 'bout time ya knew. 'Specially now that all our necks are on the line, includin' yours."

"Who is this?" she demanded in spite of her suspicions.

"What'd ya say we keep it friendly? Just watchin' your back for ya."

"Bullshit. The only back you're covering is your own."

"Ya really think Harper believes ya? Bet his goons are watchin' your house right about now."

She yanked back the kitchen curtain. With a sharp turn of her head, she looked up one side of the darkened street and then the other. Thick catalpa trees branches hung precariously above Pigeon Road, swaying with each gust of wind. Their young tender leaves had sprung to life since the recent rains and had nearly reached their full size of twelve inches. In the next few weeks, the lush green canopy above the street would flaunt white lily-sized blooms that would eventually fall like a cover of snow. She squinted to make out the shapes parked beneath their shadows.

"He won't stop doggin' ya till ya confess," he told her, "and ya will, just to get him off your back."

"You're out of your mind." She allowed the curtains to fall back into place.

"Ya and me, we got a mutual interest in lettin' Harper know the truth."

"Don't you even pretend to know my interests."

"Neither one of us should go to jail for somethin' we didn't do."

"You killed her didn't you, Joe? And you expect me to protect you?"

The connection broke off with a slam.

"No!" she gasped, startled by his abruptness. She quickly returned the receiver to its cradle and covered her mouth. Tears welled in her eyes again. Her chest heaved with each shallow breath. She had started to walk away when the phone rang again making her jump. "Don't hang up!"

"Ya want the guy's name or not?" he asked her.

Roxanne's mind raced. Regardless of her disgust, Joe was all she had to fill in her gaps of memory.

"Shit, girl –"

"No. Wait." She looked around the corner toward the steps

then returned to the kitchen. "I'm listening." She took in short shallow gulps of air and raised her hand to her lips again. "Yes. I remember. Hold on." Her fingers tore through the drawer next to the stove to find a sharpened pencil amidst old rubber bands and discarded twisted bread sack ties. "Go on."

She looked blankly at the wall and paid close attention to each word he said. The caller knew too many details about that June night. She had to think. She had to calm down, believe him, and think. When he hung up, she lowered the receiver in its cradle and stood motionless for several minutes. She allowed the images of that night to flood her mind. She remembered Joe, the babies, the landlord, and the other man the caller had identified as Chuck Toomey. What had she told Harper about Chuck? The tattoo, that's all. She did tell him about the tattoo. That was a start.

Memories of the rape gushed in too. She'd never forget her terror or repugnance of the man's sweat against her skin. She could close her eyes and still feel the force of his body thrashing against hers and the pain. There was always pain. Above all, she remembered the lifeless, cold tone of his voice after lust's fire was doused and disgust sank in with a heavy dose of reality. That's when he'd beat her; a just penance for his sins he had once told her. What woman would ever forget that? She lived with the memory each time she looked into Caitlin's pale eyes.

Why couldn't her daughter's eyes have been green like hers? "Son of a bitch."

It was only when she heard the front door slam and the car pull out into the street that she became aware of Ned's absence. Roxanne drew in a breath and cracked the living room door slightly open.

"I hate you, Ned Lewis. You're all the same. Take what you want. Toss it out when you're done. Never mind me – my needs." She whispered at first then flung the door open and yelled, "Well you're not getting Caitlin! You hear me? Should have gotten rid of you years ago." She savored the thought of seeing him dead. She had killed him often in her head each time they had argued. Thoughts of rat poisoning to asphyxiation had entered her mind, but it was all a mute point. She'd never have the nerve to go through with it. Still, she indulged herself in the pleasure of plotting. "It would have been so easy to mess with your blood pressure pills. No one would have ever been able to prove you didn't screw with the dose yourself. Still, it would have been messy; the body and all." She closed the door, flipped the lock, and returned to the kitchen.

Detective Harper's business card was still where she had left it, pinned to the bulletin board next to the phone. Worry lines settled between her brows as she ran a finger across the black embossed lettering. Maybe Joe had it right this time, but why didn't he tell Harper himself? He was always in trouble with the law and, if he was a suspect in Britni's death, he had more to lose than she did. The question was, would Harper believe her? Mr Harper, she could say, I know who killed her. I thought you should know. It's … No, daughter or not, she had no reason to help Harper or any other cop – ever. Besides, she had spent hours insisting she didn't know what had happened to Britni. If she called him now, he'd think she lied and would suspect her of Britni's murder.

"Then again, maybe he doesn't care." Why should he bother with an old murder anyway? No glory in it for a young man like him. She ripped his card in half then in quarters and again and again until she could tear it no more.

32

Six months of undercover and careful planning had gone into the sting. No matter how often Di Napoli did it, the adrenaline rush was the same. Nerves twitched, his pulse raced, and something in the pit of his stomach needlessly reminded him to watch his step. His instinct to stay alive didn't need any prodding.

Di Napoli eased his car onto the shoulder of the road in Willow Park. He turned off the engine and waited while he focused his sight on the entrance to the playground. The Puerto Ricans would be along any minute. If the sting worked, the trafficking bust would be a few days away. They'd get the Puerto Ricans at their own game but they were the cherry topping on the vanilla ice cream. The point was to capture the elusive Owens who had been too careful in recent months to do anything wrong. They had nothing on him to justify an arrest, and without an arrest, they wouldn't have cause to question him.

Holloway had plans for Owens; Di Napoli didn't care to know what. All he knew was he had to be careful. One wrong move and he'd be taking a horizontal ride to the city morgue if he was lucky enough to escape the frigid depths of Chandler Bay courtesy of the Puerto Ricans.

With few exceptions, no one had earned Di Napoli's trust. There were enough worries out on the streets without looking over his shoulder at the screw-ups from City Hall. At least if he died, it'd be on his terms.

He slipped on a pair of leather driving gloves as he scanned the park in all directions. Aside from the sunshine, he saw nothing out of the ordinary. The squeal of children came from the playground across the way while parents guarded them from nearby benches. He flipped open his cell, dialed, and waited.

"Holloway? I'm in the park. Everyone in place?"

"Just like we planned," said the Captain. "The minute things get out of hand, you get the hell out of there and let the others handle the Puerto Ricans."

"I'll be fine. These spics are gluttonous bastards. I've been around them long enough to know they wouldn't screw up a deal like this."

"I don't care. Things can go wrong."

"The carrot's too big this time," Di Napoli laughed. "Won't let this one slip through their greedy fingers."

"I don't like you out there without a wire," Holloway reminded him.

"What do you wanna do? Get me killed? I'm touched, Captain, but I'll be fine. I rigged up the camera in the trunk, busted out the taillight, and taped it back up except for a small hole for the lens. Can't even tell the thing's in there. Damned car looks like all the rest of the trash I hang around with these days. I'll make sure he stands in front of the lens. You'll have the whole thing on tape. Between it and the fingerprints on the cash envelope, you'll have your case. They're here." Di Napoli had a few minutes before the black Lincoln drove around the playground.

The sleek car with its polished chrome spinners and tinted windows made heads turn as it paraded through the park. Di Napoli was certain their eyes were on him. So far so good, he thought and glanced at his watch. Right on time. He didn't move.

The Lincoln eased around the winding road and stopped several feet behind his car, exactly as he had hoped the driver would. One of the men rushed out of the car and frisked him.

"Hey! What the hell? I'm clean, I'm clean," Di Napoli growled, holding his arms stretched out. "Maybe I should check you out, huh?"

The man curled his lip and turned around. He motioned the all clear to another man who was waiting to open the back passenger door of the Lincoln for the Puerto Rican they called Raul.

"What's the word, man?" Raul raised his hands to his hips and deliberately pulled back his overcoat to reveal the short, black handle of his Glock.

Di Napoli responded with a nod, keeping an eye on the G-20 tucked into Raul's holster. "The supplier's in," he told him.

"He agreed to our demands, no?" Raul asked.

"Yeah."

"Yeah? You sure he won't screw with me."

"Yeah, I'm sure." Di Napoli frowned. "Hey I don't mess with jerks. You think I'm stupid or what?"

"Nah, you're not stupid, just psycho, man. Give me stupid any day."

"I'm doing you a favor. First rule of the game is trust. It's real simple. If you don't, I walk and you can figure out where to get your next shipment." Di Napoli waited for an answer that took too long in coming. "Ah, the hell with this." He made a half turn toward his car and prayed he hadn't breached the fine line between a show of strength and stupidity.

"Hey. Come back here, *hombre*."

Di Napoli stopped. "We got a deal or not?" He glanced over his shoulder. Raul wasn't a tall man but he stood erect with his shoulders pulled back, his chest out, and his head up giving him a presence even Di Napoli couldn't deny.

"Where's the sample?"

Di Napoli offered a sample of the finest from Chandler's police evidence stock for Raul to taste.

"Yeah, you stupid *dago*." He nodded. "We got a deal. So where and when?"

Di Napoli motioned with his hand for the payoff.

Raul pulled out an envelope similar to the one Owens had given Di Napoli days before. "It's all there. Count it if you want."

"Difference between you and me, *hombre*," Di Napoli mocked, "is that I believe in honor among thieves." He grinned and slipped the package into his breast pocket without counting it. The amount didn't matter. Raul was on tape and the dough was going into evidence along with Raul's and Owens' fingerprints each had left on the envelopes. "You know the warehouse on Plum Street?"

"Yeah, I know it."

Di Napoli gave Raul the same instruction he had given to Owens about Warehouse C.

Raul said nothing. Instead, he pulled up his coat's collar, slipped his hands in the pockets, and turned to gaze out onto the bay. "So who is this guy? Where's he come from?"

"What do you care?"

"I want to know who I'm dealing with," said Raul.

"You're dealing with me, all right? If I say he's okay, he's okay."

"So what gives? He some sort of secret or something?"

"Gotta protect my interests," said Di Napoli.

"Your interests? Hmf. If his stuff is so good, why haven't I ever heard of him before?"

"He'll bring the goods – you bring the money. That's all you need to know." Di Napoli started back toward his car.

"I don't deal with no one I don't trust," yelled Raul.

"Suit yourself. You're not the only one in the market for the goods." Di Napoli opened his car door and slipped behind the wheel. He raised his sight to his rearview mirror. Raul hadn't moved. His hands were on his hips, feet apart allowing his heavy overcoat to flap in the wind. "Hey, *hombre!*" Raul shouted. "If your man doesn't show, your ass is mine, man."

33

Narcotics Division was down the hall and to the left. Harper didn't know and didn't care if Stewart Martin was still at his desk. In spite of Holloway's earlier warning, he had no choice but to go after Owens again. All he needed was another look through Owens' file. He and Quinn had more than a deal going and whatever the link, it was binding Quinn to a code of silence.

Except for the five detectives left in the bullpen, who were too busy to notice him, the south end of the fourth floor was empty. Harper scanned the area for Martin's desk in the third row to the back. It was easy to spot the desk with papers strewn about its surface. He pulled open the lower left hand drawer allowing his fingers to fan through tattered file tabs until he found the one he needed. At a glance, he could tell it wasn't the same folder. He frowned as he leafed through the pages. The reports he and Gillies had typed were missing. He didn't have time to worry about the discrepancy and took it anyway. He glanced at one side of the room and then at another as he shoved the drawer in and started back toward his office.

"What the hell do you think you're doing?"

The muscles around Harper's neck tightened when he heard the snarl in Martin's voice. He stopped without turning, swallowed hard, and said: "Holloway will fill you in." Harper wanted to forget himself again and the high standard of conduct expected of an officer. He wanted to belt it out with him. He'd missed his chance to finish him off a week ago, and right now, he had bigger problems to worry about than Stewart Martin's ego.

"Hey! I saw you going through my desk. Who the hell do you think you are?" Martin yelled again.

Harper kept walking.

"I told you to stop!"

Harper didn't break stride. He could feel his anger reach a boil. If he stopped they'd both be sorry.

"You want an explanation, talk to Hollo–"

The tight grip on his arm spun him around.

With a blinding thrust from his fist, Martin's aim stung sharply against Harper's mouth and drew blood. "I told you to put the damned file down!"

Harper raised the back of his hand to his lip. He could feel his anger burn across his cheeks. One look at the blood on his hand made him lunge toward his attacker. His fist slammed into Martin below the rib cage. The blow hammered him to his knees and curled him into a ball. Harper glared down, conscious of his rapid, shallow breathing. He reveled in the moans Martin was making.

"You forgot to say, please, asshole." He wiped his bloody lip again, snatched up the papers that had scattered across the floor, and walked away.

The sting from Martin's fist forced a throbbing ache up the side of Harper's face toward his temples. He lumbered into his office. He raised his hand to his lip again. It had quit bleeding, but it was tender and swollen. Blood droplets had soaked onto the front of his shirt and made him think of the baby blanket again. He turned off the overhead lights, closed his eyes, and drew in a breath. He was disgusted with what had just happened.

The light from a single lamp illuminated a circular area on his desk. The place was quiet for a change and he was glad to have it to himself. He sat down and flipped open the fought-over folder. Aside from Owens' arrest record, the file contained none of the details of his and Gillies' work. Their reports of the drug busts were missing and Martin had clearly not taken the case any further. He tossed the file down. A quick scan of his desk assured him everything was just as he had left it earlier in the day, before the interrogations ate away at the hours and his patience. The answers were there, among the list of facts each suspect had tossed out to them days before. Quinn and Owens were both involved and all he'd have to do is find the connecting pieces of the puzzle and make them fit together.

It was the third evening since Roxanne's and Quinn's interrogations. Harper still needed answers to questions and the DNA results were not yet conclusive. Hours lapsed without fulfilling a promise of disclosing any new facts on the Baby Doe. It seemed as if Owens' capture was as improbable as it had been on the night Gillies died.

Mann had left the office at six o'clock to pick Abby up for dinner. That was nearly two hours ago. Rapt in his work, Harper didn't notice the time nor remembered he was one of a handful of officers left on the floor. He stood by his window and gazed down on the river of lights flowing through the streets below. The northbound traffic stalled along Hampton Drive near exit 41. Drivers seemed eager to get out of the city on a Friday night and get on with the weekend. Dusk slowly turned into a golden thread of light along the distant horizon.

Harper crushed an empty pop can he had left on his desk earlier in the day and gave it a toss landing it in the trash on top of the wrapper from his egg salad sandwich. He'd wait for the traffic to thin before leaving.

A bad excuse, he thought, *for a thirty-two year-old man on a Friday night*. But there was no one waiting on him and no reason to hurry home. He ran his fingers through his hair refusing to dwell on his barren existence.

Mary Kemp was right, he thought, remembering her comments. Roxanne had been a victim after all. Someone stripped her of her youth and innocence in a single act of violence.

Harper knew every detail of the events that had culminated in the horror he was trying to solve. He could recite the facts in the case from memory without fear of being far from either of the witnesses' accounts of what had happened. He placed Roxanne's and Quinn's statements squarely in front of him – side by side, and began to pore over each handwritten line. The statements nearly agreed. Roxanne, Quinn, and Owens, also known as Joe and J O depending on who was talking, were in the apartment with the twins on the evening of June third. Harper circled her statement about the third man with the tattoo in red. He returned to the words Roxanne had penned onto the page about the man with the tattoo she claimed had taken Britni.

Harper switched on the tape recorder and played back Quinn's interrogation. He ran the tape, stopped it, backed it up, and played it again. Each time, checking Quinn's words against his written statement. When he was satisfied of an accurate account, he went on to the next set of questions and answers. Intent to hear every one of Quinn's statements, he continued the process for several minutes before he came to a snag in Quinn's account. The tape hummed as it wound in reverse, stopped with a click, and resumed.

Harper concentrated on Quinn's voice:

"He wanted favors done for him all the time."

"What kind of favors?"

"Favors. One day he tells me he owed this friend of his a wad of dough; Skipper owed someone else, and well, ya know how that goes. Said that gettin' rid of the little brats would make things right."

"Who's Skipper?" Mann had asked him. Quinn claimed he didn't know. Just one of J O's contacts.

"Was Skipper there that night?" Mann asked him. "Was he in on the deal to sell the girls?"

"I ain't sayin' it again. No. It was just me and J O and them kids weren't gonna be sold."

Harper flipped through the pages of Quinn's statement. There was no mention of Skipper – not a word of reference and thus no clue to the man's identity. He played the recording back several times until he was sure of what he was hearing. Roxanne was certain the tattooed man in the room was the dealer. Harper ran a hand over his mouth.

"Quinn you weasel," he mumbled. "Did you really think we wouldn't notice?" Had Quinn let a piece of information slip or did he intentionally omit Skipper's name from his written statement?

In the heat of the interrogation, Harper had drawn only one conclusion, the one he had wanted to hear; Owens was guilty. This he believed blindly, unwilling to hear the facts. Now in the solitude of his office, devoid of phone calls and interruptions, he admitted with a clear mind to his error. Mann was new to the case. He wouldn't have caught the glitch, how could he? But there it was, looming before Harper's eyes; he couldn't ignore the fact that Owens didn't have a tattoo. Nothing could alter that, not even Harper's desire to make it so. He wanted to kick himself for not having been in Interrogation Room 3 when Quinn made his statement. Frustration at the thought of not being able to charge Owens with murder replaced his past elation. All they had now was an omission – nothing less than a critical discrepancy. They were right back where they had started and so the question remained: Who else was in Roxanne Lewis' apartment on the evening of June third?

Harper rubbed his brow and frowned.

Skipper.

He'd heard the name before, not more than a couple of nights before at the Roving Dog Saloon. That's what the old guy at the bar had called Chuck – Skip. The nudging in his gut was the hope his hunch would pay off knowing he'd need a lot more than a guess to tie it all together. His thoughts about Chuck and his bar made him think about Gillies again. He was the last person he wanted to think about now, but no officer on duty at the time of Baby Doe's death was above suspicion of rape or murder. He closed his eyes to suppress the image of a sixteen-year-old runaway being raped by one of their own.

"Jesus, Gillies," he whispered.

There was no connection that Harper could see between Gillies' death and Baby Doe, or Roxanne Lewis, for that matter. No connection at all except for the tie to the mutual scum they all had in common. That alone was cause for unrest. He paced in front of his desk and thought of something else about the night his partner died. He'd have to check on the 911 call Chuck claimed he made when he heard the shots to prove his hunch, but he needed to talk to the bartender first. Harper unfolded the slip of paper he took from his wallet and dialed the number of the Roving Dog.

"Chuck? Sam Harper here."

"Ah, guess ya haven't heard. Charlie's ticker went out on him yesterday afternoon."

"He's dead?" Another frown creased Harper's brow. Rubbing the spot between his eyes didn't help the tightness that raced across his forehead.

"Yeah, right here behind da bar, just before he opened da place. Anything I can do for ya?"

"No. I'm … Thanks anyway." He dropped the receiver into its cradle. "Damn it." He made up his mind to pay the man on the other end of the line a visit when the sound of Kay's voice made him look over his shoulder.

"Are you busy?" she asked.

Kay shifted her weight to one hip and threw her head back enough for the light to capture the sweet honey tone of her lipstick. She held her briefcase and jacket in one hand and seized the doorknob with the other. Harper's gaze dropped to the slender contour of her legs then followed them up to the hem of her tailored skirt. His eyes skipped from the four small buttons on the front of her blouse up to her lips again. He pitied the poor sucker who fell for her smile – it was as inviting as it was dangerous and part of one hell of a tempting package. Harper decided that aside from the blonde hair, Kay Terrill was nothing like Deanna. She was sharp, bold, and unpredictable. The proof was that in spite of their heated argument about Roxanne Lewis, she was in his office asking permission to come in. He leaned against his desk and wondered what she could possibly want now.

"What happened to you?" she asked, nodding at the swollen cut on his lip as she nudged the door shut. She walked the few steps toward Mann's desk and let her briefcase and jacket slip out of her hand.

His glance instinctively swept to the swing of her hips as he stroked his lip. "Nothing." It was after nine. The last person he expected to see tonight, any night, was the assistant prosecuting attorney. "What are you doing here?" He watched her, curious to know what was so damned important to prompt her to come looking for him after hours.

"Just left a client in interrogation. Took a chance you might still be here. We need to talk." Kay slipped into the only armchair in the office. She crossed her legs and met his glance. "Come on. Sit down," she said, tapping the toe of her shoe to the leg of the other chair.

She had his undivided attention.

"Attorneys don't make social calls, least of all after hours. I'm almost afraid to ask," he said. "What's wrong?"

"I've been thinking about your case."

"What about it?" He straddled the side chair, leaned forward to meet her gaze, and noticed the spark in her eyes. Her glance was as deliberate as the way she crossed her leg just high enough to make him curious. Sure, they could discuss the case and anything else Kay had in mind.

"Roxanne's allegation about the rape."

"Damn it, Kay, let it go. Evidence or not, she can't be lying. She was sixteen-years-old."

"Listen to you. You don't even know what I'm going to say. Are you always this quick to jump to conclusions?"

He rolled his eyes and briefly looked away. "All right. Go on."

"I think she's telling the truth. That's why I'm here. When I first hired as the assistant prosecuting attorney, I made it my business to dig into old case files. I couldn't believe how many had gone cold. Anyway, Roxanne reminded me of a series of them."

"As in a series of rape cases?"

"Exactly."

"A serial rapist? You think there's a connection between Roxanne's attacker and a serial rapist?"

"I'm only speculating, but it's possible," she said. "There were five teen rape cases in and around the Rock Hill area in four years; two in 1980, one in 1982, and two more in 1983."

"Five? Hell, that's nothing compared to what we deal with on a regular basis." Harper wasn't familiar with Rock Hill except to say it was a small community in the northwest corner of the county with a police force of three. "Wish our crime rate was that low." The slight curl of her lips told him she didn't like interruptions. "Sorry, go on."

"What's unique about those five cases is each girl claimed she was raped by a police officer. They all told a similar story. Each rape happened at night. The rapist picked them up while the girls were walking alone. The creep evidently lured them into an unmarked car and gave them a line on safety before he attacked them."

"Little town like that, everyone knows their neighbor and their neighbor's business," he said. "What's more, you can count the number of officers in Rock Hill on one hand."

"According to the sheriff's report, each of the three officers had an alibi during the time of the rapes."

"Anybody check the sheriff's alibi?"

"You said it yourself. It's a small town and everyone knows everyone. No. It wasn't any of the locals, including the sheriff. The girls attested to that."

"What about a description of the guy?" he asked.

"That's where the case reached a snag. Each of the five gave a different account of what she saw. One said he was blond, another said he had dark hair; one claimed the guy had a mustache the others said he didn't. The police concluded the rapist disguised himself."

"Well weren't they a sharp bunch," he said.

"Quit being so cocky. The thing is," she continued, "the rapist had to have known what he was doing or at least understood what the police would look for."

"How long did the cases stay open?"

"Not very. The police had nothing to go on. According to the officers' reports, the girls were too frightened and humiliated to file charges. They were afraid to testify. You know how it goes. Doesn't take long for the trail of clues to dry up."

"And you think we're dealing with the same man?"

"I think it's entirely possible, yes. Roxanne would have conceived in September of 1989. We're talking about a nine-year span between the first Rock Hill rape and Roxanne's. You know as well as I do there are crimes on the books that span fifteen – twenty years where the killer disappeared and resurfaced years later."

"Now we're looking for a pervert passing himself off as an

officer. Thanks for making my life easier." He rubbed the back of his neck. "It could be anyone."

"I say it's worth looking into."

"Any other similar cases?"

"Not that I could find," she said. "At least not in our county. We'll have to check with the State Police."

"The last attack was six years before Roxanne's rape. Why'd he stop?" Harper asked.

"Only three things I know stop a rapist; he's either moved on, he's sitting in jail, or he's six feet under. We'll ignore the latter for now and concentrate on the possibility he's moved on."

"What about a trademark – calling card?" he asked.

"None."

"Trace?"

"The file didn't indicate that trace evidence was secured from any of the girls. The only similarity between the cases was the rapist's clothing."

"Where did he get the uniform? Anybody question the costume shop owners in the area?"

"Yes, and they came up with nothing."

"So what are you telling me? That the guy knew a cop and used his uniform?"

"I don't know how he got his hands on it. It looks like the police went over everything. Never found a connection to anyone," she said.

Harper lowered his glance as he mulled things over. "Kay, those rapes were committed before DNA was admissible in the courts. You have no positive ID, no calling card, and no trace. What do you expect me to do with this?" he asked. "What's your angle?"

"A hunch. You act on hunches, don't you, Harper?" A smug smile slipped across her face then quickly faded. "I don't care what the reports say, a couple of the girls were from well to do families. I'm betting the parents had their daughters examined and forced the authorities to retain and preserve semen samples."

"Even if they did, it's a gamble at best," he said. "Without someone to match to the specimens, they're worthless."

"It's a damned good lead and you know it."

Harper frowned. Holloway's orders to him were not to involve anyone else in the rape investigation. *On the other hand*, he thought, *Kay's the assistant P.A., she heard Roxanne's statement first hand, and stuck her neck out to find a possible connection to another crime.* "We're putting in overtime as it is. I don't know when I'd be able to get up to Rock Hill," he told her.

"I can go." She tilted her head again. "You've got this look on your face." She mocked his frown and placed her finger on the spot between her eyes. "What's this all about?"

"I need your word."

"On what?"

"If you're right about this, anything you find, and I mean anything, you give directly to Holloway and me. Understand? Not a word to anyone else, including your boss, until we have all the facts. Holloway's orders."

"I figured as much. Why do you think I'm here? If this guy is still on the loose, I want him. I'm not about to let anything screw it up."

"You have any connections in Rock Hill?"

"No. Not yet. I'll work on it though."

The smile that eased across her lips again told Harper she was used to getting her way. In that sense, she and Deanna were identical, except he had no choice but to trust Kay's instincts. "Let's hear your plan."

She inched closer to him. "If the DNA from the semen matches the baby's DNA, we'll at least know we're looking for the same person. With luck on our side, we could nail him on six known rape charges." She paused and waited for his response. "What do you think?"

"Those are big *if's*."

"Bullshit. You know I'm right."

He had to admit she also had a point. The hitch was the five-year statute of limitations on rape. They were screwed without DNA. Then again, if the authorities had collected and preserved the semen, he could search the DNA databank for a match to known rapists. "It's a long shot. You know that, don't you?"

"Long and crazy enough to be worth investigating."

"How soon can you get on it?" he asked.

"I'll make some inquiries first thing in the morning." She rose to her feet and gathered her belongings. "Holloway will need to talk with the sheriff. If they won't release the evidence, I'll get a warrant and let you know as soon as I have something." She slipped on her jacket and started to leave then stopped. They were both near the door when she asked: "Harper, you ever eat anything that doesn't come hermetically sealed from a vending machine?"

"What did you have in mind, counselor?"

"What do you think?" She ran her hand down his arm and laced her fingers through his. "Dinner. Tomorrow, eight o'clock. Your treat of course."

"Sure, why not." *What's wrong with tonight*, he wondered. The investigation could wait a few hours.

"Good." She squeezed his hand then pulled away as unexpectedly as she had arrived. "I'll call you when I get back from Rock Hill."

"Kay, wait a minute." He stepped between her and the door. Words hung on the tip of his tongue. He looked into her eyes hoping to find a hint of warmth. Instead, he detected the cold determination of a professional mixed with a delicate scent of perfume. It swept past him as fast as he had blocked the urge to kiss her when he saw her standing in his doorway. The ugly reality was a relationship, even a casual encounter, right now would complicate matters. Instead of a plea, he reluctantly pulled the door open. "Thanks."

"You're welcome." She slipped her hand over his belt and pulled him near.

He was trained to expect the unexpected but the law enforcement manual never mentioned a thing about Kay Terrill. He leaned in and wrapped his hands around the small of her back as they kissed. Maybe he should take her home. He'd go with her to Rock Hill; they could make a day of it.

"I need to go." Kay whispered and pushed herself away. She raised the strap of her purse to her shoulder, turned, and drifted down the hall. "I'll call you."

"Wait a minute. Kay?"

"Tomorrow, Harper. In the meantime, be careful. If it does turn out to be a police officer, things could get ugly."

34

Harper's third stop at the Roving Dog Saloon made him feel like a regular. Inside, the room was thick with smoke. He strained to see past the first few figures sitting at the bar nearest the door. His first observation was that little had changed since Chuck's death. The beer and bourbon flowed as freely as it had before and, from the looks of things, it hadn't made the hookers frigid with sorrow either.

The man behind the counter was younger than Chuck by at least thirty years and a good forty pounds lighter. He nodded and pointed in bartender language for: what'll it be?

"Scotch and soda," replied Harper. He pointed to his favorite red label brand and took a seat at the far end of the bar near Chuck's collection of photographs. He pretended to give the ten or so framed pictures hanging randomly along the wall a casual glance while he scrutinized each within his immediate view. Harper inventoried his memory of facts about Chuck; he knew Owens, he bore a naval tattoo on his arm, and people referred to him as Skipper. Incredible coincidences he couldn't believe he had missed. Maybe he was grasping at straws, but right now the straws were his only leads and he wasn't leaving this place without answers.

"There you go. That'll be three and a quarter."

"I hear Chuck passed away."

"Yeah, yesterday. Can ya believe it? Ya knew him?"

"No, not really. I've been in here a few times." Harper showed him his badge. "He helped me out on a case once," he lied. "What happened to him?"

"I wouldn't know, man. The story I got was it was a heart attack. Guess he was setting things set up for the happy hour crowd." The bartender thumbed over his shoulder at his customers and laughed. "Like ya have to tell these jokers it's happy hour."

Harper raised his glass and stopped short of taking a drink. "Anybody with him?"

"One of the other guys was here, the bookkeeper. Said Charlie was fine one minute and the next thing he knew he was sicker than a dog."

"This bookkeeper, does he have a name?"

"Hospital said Charlie died of natural causes. Why are the cops getting involved?"

"Never said this was official," he lied again. Lies were starting to roll off his tongue a little too easily these days. "Just curious to know what happened, that's all. Seemed like an okay guy. Any reason you can't talk about him?"

"No reason. Just seems strange is all. Cops don't come around asking questions for no reason."

"I'm off duty and just paid for a drink. So how about it?"

The bartender dropped his glance and wiped a spot off the counter. "Lonnie. His name's Lonnie Powers. He wanted to take Charlie to the hospital. Guess he was a mess, salivating, puking. Charlie told him it felt like he had a fire in his belly." The bartender ran his hand up and down along his chest to indicate where Chuck had felt the sensation.

"Heart attack?"

"That's what the doc said. Anyway, Charlie wasn't much for hospitals. Hell, in the time it took him to argue with Lonnie about it, he dropped dead."

"That fast, huh?" Harper wasn't about to mention Chuck's symptoms were inconsistent with a heart attack. "Did he have a condition?"

"Beats me. Didn't know him well enough to ask. Looked as healthy as the next guy. But hey, what'd I know, right?"

"I take it you two weren't close then."

"We got along fine." The bartender rested his elbows on the bar and leaned in. "Charlie was all business around here. Never got close to the hired help." He paused for a moment and glanced over his shoulder then turned around and whispered: "A few days ago. I was in here stocking the cooler when I overheard him on the phone. He said war and prison have a way of changing a man forever and he didn't intend on going back to either one in this lifetime. Said he'd rather die."

"Any idea who he was talking to?" asked Harper.

"Nah, but he seemed real upset about something. Anyway, he hung up right after that. Seemed fine later. Didn't think too much about it at the time, but after he croaked, well that's the kind of crap that sticks with a guy, ya know?"

"What struck you as odd? That he served in the military or time in prison?" Harper added a prison stay to the short list of things he knew about Chuck. He could only assume that was Chuck's connection to Owens.

"What do ya think?" the bartender asked. "Around here, ya get to know plenty of guys who were in and out of the joint but Charlie didn't look like a criminal."

"Did you ask him about it?"

"Do I look like an idiot? Hell, I just started working here a couple of months ago. Wasn't my place to ask him. Besides, he wasn't exactly talking to me. Last thing I needed was for him to know I was eavesdropping. Hell, the guy signed my pay checks, if ya know what I'm saying."

Harper nodded and motioned for a refill.

"The way I see it, it was none of my business. Guess we'll never know what he did now."

"Hey Tiny. Fill it up!" The man calling held up an empty beer pitcher.

The bartender tossed the towel over his shoulder, took care of the order, then came back to finish his story. "Charlie liked to think he was tough. Goes to show ya never know when your time's up."

This bartender didn't need prodding to talk, but it seemed Lonnie was the person Harper needed to speak with next. "All those Chuck's?" he asked, thumbing at the photographs hanging on the wall.

"Yeah. He was real proud of his Navy days. In fact, some of the old timers still called him Skipper. Not that he was or anything – enlisted man. But that's all Charlie talked about. The gunnery."

Harper was pleased with himself. The bartender had just confirmed his suspicions. He tossed his glass back and let the sweet burning feel of the Scotch ease down his throat. It was good. Too good in fact and he immediately knew he needed a third.

Harper thought of the day he and Mann had responded to the call at the Harbor View Apartment building. From the beginning, the case was earmarked in need of a miracle. They had stripped back the layers of clues only to find a snarled, tangled web of lies and even darker secrets beneath each one. Ironically, the unlikely deliverer of a miracle was Alvin Quinn. Without Quinn's slip of the tongue, Harper would never have linked Chuck to the case.

Dead or not, Harper needed to match Chuck's blood to the blanket. He tipped his glass back again, lowered it, and glanced across the room. The couple kissing in the back booth caught his attention. He watched them until his stare became uncomfortably apparent to him. He thought about Kay; her sexuality, her appeal, and her ease. Women like her were the type men dream of but they're nothing but trouble in the flesh. Maybe he should have taken Abby up on that blind date. He swirled his stool back around and quickly put the thought out of his mind. Tiny was busy serving up drinks when Harper motioned for his attention.

"Ready for another?"

Harper nodded and pointed to the wall. He remembered Chuck had taken a picture down while they were talking and placed it beneath the counter. "There's a picture missing."

"Where?"

"There. You can see the mark of the frame where it hung on the wall. I was just here a couple of nights ago. I'm sure it was there."

The bartender looked around beneath the counter and along the backside of the bar.

"The nail must have fallen off," said Harper.

"Ah, here it is. Must be one of his war buddies." He grinned. "Look at this. He still had dark hair."

While the bartender stepped away again to fill orders, Harper angled the picture toward the light and narrowed his eyes. The yellowed snapshot was out of focus, but it was clear enough for Harper to make out the faces. A young Chuck Toomey was standing, smiling broadly beneath the sign of the Harbor View Apartment. But Harper's attention focused on the man standing off center a few steps behind him to the right. Alvin Quinn. He mentally recapped the suspects' statements and decided Roxanne hadn't lied about seeing a tattooed man. Quinn hadn't lied either, at least not completely. Someone had wanted favors from him and the use of the building and someone had shaken the baby to death. Why then, had Quinn fingered the wrong man?

Harper slid behind the wheel of his car and checked the time. It was after one in the morning when he reached for his cell phone.

"Never too late for good news," he said as he dialed Holloway's number. It rang several times before the Captain answered. "Are you ready for this?" Harper asked him.

"Probably not. What time is it?" The Captain's voice was groggy with sleep.

"One twenty-three."

Holloway grumbled something under his breath. "Harper, don't you have a life? You're not still at the station, are you?"

"No, just left the Roving Dog." He could hear Holloway draw in a gulp of air. "Chuck Toomey's place."

"All right, do I want to know why?"

"You remember Quinn's statement about everyone owing somebody else money?"

"Go on."

"Remember he mentioned someone by the name of Skipper?"

"Not at the moment," said Holloway.

"He was talking about Chuck Toomey. Do you know him?"

"I know the name. The guy has a police record, a DUI – killed a guy years ago."

"Did you know he had a tattoo? He fits Roxanne's description of the third man in the apartment."

"And you think he's the one? Can you prove the connection

between him and Quinn?" asked Holloway.

"Found an old picture of the two of them tonight in the bar."

"You sure about the nickname?"

"Anybody at this bar can testify to it. Hell the bartender is new and knows it."

"So where is he now?"

"Dead."

"Ah, Jesus. When?"

"Yesterday afternoon. There in the bar."

"What happened?"

"The bartender claimed the docs in emergency called it a heart attack. No heart attack I ever heard of left people puking their guts out."

"Have you talked with the doctors?"

"Not yet. His death seems too convenient though."

"A misdiagnosis?" Holloway suggested.

"Or a cover-up." He waited for Holloway's reaction. "Are you there?"

"Yeah. What are you thinking?"

"So far, the blood type on the baby blanket doesn't match any of the suspects. I'm willing to bet it'll match Chuck's."

"I'll call the medical examiner, have them run blood work before they release the body," said Holloway. "The ME will question the request. They don't run them when the death certificate indicates a natural death."

"Tell him the truth. We have reason to believe Chuck Toomey was murdered."

"By who?"

"Owens or Quinn, take your pick. They were both in the apartment on the night the baby died and were both mixed up in whatever was going on in there. Now they're scared and covering their tracks. In my book, it gives them each a motive and opportunity. Can't understand how the hospital could have screwed up the diagnosis though."

"Wouldn't be the first time a doctor took a bribe," said Holloway. "They only autopsy the suspicious deaths and calling it a heart attack doesn't qualify. If you're right and Toomey was involved in the baby's case, someone went to a lot of trouble to make sure his death went unnoticed." There was a long pause while Holloway drew in a breath and let it out.

"One more thing," said Harper. "I need a warrant."

"For what?"

"The Roving Dog. We need the photograph of Quinn. Maybe there's a date on it; something we can used to establish a connection to the case."

"Anybody else in the bar besides Toomey when he died?"

"Yeah, a guy by the name of Lonnie Powers."

"You believe the bartender's version of things?"

"I believe he believes it."

"No judge is going to grant a warrant without probable cause. We'll wait for the lab to run the usual tests on the body before I call for one. I'll get a hold of the ME right now and then, if you don't mind, I'm going back to sleep."

"What about Gillies?" asked Harper.

"What about him?" Holloway growled.

"Roxanne's allegation, the rape."

"Christ, Harper," he moaned.

"Hell, he was close to Chuck and Owens. Do you think he was mixed up in any of this?"

"Do us both a favor. Go home."

The morning sun peeked through a narrow gap in Harper's bedroom curtains. It was the shrill sound of the alarm though that forced him awake. He moaned, buried his face in the pillow, and reached for the switch. Dry-mouthed from the Scotch, he rolled over and glanced through half opened eyes at the empty pillow next to his. Kay crossed his mind again. He'd see her tonight, right now he needed to get his head on straight and attend to some unfinished business. He swung his legs out of bed, grabbed his jeans that had landed on the floor, and left.

The morning air was fresh and warm for a change, the kind of day that brought out the convertibles. He gripped the wheel of his Jeep, dropped the driver's side window, and reveled in the sunlight. For all he knew this might be all he would see of the sun today. The mental list of contacts he needed to phone was getting longer, but they would have to wait. Right now, answers were waiting for him inside the morgue.

35

Locked doors lined either side of the empty corridor that led to the morgue. Except for the faint rhythmic sound of Latin music coming from the door near the end of the hall, there was no sign of activity in the lower levels of the hospital on this Saturday morning. A light filtered through its frosted glass panel and spilled onto the hall. The dull echo of Harper's measured steps on the polished, tiled floor reflected his sentiment. He turned the knob and swung the door open. Yolanda Cruz was still in her scrubs cleaning up from a recent autopsy, bobbing and humming to a Cuban beat.

Harper darted a glance at the instruments on the stand covered in blood and tissue. Chuck Toomey's washed corpse was face up on the slab. His flesh looked pasty white under the florescent light; his lips were drained of color. A white sheet covered him from below the rib cage down to his feet. Harper's sight went directly to what he could see of the sutured Y incision that forked upward from his sternum.

"What's going on?" he asked her. "All I needed was blood work." A subtle wrinkle lined his brow.

"Morning sunshine." Yolanda looked up and smiled. "Long night? You look about as pale as our friend here." She nodded toward the corpse.

"Couldn't sleep thanks to him and a whole lot of other things. I see you got Holloway's message."

"Do you really think he did it?" she asked.

"I'll let you know when you tell me his blood type. Do you have it?"

"As you can see, I got sidetracked. I'll call you as soon as I do." Yolanda pulled the sheet up over Chuck's face, let it drape down, then peeled off her gloves.

"You're a gem for doing this on short notice," he said as he followed her to her desk and sat in a chair across from her.

"I did it for Britni. She deserves justice."

Harper nodded. "That's the first thing I've heard in days that makes sense. So what's up with Toomey?"

"You know, you're lucky we still had him. The doctor in the ER pronounced him dead of a heart attack – idiot."

"It didn't make sense to me either," he said.

"If Holloway hadn't called last night when he did, I'm not sure we would have gotten to him. He was scheduled to go to Flannery Funeral Home at eight-thirty this morning." She glanced at her watch. "He just missed his ride."

It was a statement spoken in her usual matter-of-fact style, but her eyes said more than her words. Something in the way she had said it and in that knowing glance of hers, made her statement anything but trivial. "Why the autopsy?" he asked again.

"Aren't you going to ask me what I found?"

"I'm all ears."

"I ran a blood analysis like you asked, also ran a sample of his urine. Came up with, let's say, some unusual results."

"Yolanda, I haven't slept all night. Don't play games with me. What did the man die of?"

"Found concentrations of aconitine in the postmortem femoral blood and urine that shouldn't be there."

"Acon what?"

"Aconitine. Chuck Toomey was poisoned. Aconite is a fast acting toxin found in several plants belonging to the buttercup family, Ranunculaceae. The most potent in the group is monkshood; the entire plant is highly poisonous especially the roots and young leaves. The only good thing about dying from it is that it's quick."

"How quick?"

"Anywhere within minutes to an hour from the time it's ingested depending on the dose."

"The guy I talked to at the bar last night said Chuck got violently ill."

"It doesn't surprise me, but he'd still be alive if he had gone to the hospital instead of staying put," she said. "Not the best way to die, especially since the poison doesn't affect the cerebrum."

"Which means what?"

"The mind remains completely unaffected. He was conscious to the end and was most likely aware his body was shutting down."

"What exactly does this stuff do?"

"It causes epigastric pain, burning, tightness in the throat, blurred vision, and a whole mess of other unpleasant side affects. In essence, the poison affects the circulatory and nervous systems and shuts down respiration. The victim ends up dying of asphyxiation. Must have been a hell of a night at the ER if they this missed this one."

"How much of the stuff does it take?"

"A smidgen. The roots can be processed into a liquid form. Five drops will do it."

Harper glanced back at Chuck's body. Murder had crossed his mind, but neither Owens nor Quinn seemed like the types who would know anything about poisonous plants. "So how hard is it to get a hold of this plant?"

"Not very. It's more common than you think. It'll grow in most gardens. Go to the internet sites that sell perennials, not a big deal. You just want to make sure you don't have any pets or young children running around in your garden. The stuff is so toxic it can be absorbed through the skin."

"Why would anyone want it around?" He shook his head and she shrugged her shoulders.

Yolanda motioned for him to wait while she answered her phone. "Cruz, Medical Examiner's Office." She paused for a moment then began jotting down some notes.

Harper rose to his feet and stepped away. He speed dialed Holloway's number and gave him the news. The blood work gave them the proof they needed to request a warrant. By the time she hung up, Harper was back in his chair.

"He died at work," he said. "If it really takes minutes to kick in, he must have ingested it while at the bar. Any thoughts on how he got it?"

She leaned back in her chair and smiled. "Good question. Deserves a good answer. But you, Detective, will have to come up with that one on your own. I can tell you this much. His stomach content had trace evidence of pretzels, cheese and coffee."

36

"Christ, Harper. It's Saturday morning. Don't you ever give it a rest?" Mann's voice was thick and sluggish with sleep.

"We need to talk – about Owens."

"Can it wait?"

"Sure. I'm just leaving the morgue. See you in the office in twenty." Harper tossed his cell onto the seat next to his and maneuvered through traffic. Chuck's death put a new crimp in the case, but Harper didn't have to look hard for a suspect. The ammo didn't fit the male killer's profile. A man would have used direct physical contact; knives and strangulation. Women, on the other hand, prefer to keep their distance.

The usual skeletal weekend crew staffed the police station and for the next thirty minutes, he had it all to himself. The sound of the elevator stopping on his floor and tennis shoes squeaking against the polished tiled floor announced Mann's arrival.

"Here, thought you could use one," he said, handing Harper one of the cups of coffee he had picked up from the shop around the corner. He wiped his hand on his jeans and rolled up the sleeve of his sweatshirt. "Now, you want to tell me what's so damn important?"

Harper took the cup and flipped off the lid as he motioned for Mann to sit down. "I screwed up the other day, with Quinn."

Mann glanced at his watch. "You got me out of bed for that? Damn it, so what if you blew up? The little weasel deserved it."

"That's not what I'm talking about."

"What then? Quinn's statement confirms Roxanne's account of what happened. He gave us Owens. What more do you want?

That's what you've been after, isn't it? All we need is a match of Owens' blood to the stains on the blanket and we've got him on murder." Mann grinned as he propped his feet on his desk and took a drink. "It's an open and sh–"

"It's not going to match."

Mann threw his head back and closed his eyes. "How do you know?"

"Owens doesn't have a tattoo – anywhere. Only distinguishing marks he has are three scars on his chest, four on his right arm, and one on his left thigh, but no tattoo." Harper handed him the file he took from Martin's desk. "Take a look for yourself. That's not the file Gillies and I had, but the information from Owens' last arrest is legit." Harper waited while Mann thumbed through the pages. "According to Roxanne, the man who took the baby from Quinn had a tattoo on his arm, remember?"

"So, Quinn fingered the wrong guy. Who's he protecting?"

"Chuck Toomey."

A sour look washed over Mann's face. He lowered his legs and leaned in. "Who the hell is he?"

Harper filled him in on how he had met Chuck on the night Gillies died. That he remembered a bar patron had called him Skip, the same name Quinn had let slip on the tape recording and a fact the new bartender had confirmed the night before. And now Chuck's body was chilling in the morgue.

"But Quinn said this Skip person was one of Owens' contacts not his."

"Wouldn't be the first time Quinn lied to us. I found a picture at the bar that tells a different story," said Harper.

"Let's say the blood type confirms this guy's the killer," said Mann. "What does his death have to do with anything? If you're right, he just saved the state a pile of money."

Harper explained the connection as he saw it.

"Now I know where they get the old cliché, a web of lies. Damned thing is going in all directions. All right. You've got my attention," said Mann. "What's next?"

"We need to talk with the guy who was with Chuck when he died. The cause of death was a quick acting poison which means he would have ingested it there at the bar."

They were ready to leave when Harper's phone rang. The news from dispatch didn't surprise him, but he had hoped it wouldn't be true. "Thanks." He snapped his cell shut and drew in a breath.

"What's the matter?" asked Mann.

"That was dispatch confirming another hunch. Gillies' death was a set up." Harper gave Mann a detailed account of his suspicions of Gillies on the night he died; how Gillies had lied about Mellow killing a man near the Trenton Overpass, that Chuck had known of the false shooting, and that Chuck had sent Owens away hours before they arrived. "Chuck made the 911 call to report the shooting and to request an ambulance at 1:09 in the morning."

"What's that prove?" asked Mann.

"I looked at the dashboard clock as I opened the car door to go after Mellow," said Harper. "It was 1:18. Figure the chase probably took another five minutes. How the hell did Chuck know we'd need an ambulance more than ten minutes before the first shot was fired?"

Weeks ago, Harper had asked himself why the bartender had sent Owens away on the evening of March 3. Now he knew. Chuck had other plans and they didn't include Owens' capture. Gillies had been his target. To keep quiet? About what? Maybe Chuck was thinking dead men couldn't talk. What he hadn't considered is the dead don't tell lies either.

"Look, Sam. I know your partner's death has been tough to swallow, but there's nothing you can do about it now. We know who killed him. Except for you, the guys involved in the shooting are dead. Close the book on it and move on. It's not the first time a cop got killed by a dealer."

"It's not just Frank Gillies' death. This," he said pointing at his stomach, "tells me there's a connection to Baby Doe."

"That a stretch, even for you."

"I can't see it yet, but I do know one thing, his death had nothing to do with drugs."

"Let's say you're right. How are you going to prove it?"

"Go after the only other person in the ring who's alive and can fill in the gaps about Gillies and Baby Doe."

"Owens?" asked Mann.

"The same perps are involved in both cases. What are the chances of that happening? Here, take a look at this." Harper handed him the printed copies he had made of Gillies' CD files. "Look halfway down the page." He pointed to a name he had circled in red pen.

"This Tommy Di Napoli?"

"He's an undercover cop in Narcotics; been around a while. We both worked the Owens case. I hear he's still working it."

Mann placed the pages back on Harper's desk. "Good. Let Di Napoli get him then."

"Di Napoli is after Owens on drug charges. We have him in connection to the baby's murder. Maybe Chuck's too."

"We have nothing on him and you know it. You just said Owens couldn't have been the baby's killer. If Chuck's blood type matches the blood on the blanket, we're going to stamp the damned thing closed and move on. All we have on Owens are statements from two witnesses who claim he was in the apartment on the night in question." Mann tossed his empty cup in the trash then raised a hand to the back of his neck. "You're obsessing over this, you know that? Who exactly is this Owens character anyway that everyone's tripping over each other to get to? He's just a pusher. Nothing but a hop-head. Why are you making him out to be the key to this investigation?"

"Owens is responsible for …" Harper frowned. "What did you say?"

"What?"

"Just now. The last thing you said."

"That he's the key to this invest–"

"Damn. I almost forgot. Come on."

"What's with you today?"

"I'll explain on the way to the subway." Harper recalled his conversation with Abby about the man in her office who kept his work in a locker. He hurried to grab the key from his drawer. The one with the funny round bow Emma had given to him; the one that didn't belong to the Chandler Police Department.

37

Harper pulled hard on the doorknob of the Roving Dog Saloon.

"How many bars do you know that are closed on a Saturday afternoon?" he asked Mann. He pressed his face against the diamond-shaped glass of the red door and cupped his hands around his eyes to block the sun's glare. Inside, save for the glow from a small gooseneck lamp at the far end of the bar, the place was in complete darkness. A man sat hunched in a writing position near the light. An assortment of papers and books lay scattered before him. Harper made a fist and hammered hard on the door. "Open up. Chandler PD."

Harper was about to knock again when a man's thin, pale face appeared in the window. Dark eyes beneath a set of thick brows looked back at him and frowned.

"We're closed." The man's muffled voice was barely audible.

"Detectives Harper and Mann, Chandler PD Homicide." Harper pressed his badge against the window. "Open up." As soon as Harper heard him unlock the door, he pushed it open, walked in, and took off his sunglasses.

"Did you say Homicide?" the man asked as he brushed down his mustache. "I don't get this."

"Take a number," Mann muttered.

"And you are?" Harper asked him.

"Lonnie." He frowned and swept back the hair from his eyes then crossed his arms.

"You have a last name, Lonnie?" asked Harper.

"Powers. Lonnie Powers. What's this all about?"

Harper looked around the dark room, reached for the light

switch, and locked the font door. "What exactly do you do here, Lonnie Powers?"

"Now wait a minute." The man's eyes widened. "Aren't you supposed to read me my rights? Shouldn't you have a warrant or something?"

"Sounds guilty to me," said Mann. "What do you say we take him downtown and get this over with?"

Harper reached into his breast pocket for the warrant and pushed it against Lonnie's chest. "Sit down. You haven't given me a reason to arrest you – yet." He pointed at a stool and waited for Lonnie to take a seat. "Now, what do you do here?"

"I'm only part time while I finish up a night class." His glance darted between the two detectives.

"You get to the chapter on how to give a straight answer yet?" asked Mann. "What's your job here?"

"Christ. I keep the books, all right?" Lonnie thumbed over his shoulders at the papers he had left at the other end of the bar. "I keep track of the inventory, place the orders, stuff like that. What the hell's going on?"

"Turns out your boss didn't have a heart problem. Toomey was murdered."

"You're kidding, right?" Lonnie blinked and then started to grin. "Okay, I get it. A late April Fool's gag. Someone's idea of a joke, right? You guys aren't really cops, are you? Who sent you? Was it –"

"Do you see us laughing?" Mann leaned in within inches of the man's face then turned away and walked behind the bar.

Lonnie gave Mann a guarded glance as Mann eyed the items beneath the counter. "But the doctors said it was a heart attack. I was in the emergency room. Heard it with my own two ears."

"You were with him when he died too, right? Here, on the afternoon of April 5?" asked Harper.

"That's right. I tried to get him to go to the hospital, but he was a stubborn old goat. Jesus, he wasn't murdered. He just keeled over and dropped dead."

"Where'd you get your medical degree?" Mann asked him.

"Go through your day for us," said Harper, "from the beginning when you first arrived."

"Am I a suspect?"

"You want to be?" asked Harper.

"Hell no!" Lonnie's eyes opened wide again.

"Then start talking," said Harper.

"Yeah, but –"

Mann reached for his handcuffs and slapped them on the counter. "Here's how this works, Lonnie. We asked the questions and you give us what we want or we haul you in."

"Jesus Christ, all right!"

Harper raised his foot to the rung of the stool without taking his eyes from Lonnie. "The official time of death was two-twelve p.m. on Thursday, April 5. Let's start with what time you walked through those doors and who was in here."

"I got here about quarter of eleven that morning. Chuck was already here," he said, watching Mann take down his statement.

"I'm over here," said Harper. "You talk to me. Anyone else in the place?"

"Nah. He was alone. We always did the inventory together; placed the order early on Thursdays for the following week." Lonnie explained they normally open for business at eleven o'clock sharp throughout the week except on Thursdays when they order supplies.

Harper glanced around at the empty establishment. "What about today? It's after one on a Saturday afternoon. Why's the place closed?"

"I do the books on Saturday. Don't open up until three."

"What happened after you got here?"

"Like I said, I came in just before eleven. Chuck had already started inventorying the stock. We finished around noon and then I started filling out order forms. He was working on the books pretty much the rest of the time."

"Seems Chuck liked cheese and pretzels."

"Yeah. He finished off an open package of cheese and a couple small bags of pretzels."

"Did you see him eat or drink anything else?"

"No. Not that I can remember." He paused for a moment. "Except, he did make a pot of coffee."

"What time was that?"

"I couldn't tell you the exact time."

"Was it made when you got here, did he make it right after you got here, what?" Harper pressed him for details.

"After I got here; closer to two."

"You're sure about the time?"

"Damn sure."

"Why? What happened to make you so *damn sure*?"

"A woman stopped by to use the phone. Heard a knock on the front door. I remember thinking we still had an hour before we opened. Couldn't figure out what she was doing here. Especially someone who looked like her."

"What did she want?"

"Had a flat. Needed to call for a tow truck."

"Describe her."

"Nice looking. Average height, slender. Sexy southern accent," he said.

Harper exchanged glances with Mann. He pulled out the police photograph of Roxanne Lewis and flipped it in front of Lonnie's face. "Have you ever seen this woman here before?"

"That's her. That's the woman." He reached for the picture to examine it closely. "Holy shit. This is a police photo. What'd she do?"

"Ever see her here before last Thursday afternoon?"

Lonnie shook his head and gave the snapshot a tap. "No. Then again, I don't come in except to do the books."

"What happened after you let her in?" asked Harper.

Lonnie shrugged his shoulders. "It's a crummy neighborhood. Chuck told her she could wait in here until the tow truck showed up. He handed her the phone and poured her a cup of coffee."

"A real gentleman, huh?" said Mann.

"We don't get any ladies around here, if you get my drift. Didn't see any harm in letting her use the phone. I had things to finish. Didn't pay any attention to her after that."

"Let's go back to the coffee. When did you see him pour the last cup?"

"Just before she came in."

"You say she drank from the same pot?"

"Yeah."

"What did he do with his cup?"

"I don't get what you mean."

"Where did he leave the cup while he was talking with her? Did he leave it on the bar or what?"

"Yeah. Left it right here." Lonnie tapped his hands down on the bar. "She sat on a stool right in front of him."

"You think Chuck knew her?" asked Harper.

"Didn't act like it to me. He struck up a conversation with her like he would with any other customer."

"What'd they talk about?"

"Ah, you know. They just shot the breeze, weather, crap like that. Nothing worth listening to."

"So he was standing there, the coffee mug in front of him, right?"

"That's right." Lonnie nodded.

"And he took a drink."

"I guess. He was always drinking coffee."

"What about her? What was she doing all this time?"

"She didn't do anything. Tried to call the towing service; said the line was busy so she sat there, drank her coffee, and talked with Chuck. What's the big deal?"

"Did you see her touch his cup or go near it at any time?"

"Nah, why would she?" He paused. "Except when she had to clean up her spill. Other than that, she didn't touch it."

"What happened?" Harper leaned in and fixed his attention on every word Lonnie Powers said.

"No big deal. She was talking with her hands and almost knocked over her cup. Some of it spilled on the counter and ran all over the place. While Chuck turned to get a rag, she started wiping the mess up with some napkins. She picked his cup up and wiped off the bottom. That's it. Nothing out of the ordinary."

Harper could feel a grin tugging at the corners of his mouth.

That was it all right. His first thought was she had lied about knowing Chuck Toomey. How else would she have known he would be here last Thursday and know when to slip him the poison?

"She must have had it in her hand; slipped it in when she picked up his cup," said Mann.

"Slipped what in?" asked Lonnie.

"How long was she here?"

"Twenty minutes, maybe. I don't know. She was still around when Chuck got sick. That's all I remember. She left before the ambulance got here though. Could have used some help too. I had my hands full with him. He barely made it into the back room. Never seen anything like it. I'm telling you, he was a mess."

The detectives exchanged glances again. A search of Chuck's back room didn't offer any evidence he and Roxanne had been in contact before the afternoon of his death. Harper grabbed the photograph of Quinn and Chuck from behind the bar. He gave it another look. There was nothing routine about this case. What appeared to be so, wasn't. Why should Chuck's murder be any different?

38

Harper watched as a uniformed officer escorted Roxanne out of her home. When she disappeared into the back seat of a city car, he reached for the door of the black Chevy sedan she had parked in her driveway. Her dry cleaning hung on the hook above the rear window and the bag of recently purchased cosmetics from Oakley's drug store was sitting next to the grocery sacks on the back seat. Harper eyed the wrappers of take-out food scattered on the front passenger seat. The condensation on the outside of the soft drink cup told him it hadn't been long since she had stopped for carry out.

It was late Saturday afternoon and Roxanne Lewis had spent her day running errands like any other suburban housewife. She had been going about her business for the past several hours as if nothing had happened, as if she didn't know Chuck Toomey, as if she hadn't prepared the deadly concoction, and as if she didn't commit a cold-blooded murder two days before.

Mann was waiting inside the house. Yolanda Cruz, the assistant medical examiner, had come along too. Her familiarity with monkshood and its poisonous properties made it imperative she be there.

Harper snapped on a pair of gloves and headed toward the house. Inside, the home was as tidy as he remembered from the quick glimpse he gave it on the night they knocked on her door. "What's this plant look like?" he asked.

Yolanda pulled out a photograph from her kit. "That's it."

"Pretty. Looks harmless," said Mann.

She shook her head. "Pretty deadly. One of nature's most lethal weapons. It's been around for centuries. Folks have used it for everything from an external painkiller to an effective way to bump off their neighbor. Trust me, Roxanne isn't the first one to try it." Yolanda pulled back the kitchen curtain and looked out toward the Lewis' back yard. "In ancient Europe and Asia, monkshood was used to poison the enemy's water supplies during war time. It was also used by hunters to poison arrowheads and trap baits," she said as she opened the back door. "Let's see what Mary Mary Quite Contrary is growing out there in her greenhouse."

A uniformed officer wearing protective gear followed the partners and Yolanda across the yard.

When Harper opened the structure's glass door, warm, humid air and the scent of moist soil brushed against his face. Lush ferns, orchids, and an assortment of spring bulbs packed two tables along the west wall. Harper knew nothing about plants. He knew even less about poisons. He was glad to let Yolanda walk ahead of them and watched as she carefully studied each specimen.

She stopped and held out her hand. "There it is. Whatever you do," she said. "Don't touch it."

Harper instructed the uniformed officer with the protective gear to gather the potted monkshood plants and take them back to the lab. While the officer removed the plants, the three returned to the home to search for more evidence.

Yolanda looked on as Harper systematically opened kitchen cabinet doors and drawers. "Sam, what are you doing? The stuff is too toxic. She wouldn't keep those seeds in the kitchen." Yolanda opened another door that led into the garage and eyed the gardening tools kept to one side and the shelves above them. "My guess is she keeps it out here, in the garage – some place out of sight and out of reach. One seed would be more than enough to kill a person the size of Mr Toomey."

Harper pulled a stepladder from its hook on the wall and positioned it beneath the shelves. Containers of pesticides, plant food, potting soil, and other gardening tools and supplies lined the narrow wooden ledges. "Is this what we're looking for?" He asked lowering a shoebox with a collection of old spice jars used to store different varieties of seeds, and dried crushed leaves.

Yolanda took one of the jars from the box. She turned it and examined the seeds.

"Well?" Harper asked her.

She smiled and raised her brows.

Harper was a mile from home when his cell phone rang. He glanced at the clock on the dashboard and immediately thought of Kay. He was supposed to pick her up in two hours for dinner. He assumed she was calling to fill him in on her trip to Rock Hill, but it wasn't her number reflected on the LCD screen.

"Harper?"

"Commissioner."

"Holloway seems to think this baby case of yours is cold and can't be solved. What's your take on it?"

The question left Harper with an issue of his own, like why Flanagan would doubt the Captain's opinions?

"We really don't have much to work with; not many clues and no trace evidence," he said guardedly.

"He told me an eye witnesses fingered Owens as the killer. When are you picking him up?"

"We're working on it, sir."

"You've got an eye witness, Harper. What's there to work on?"

"The witnesses can only place him at the scene. There is absolutely no evidence that marks him as guilty."

Harper waited a second or two in silence before Flanagan spoke again.

"Do I have to remind you about the press – public opinion?"

"No sir. You don't."

"I can't go to a public restroom without someone asking me about this baby killer."

"All the more reason we're being cautious. The minute we find solid evidence, we'll go after the guilty. You have my word on it."

"What evidence do you have?"

"The only thing we have is the blood on the baby blanket. So far it hasn't matched any of the suspects."

"You can't say that until you compare it to Owens'. I want him picked up and charged."

The Captain's order to keep things quiet about Roxanne's rape came back to him as he wondered why he, a plain-clothes cop, would get such a call from the Commissioner himself. And why was Commissioner Flanagan so interested in nabbing Owens for a murder Harper knew Owens didn't commit?

39

The path of deception leads straight to the gates of hell.

By late Saturday afternoon, Harper had solved two murders with one quirky sweep of luck. Chuck's blood type matched the stain on the baby blanket and the traces of monkshood found in his system had led them straight to Roxanne.

Any other time, the Commissioner's call would have been a thorn to pick at, but not tonight. Aside from whatever news Kay brought back with her from Rock Hill, his plans didn't include any talk of the case or the growing list of suspects.

The Islander, a landmark in Chandler Bay Harbor, was an old converted ferryboat; Harper's favorite seafood place. He and Kay talked about Roxanne over drinks. As they cracked open the crab legs, she filled him in on the Rock Hill rape cases. The authorities had preserved semen samples as Kay had suspected. Better yet, she had told him, two of the five victims were still in the Rock Hill area and were willing to testify against their attacker. Harper had changed the subject a number of times but had underestimated Kay's gritty pursuit for the truth. By morning, she had outlined his plan of action.

"Now all you have to do is find him," she said. "How do you like your eggs?"

Harper kept his eye on the clock. What was left of the weekend had blurred into Monday morning and Holloway was waiting to see him and Mann. They were late and his partner was still on the phone. It was ten after ten before they entered Captain Holloway's office.

"Dad?" Harper held a black and white duffel bag in one hand. "What are you doing here?" His glance swept from his father to Holloway and back to his father.

Silence clung to the air like the crisp chill of a blue winter morning. Walt Harper sat in an armchair in front of Holloway's desk. He cut a glance toward the bag before meeting his son's eyes. Captain Holloway stood facing his office window. His posture, hands clasped firmly behind his back, predicted an impending snag.

"Shut the door," said Holloway.

Without taking his eyes from his father, Harper placed the duffel bag on the Captain's desk. The one he and Mann had found inside the locker at the subway terminal two days before. Gillies' odd looking key had slipped easily into the padlock of locker 317.

"Brought you a little something, Captain."

Holloway forced himself from the window to look at it. Straight-faced without balking or batting an eye he returned his attention to the traffic six stories below. "I was wondering what Gillies did with the key. Have a seat, men."

"You were wondering? You knew Gillies had this?" Harper asked, pointing at the bag. "What was he doing with copies of Flanagan's phone records and bank statements? What the hell was he into?"

"Settle down, Sam," said Walt.

"My partner is dead, Dad. Don't tell me to settle down. I'd like some answers."

"We couldn't tell you. Not right away. Sit down." Walt glanced up at Mann. "You too."

"You men understand this conversation doesn't leave this room." Holloway slipped his hands into his pockets and nodded a go ahead signal to Walt.

Walt gave the arms of his chair a gentle tap. "When Lou, Flanagan, and I were still in uniform, we were in on a raid of a topless club down on the strip. The detective unit had been watching the owner for weeks. We arrested him and several others on charges of narcotics, prostitution, and pornography. They had a whole system of racketeering going on in there. The FBI got involved at that point."

"Dad, what's any of this have to do with Gillies?"

"I'm getting to it," he said. "I caught Flanagan taking a slip of paper from the owner's desk."

"What was it?" asked Harper.

"I don't know. It was a big place and I was standing several yards away. He destroyed it before I could get to him. There was an investigation but without evidence or any other witnesses, Internal Affairs dropped the charges against him. He never forgot it though."

"So his beef with you is you were doing your job?"

"You might say that. The FBI turned up evidence against the owner of the club. Seems he and his money were tied to the political corruption that was going on in the late 1970's. Whatever Flanagan took must have been incriminating evidence either against him or against someone higher up. Next thing we know he gets promoted to sergeant and, well, you know the rest."

"You're saying he bought his way up?"

"I'm saying someone has always covered his back. Every time there was a rumbling of bad blood, Flanagan's name popped up but that's as far as it ever went. Seven years ago, Lou and I went undercover after evidence from a drug raid disappeared from the evidence locker. Flanagan was one of the officers we were assigned to watch. We were close to making an arrest when several of us responded to a non-related hostage situation." Walt relayed a detailed account of that particular event. He, Holloway, and several other officers were moving in close to the building when the shooting began. When it was over, they had three fatalities at the scene in addition to Walt's critical back injury that had forced him into an early retirement. "We had our suspicions of who shot me and why."

"It was an accident." Harper frowned, unable to take his eyes from his father. "You told us it was a stray bullet – friendly fire."

"The bullet's trajectory proved only one person could have taken the shot. It also proved the shooter had aimed directly at me," said Walt. "Evidence conveniently disappeared. The whole thing went away under the guise of friendly fire. You know how it goes."

"No." Harper tried to let his father's words sink in. "I don't know how it goes. Are you telling me a police officer shot you intentionally? Who was it?" Harper paused briefly, lowered his gaze, and glanced back at the bag. As he mentally sifted through the bag's contents, his thoughts honed in on the racehorse, Great Fire and the irony of its initials. No wonder he hadn't been able to find the horse. Those weren't race dates; they were meetings between Gillies and the Commissioner. "You're accusing Commissioner Greg Flanagan of being the shooter?" His father didn't answer. He didn't have to. Harper could read every expression on his father's face.

"What's important," said Walt, "is for you to understand that this wasn't an isolated incident. Lou and I knew about his other activities but couldn't prove any of them. The guy made sure to keep things clean." Walt dropped his gaze.

"Jesus, Dad. Why didn't you tell me?" he whispered as if he and his father were alone in the room. "Why did you wait until now?"

"The little evidence that was available from the shooting was suspiciously misplaced. We couldn't accuse a fellow officer of that type of crime without evidence. All it would have taken was for us to accuse him without proof and the whole thing would have blown up in our faces. The entire police force would come down on us," said Walt. "Friendly fire; that's all you and your mother needed to know."

"With the changes in the political arena, Flanagan had to clean up his act before he became chief," said Holloway. "Good thing 'cause there was no touching him after he made commissioner. We thought we'd seen the end of his activities until about six months ago. Do you remember when you and Gillies had to let Owens go on that technicality?"

Harper remembered his anger and frustration at the thought of the months he and Gillies had wasted making their case. The judge had ordered half of the evidence thrown out of court as inadmissible because someone had screwed up the chain of custody.

"It wasn't long after that Flanagan called Gillies." Walt leaned forward in his chair, folded his hands, and took a longer than normal pause before saying: "Sam, Flanagan ordered Gillies to kill Owens."

His father's words struck Harper silent. They hung suspended in air waiting for his reaction to pull them down and make sense of them. "That's crazy. Why would Flanagan risk something that stupid?"

"He's arrogant. Thinks his badge places him above the laws he's supposed to uphold. It happens – power corrupts some men."

"How does Owens fit into the picture?"

"Flanagan became the protector, covering the backs of those who did favors for him. Owens has something on him, but evidently, things soured between them. So in order to legally retaliate against Owens, he made damned sure everyone knew he blamed Owens for his son's death."

"Patrick's overdose? He never cared about Pat when he was alive." Harper had known Patrick Flanagan most of his life. They were close in age and their fathers were cops. That's where the similarities ended. Patrick hated his father. He had told Harper of the beatings, the fights followed by endless silence. Drugs were Patrick's escape from his father's abuse. Harper didn't understand it when he was young. He hadn't thought about it again until now, but he had seen the scenario too often when he worked in Narcotics to not recognize the escape drugs offer their victims.

"But Flanagan knew we had Owens," said Harper. "He'd be in prison right now if someone hadn't screwed with the evidence."

"We don't think the mix up in the lab was an accident," said Walt. "While Owens was in custody, he got the standard one call; got belligerent with whoever he was talking to on the phone. Gillies overheard Owens threatening to expose the person on the other end of the line so he had the call traced. He was expecting to get a lead to Owens' supplier."

"Did he?" asked Harper.

Walt pursed his lips. "The call went directly to Flanagan's

private line. Whatever connection Owens has to Flanagan, it goes back a ways. Gillies concluded Flanagan was tipping Owens off, protecting him. That's why you two could never catch up to him."

"It confirmed our suspicions that Owens knows things about the Commissioner," said Holloway, "and that's why we need him."

"The Commissioner, the Chandler Police Commissioner, made the evidence disappear from the lock up?" Harper asked. "Are you two insane?"

"We have a record of the phone trace, and these," said Holloway, pointing at the bag on his desk. "There were several calls made to Owens from Flanagan's phone and several large sums of cash getting moved to different accounts. Owens knows too much. That's why Flanagan doesn't want him anywhere near a courtroom."

"Then why did the Commissioner call me two nights ago to make sure I was going to pick Owens up?"

"It's a front. Trust me. He doesn't intend to let it happen. Owens' only defense in court would be to expose Flanagan."

"What about Martin? Why did Flanagan order you to put him in charge of the Owens case?"

"Aside from being Flanagan's nephew, he's his stooge. Does whatever Flanagan tells him to do. Only reason he ordered me to assign him to the case was to make damned sure it stayed inactive." Holloway placed his hand on a familiar thick file folder he had sitting on the corner of his desk. "I gave him the case, but not the whole file."

"Gillies ever figure out what Owens has on Flanagan?" asked Harper.

Walt shook his head. "If he did, he never had a chance to tell us."

"But why Gillies?"

"Flanagan found out about Gillies' gambling debts. He looks for the weak points in people and uses them. Thought he could be bought," said Walt. "Flanagan would get what he wanted. Owens would be out of the way and in return, Flanagan would cover Gillies' debts. That's how the bastard plays his game."

"The gambling thing was a guise." Harper took an envelope with his name written across the front from inside the black and white duffle bag and handed it to his father. "That's the money he borrowed from me. Gillies never used it." He paused. "There's a twenty in there with something written along the edge in a red marker – I remember giving it to him."

"But why?"

"Maybe Gillies knew more than he was willing to tell and made up the gambling debt to lure Flanagan out in the open." He looked at the letter size envelope. "He wanted me to think he gambled so I wouldn't have to lie for him."

"Flanagan's problem was that he never counted on Gillies letting me in on their arrangements," said Holloway.

Harper tried to process all he had heard in the twenty minutes since he and Mann had entered the room. "Let me get this straight. You suspect Flanagan of two counts of attempted murder; Dad's and Owens', and now bribery and murder for hire?" He closed his eyes. His head hung with the weight of the assumptions he had made about Gillies. As Holloway's words rolled around in his head, shame slowly smoldered into a flame of indignation. "Then why didn't you arrest him?" he demanded. "Why the hell didn't you get Flanagan before it went any further? Christ, you might as well have put the damned gun to Gillies' heart and pulled the trigger yourself. You used him. Gillies was nothing but a pawn."

"You don't understand," said Holloway.

"You're damned right I don't. Only thing I know is you let Flanagan get away with it again."

"I had to. It would have been his word against Gillies' and who do you think would have come out on top again?" Holloway clenched his teeth. "You think Gillies' death doesn't eat at me every goddamned minute of the day? We couldn't prove a damned thing. Nothing in writing, no money exchanged – nothing." Holloway rammed his fist onto his desk. "I couldn't do a damned thing about it, but I'm not about to blow it this time. I don't care what it takes; I don't care how many hours we put into it. We need rock-solid evidence against him. He's an executioner and I want his ass nailed to the wall." Holloway narrowed his eyes. "Do you understand the magnitude of the situation?"

"Magnitude? What do you think?" Harper hissed. "That I don't get the fact my father could have died, like Gillies, because he was trying to clean up somebody else's mess? That we're accusing the highest-ranking official in the department of attempted murder and bribery? Just how stupid do you think I am?"

"Now that's enough." Walt snapped. "No one thinks that and you know it."

"How the hell am I supposed to feel? You lied to me – you both did. How long was Gillies into this?"

"Six months. The only way to get to the truth was for him to play along. He knew the risks; he wanted to do it," said Walt.

"Then why wasn't I told? Goddamn it, I was his partner."

"It wasn't your battle," said Holloway. "Gillies insisted on keeping you out of it."

Harper raised the heels of his hands and pressed them against his forehead. He thought back to those final days with Gillies. He had never noticed anything unusual. Even the trips to the subway terminal seemed inconsequential. He was suddenly aware of the thick silence closing in on him and the weight of responsibility that had fallen on his shoulders.

"How widespread is the corruption?" he asked.

"We suspect four other officers," said Holloway. "When he falls, you can bet he'll take his cronies with him."

Harper drew in a breath and let it go. "What else do you have on him?"

"Flanagan and Chuck Toomey grew up in the same neighborhood." Holloway pulled his chair out away from his desk and sat down. "Chuck went to Nam, came home a junkie; was arrested on charges of a hit and run fatality – he served his time – got clean. Flanagan gave Chuck the down payment for that bar of his.

"One night, Lou and I were doing our third shift rounds and caught Flanagan coming out of the place with a hooker wrapped around his arm. Couple of nights later we spotted her again and picked her up. She was a mess; had a black eye and bruises on her throat and upper arms. Seems Flanagan liked slapping women around. According to her, it wasn't the first time he had threatened to kill her."

"And you didn't arrest him?" Harper glared at them. "What the hell was wrong with you?"

"Damn it, Sam. You weren't there." Walt shook his head. "She wouldn't press charges. We told her to think it over, that we'd be back. The following morning, a couple of kids found her in the park with her throat sliced open from ear to ear. All we had was the word of a dead hooker and not a damned thing to link him to her, not even semen."

"That one slipped through our fingers just like the others," said Holloway. "All we could do was keep watch and pray he'd make a mistake. That was the last incident until a few months ago when he called Gillies." Holloway swallowed hard. "We suspect Gillies was getting too close to the truth about Flanagan's crimes. That's why he was killed."

"No." Harper frowned. "Mellow's the one who shot him, he fired on instinct. The guy was drunk out of his mind; he couldn't have aimed for Gillies. Hell, I was right there inches in front of him. If he aimed to shoot, he would have shot me."

"But he didn't – did he? You were on top of him, had your weapon aimed right at his chest yet he turned his focus and aimed for Gillies who was twenty-three feet away. Got an answer for that?"

Of course he didn't. Wasn't that the very point stuck in his craw all these weeks?

"Owens is the only person standing between Flanagan and his getting away with whatever crimes Owens can pin on him. Flanagan took a chance when he bribed Gillies into wasting him," said Holloway.

"We think someone tipped Flanagan off about the sting against him," said Walt.

"Chuck," said Harper. "It couldn't have been anyone else but Chuck. Gillies must have said something to tip him off."

"After Gillies died, and with Flanagan close to retirement, Lou and I thought he'd back down again. He probably would have too if it hadn't been for you finding Baby Doe."

"All of a sudden, the minute you two find the baby's remains, Flanagan started snooping around and Owens' and Chuck's names popped back up again." Holloway leaned forward. "I want to know why the hell he's so interested in the case." The Captain curled his lip. "We've handled far more serious crimes than this. He never called to check on their progress, not the way he has with this one."

"According to Quinn, Owens and Chuck were in debt to someone else," said Mann. "Maybe Flanagan was pulling the strings."

"How the hell do you propose we tie Flanagan to the baby's case?" ask Harper.

"Absolute proof and you two are going to get it," said Holloway. "I want the bastard behind bars and Owens' testimony is going to put him there."

"Word on the street is someone wants Owens killed. We have to assume Flanagan is behind it," said Walt.

"The night Gillies and I went to the bar, the bartender said Owens had gotten beat up hours before," said Harper. "Said Owens was running scared."

"Di Napoli is on it. He's going to bring him in for questioning."

"How?"

"Owens thinks he's going to make a killing on a drug deal," said Holloway.

"And you're going to cut him a deal?" Harper cringed as he thought back to the crimes Owens had committed.

"We don't have a choice. Flanagan's a bigger catch and Owens' testimony can put him away for life. We'll have to sweeten the pot, of course, but without it, we don't have anything to offer the prosecutor. If it's any comfort, we have evidence now against a Puerto Rican drug ring we didn't have before."

"I want in on the sting."

"You stay out of it. I mean it, Harper." The Captain's eyes glared at him from under a knitted brow. "Di Napoli has it covered."

Harper heard the order and understood the seriousness of the

Captain's warning, but a brick wall had never stopped him before, he'd go around it. Nothing was going to keep him from being at the scene of Owens' arrest. Holloway's statement about the prosecuting attorney's office reminded Harper of Kay again. Her interest in following up with the five teen rapes had nothing to do with Flanagan or Holloway's objectives for Owens, but Harper had promised her he'd talk to Holloway about calling the Rock Hill sheriff.

Flanagan aside, the matter of Roxanne's rapist continued to dominate Harper's thoughts.

40

Five minutes until closing. The strip mall's parking lot was nearly empty when Harper backed his Jeep into a spot at the far end of the lot. He turned off the motor and waited. Shoppers scuttled out of the shops and quickly emptied the lot. By ten o'clock, only a handful of cars remained.

His father's accusations against Flanagan were still fresh on his mind. He glanced at the time and drummed his fingers on the steering wheel. Harper hadn't seen Di Napoli in several months; he wondered how receptive the undercover would be to his request.

The sound of a thunderous muffler drew Harper's attention toward the lot's entrance off Polk Street. He kept his eyes on the black Camero with rusted fenders, its slow approach, and the driver's half-cocked parking job next to his Jeep. The five-foot six undercover strutted in front of Harper's Jeep. Dark wavy hair hung down across the back of his black leather jacket. Sporting a black t-shirt, and jeans, his appearance was every bit Di Napoli except for the new beard and mustache. Harper's immediate thought was of Al Pacino's Serpico and grinned.

"What's up, man?" Di Napoli slipped into the front seat.

"Christ, how long are you going to drive that heap?"

"I thought about trading up, but I'm kind of attached to it now. Besides, it goes with the overall image." He tugged at his leather lapels in mockery of himself.

"No wonder you're working the streets."

"What? It's the look that keeps me alive." Di Napoli gave Harper a half-hearted smile.

"Didn't know if you'd show or not," said Harper.

Di Napoli shrugged a shoulder. "What the hell happened to you?" he asked pointing at the scab on Harper's lip. "You still dating crazy woman?"

"This," he said, licking his lower lip, "was courtesy of Stewart Martin."

"I hope you beat the living shit out of the prick."

"Last I saw of him he was rolling on the unit's floor clutching himself."

"I knew there was something I liked about you even if you're not Italian. He's such a worthless ass. So what's up? You didn't call me out here to shoot the breeze."

"Owens."

Di Napoli looked away and tilted his head in a gesture that said he wasn't surprised. "I told Holloway you'd try to get back into the game."

"I didn't try," said Harper. "Owens just happened. I hear you're going to bring him in."

Di Napoli watched him in silence.

"I know about Flanagan," said Harper.

"Then you know it was Flanagan's idea to put Martin on the Owens' case. Gillies wasn't cold yet when he ordered Holloway to assign the case to him."

"You get anything out of Owens yet?"

Di Napoli focused his sight directly ahead and said nothing for several seconds. "What's going on, man?"

"The stakes just got bigger."

"How big."

"Murder."

"Owens involved?"

"I need his testimony."

"Take a number."

"I'm talking about a baby who was killed and stuffed into wall."

"Word is," said Di Napoli, "that you know who killed her and the guy's dead. What do you need Owens for?"

"The name of mother's alleged rapist. I have two witnesses who will testify Owens is the one who pimped her. The rapist could be the murderer too. I want to be there when you arrest him."

Di Napoli shook his head. "You don't want much, do you?"

"No less than you," said Harper.

"You can have him when I'm done."

"Damn, there's more at stake than a few drug busts."

"Yeah, and while the rest of you bums were sipping your coffees inside a warm, dry office, I was out on the streets, getting the shit kicked out of me, shot at, and risked my ass every night just so I could get close to him. You think I'm handing him over to you now? You're out of your mind. I've breathed that scum's air for months. What the hell have you done besides trying to pin Gillies' murder on him?"

"Shit. Gillies got screwed. Flanagan's history and his peculiar interest in the baby's murder tell me he has a secret. I'll be damned if I can figure what it is. Owens is the only one left with the answers." Harper couldn't read Di Napoli. No one could. His chiseled, stone expression was exactly what made him a good undercover.

After a pause, Di Napoli opened the car door and stepped out.

"Wait a minute," yelled Harper. "Where are you going? Is that it?"

"I'll think about it."

"I don't have time for you to think about it."

Di Napoli didn't respond. Instead, he sauntered toward his car.

"Answer me, damn it!" Harper rammed his hand against the stirring wheel.

Di Napoli glanced up at him as he slid behind the wheel of his car. "I said I'd think about it and I will." With that, he lifted the sagging car door and slammed it shut.

Harper frowned and ran his hand across his mouth. He fixed his sight on the undercover as he started the engine. "Hey! Di Napoli! While you're at it, think about this. Murder carries a death penalty and our boy's an accessory."

The steaming hot cartons of Chinese take-out felt warm through the brown paper bag in Harper's hand. The smell of pork-fried rice made him hurry to toss down his keys and tear open the cartons. He grabbed a quick couple of bites then tugged at his tie and yanked it off on the way to the bedroom. He returned his gun and badge to the top drawer of his nightstand and removed his shirt. He slipped off his belt letting it land on the bed then returned to the kitchen.

Gillies' death and Owens' involvement continued to press him for answers. It was absurd, yet that was the very thing that had gnawed at him from the beginning. Harper spent weeks convincing himself Gillies' death was an unlucky draw yet, in a matter of minutes, his theory exploded into a gruesome reality of murder.

Gillies' stint as an undercover gave credence to his reason for making up the shooting near the Trenton overpass. But Harper was no closer to understanding why his partner had lied to him. If Gillies was trying to protect him from the truth, why drag him along to the Roving Dog Saloon in the first place? That made as much sense as leaving the locker key in plain sight for Emma to find.

Harper poured himself a Scotch straight up and took another bite of the stir-fry. His mind churned over the facts. His partner had known the risks, then why didn't he wear his vest? Harper was back to the vest, the goddamned bulletproof vest. He'd never figure that one out, but it didn't keep him from asking.

As he scraped the bottom of the carton for the last grain of rice, he wished he had gotten two but quickly consoled himself with another drink. Gillies said all he wanted to do was talk to Mellow, to find out where Owens was hiding. Holloway wanted Owens brought in for questioning about Flanagan. That much he understood.

He closed his eyes and allowed Kay to slip into his thoughts. He dialed her number; she wasn't home. It rang six times before he hung up. Four drinks later, he gave up trying to reach her. Hell, she wasn't even his type, he thought as he threw himself on the bed. He closed his eyes and tried to turn off his day.

Harper tossed between dreamless sleep and wakeful awareness. Twice he rose, then returned to bed, and continued to stare at the ceiling as if the answers he sought would flash across its surface.

Neither his will nor the six Scotches could shut down his mind. Images flooded in. They flashed, zipped around, and out before he could grasp them.

Worn and unable to fight his edginess, Harper hoisted himself up on one elbow. The large red numbers on the alarm radio announced it was three thirty-two in the morning. Images of that rainy March night in front of the Roving Dog Saloon forced themselves in again. He was fighting them off when Gillies' last words tumbled back into his head. Mellow was nothing more than a way to find Owens. All he had wanted were answers. No threats. No reason to think that Mellow would turn on him. That's why Gillies wasn't worried about the bulletproof vest. Harper threw himself back down on the bed, slammed a fist into his pillow, and buried his face.

"Damn it, Gillies. First rule of the game; you don't let your fucking guard down."

41

Holloway thought of the years; how they had slipped away. The times he had failed to stop the man at his game. He thought of the ease with which he could jam the barrel of his gun against Flanagan's head and squeeze the trigger. He'd feel no remorse. The notion alone brought him pleasure, but reality and his badge pulled him back away from the other side of the line – that linear edge he could only cross in his mind.

The image of Walt Harper lying motionless in a pool of blood with nothing more than an officer's bullet between him and death was as clear in his mind as the day it happened. "Friendly fire my ass," he mumbled. They had brushed the whole thing off with a frivolous apology and shoved Walt Harper out the door.

Flanagan made captain not long after. With then Commissioner Palmer neatly tucked away in his back pocket, Flanagan had his sight on the commissioner's post and did whatever he had to do to get it.

Right now, Flanagan was waiting on him inside the Elton Room, a private dinner club across the street. No amount of procrastination would change what Holloway had to say to him. He gripped the wheel of his car and gathered his thoughts a moment longer. He knew exactly how he'd break the news to him. The question was: how would Flanagan take it?

Holloway pushed open the club's door giving the lobby a sweeping glance. The white-haired man at the front desk put down his coffee cup and glanced up when Holloway flashed his badge. The man's initial apprehension eased as soon as Holloway explained his presence. The old gent acknowledged that Flanagan was waiting and escorted him into the dining hall. The members-only club was too rich for Holloway's blood. Aside from the Commissioner, Holloway didn't expect to find any other familiar faces in the place. Flanagan was wearing his navy suit and was sitting at the table near the large paned window at the other side of the dark paneled room. The man's broad shoulders, staunch and erect, would seem more fitting on a man half his age. Only the strands of white hair that encircled the sheen on the crown of his head gave a hint to his age. He knocked a drink back, unaware of Holloway's presence.

"Greg?" Holloway pulled out a chair and took his seat across from him. "Sorry I'm late. Got tied up," he said, glancing at the mound of crushed cigarette butts in the ashtray.

Flanagan lowered his glass, looked up, and brushed off Holloway's apology. "The little server girl is here some place." Flanagan looked around the room then raised his arm to get the server's attention.

"I'm glad you called. I was just about to get a hold of you. Greg, I ..." Holloway glanced up at the server and ordered a draft.

"And you sir?" she asked. "Are you ready for another?"

Flanagan shoved his empty glass toward her. Steel blue eyes peered dead straight at Holloway. Flanagan told her, *Yes,* ignorant of the server's smile and indifferent to any courtesy he might have shown her.

"How's Harper's boy doing?" Flanagan lit another cigarette.

"Detective Harper is fine. Why?"

"Don't trust him."

"You don't know him."

"I told you, I don't want him going crazy on us."

"He's every bit as good as his old man ever was." Holloway egged him on watching for the slightest change in Flanagan's expression. "You know Walt. Good man – first class." A touch of resentment, or even anger, would have been better than Flanagan's icy stare. A ribbon of smoke curled up from his cigarette. Holloway knew Flanagan had no more interest in Harper's well-being than anyone else he had ever encountered. He looked away, afraid his eyes would expose his hatred.

When the server came back with their orders, Flanagan gently shook the glass and gave the ice a twirl. His brow twitched into a frown.

"So, how's he coming along on the case?" he asked, raising the glass to his mouth. "Does he know any more than he did the last time we talked?"

"That's what I want to talk to you about. You know how these cold ones are. Sometimes you miss the obvious just because it's too obvious. You look in one direction, when you really should be looking in the other."

"Is that so?" Flanagan's stone-faced expression remained fixed. "What's so obvious about this one?"

"We're still speculating on how the child died," he lied. "But there's another matter that came out of all this."

Flanagan took another drag from his cigarette and blew it out. He cupped his hands in front of his mouth and let the smoke rise past his eyes.

"The mother claims she was raped."

"So what if she was? You're supposed to be looking for the kid's killer, not the father."

Funny Flanagan should choose those words, thought Holloway. *They weren't looking for the father they were after a rapist.* "Greg, we compared the baby's DNA against the records in the DNA database."

"You actually believe her?"

"You weren't there to hear her."

Flanagan rolled his eyes in a show of disgust. "I don't have to hear her. Every whore screams rape when she knows damn well she asked for it." Flanagan curled his lip. "Shit. I was wondering how long it would take you to go soft."

"We found a match." Holloway looked squarely into Flanagan's eyes and waited to see his reaction.

"Jesus." Flanagan crushed out his cigarette and sat back in his chair. "What the hell is this? What do I care who knocked her up?"

"It's a match to your son Patrick's DNA."

Flanagan said nothing. Instead, he tipped back the rest of his drink and cut a glance to the other side of the room.

An uncomfortable silence engulfed them.

"Greg, I hate to –"

"What the hell is his DNA doing in the fucking database?" Flanagan growled under his breath.

"Patrick was arrested on drug charges. It's standard procedure. You know that; anyone with a record …" Holloway didn't have to finish his sentence. Flanagan knew all about the standard procedure – he had approved the measure.

Flanagan stared at him. Straight face at first, then slowly a grin tugged at the corner of his lips before he broke into a chuckle. "Patrick, huh? Hell, no wonder the kid fried his brains. Serves him right for sticking his pecker where it didn't belong." He threw his head back and laughed. "Hell, he would have still been in high school back then."

Holloway glanced around the room. A few curious eyes looked on. He lowered his gaze and frowned. "Sorry."

"Well, I'm not. What the hell do you expect me to do about it? He's dead. Can't press charges against the dead, can you?"

"There's more."

"More? Hell, bring it on. I could use another good laugh."

"Baby Doe was a twin. That makes you the grandfather of a sixteen-year-old girl. Thought you should know. You might want to stop by the station and see her tomorrow."

The smugness on Flanagan's face faded. "What the hell do you expect me to do? Cuddle with her and the whore who had her? Right, Holloway. You'd like that, wouldn't you?" Flanagan leaned forward and shoved his finger within inches of Holloway's face. "Don't you ever bring this up again. I'll have your fucking job."

"In the meantime, you and I both know DNA doesn't lie."

Flanagan drained his glass and slammed it down on the table. He clenched his teeth and motioned again for the server. "How the hell am I supposed to tell my wife about this? I suppose the bitch expects me to pay for the little bastard."

"She doesn't remember Patrick; never identified him. She doesn't know you either. I wanted you to hear it from me before it makes headlines."

"Oh no. You're going to keep it out of the headlines –

understand? It was bad enough to have to answer all the goddamned questions from reporters when the little prick took his life. I spent years trying to knock sense into him and that's how he repaid me? Frying his goddamned brains on crack? Like I gave a shit if he wasted his life after that. What the hell do you expect me to say to the press now? It's none of their fucking business what happened."

Holloway rose and tossed a ten on the table. "You're a public figure. Figure it out." As he turned to leave, he heard Flanagan call out to him.

"What about Owens? You ever going to haul his ass in or are you soft on him too?"

Holloway stopped. "We're close," he said without turning around. "Trust me. You'll be the first to know the minute we do."

42

An eerie calm settled upon dock thirty-two. Even the winds were hushed on this moonless night. Streetlights on the dock beamed down into small circles of light along the boardwalk. Stretches between each shaft of light were as black and unwelcoming as the ocean's depths.

This was it. The sting was on and soon Di Napoli's life would be back to normal. The last time he checked, it was just past midnight. Holloway and the others wouldn't be there for another fifty minutes. He arrived early, parked his car out of sight, and watched – waiting for any suspicious activity that would hinder Owens' capture.

He glanced at his watch again. The hour hand crawled. He drummed on the car door and finally decided it was time to head over to the rear entrance of warehouse C. He needed to be in place inside the building by the time backup arrived. Maybe the cool salt air would clear his mind and calm his jittery nerves.

He was within twenty yards of the building when a shuffling sound stopped him. His pulse raced as he drew his Ruger, turned, and took aim into the pit-like darkness. Nothing. All he could hear was the water lapping against the rocks below. Whatever had broken the silence was gone.

Di Napoli cased his surroundings, pulled up his collar, and lowered his weapon.

His stride quickened to the beat inside his chest. The building's back door was within reach – ten paces away. Owens and Raul would be here soon. He'd wait inside. Let them make the exchange before giving the signal. That's what he was thinking when he heard the shuffled steps again. This time the sound was distinct and close.

Inside the warehouse, stacked crates blocked his view of the entrance. Di Napoli edged toward the front of the building, moving cautiously between the rows of crates. He gripped his weapon close to his chest, cut a glance to one side and then to the other, but detected no movement. He stopped and looked over both shoulders, then straight ahead before taking another step.

Nothing.

A scattering of lights lit the front side of the warehouse too. Di Napoli leaned against the crates and tried to relax. He glanced at his watch again and rubbed his hand across his mouth. Holloway was still thirty minutes away.

"All right," he whispered, giving the place another glance. "Be cool, man. Won't be long now."

Thoughts of what he would do the minute he handcuffed Owens popped into his mind. He'd go straight home, sleep in for a week, and consider taking a leave. Holloway could interrogate Owens himself.

Di Napoli stepped out of the shadows for just a moment. Eleanor crossed his mind. He hadn't allowed himself to think of her in the months he had worked undercover. He ran a hand through his hair knowing she wouldn't want to see him looking like street trash. He'd have to shave and cut his –

"*Hombre.*"

A man's nasal tone spoke into his right ear. Di Napoli couldn't break away from for the stranger's hold around his neck.

"You should have played it straight, my friend."

That's when Di Napoli felt it – the cold steel. He felt it plunge deep. Felt its upward thrust and the concrete floor coming up to meet him. The pounding in his chest subsided into a slow erratic thump as he drifted in and out of consciousness. He tried to yell.

"Piece of shit cop."

He barely heard his assailant's remarks, but felt the blow to his side from the kick to his ribs. Faint, tiny white lights flickered before his eyes.

His shallow breathing stopped. White lights faded to black.

Harper blew into his hands. Warm air billowed through his fingers into the cool night air. At one twenty-three a.m., the wharf near dock thirty-two was deserted. It was quiet except for the rhythmic sound of waves slapping against encrusted posts and mossy embankments beneath the pier.

Backup units, the hidden sentinels of the CPD, positioned themselves out of view of on-coming traffic. Holloway hadn't been able to argue with either Harper or Di Napoli, two of his most bull-headed cops, but Di Napoli had finally made it happen. Harper was in on the sting and now he and Mann were waiting for orders.

Mann parked their car in the alley between the warehouses. He rolled down the driver's side window.

"Dead silent," he said, inhaling the salt air.

Harper rubbed warmth into his hands. The same apprehension he had felt on the night he and Gillies had waited for Mellow set in. "You know there should be a law against doing surveillance work in damp weather."

Mann glanced at his watch then looked toward the blackness of Chandler Bay. "It's almost one thirty. Thought you said Di Napoli was meeting us here at one?"

"He's here, someplace. Don't worry about him, he knows what he's doing."

Mann reached up to secure the straps of his vest. He leaned his head back and closed his eyes.

Fifteen more minutes passed before the hum of Harper's cell broke the stillness inside the car. It was Holloway calling from one of the units across the way. Harper answered and poked Mann's arm. "We're on."

Leaving the safety of their car, Harper ran to look around the corner of the building. "I see their headlights. Right on time," he said to Holloway. "Anyone hear from Di Napoli?"

No one had.

"Something's wrong. I don't like this," said Harper. "It's his bust. Not like him not to show."

"You two go in as planned, with or without Di Napoli," said Holloway. "Signal the minute the dealers exchange the goods. No one moves in until then. Let them make the exchange. Understand?"

Mann was at Harper's side. They watched a set of headlights approach, followed by another. Both cars stopped in front of the warehouse entrance. Harper recognized the man getting out of the old Monte Carlo. The lanky arms and legs and disheveled hair could only belong to Owens.

The black Lincoln with the polished spinners nosed in behind him. Owens stood with his back to the warehouse door and waited for the Puerto Rican to get out of the Lincoln.

"Must be Raul, the guy Di Napoli mentioned," Harper whispered. "Here we go. Get ready." Harper was waiting for Owens to produce the goods when a stocky man emerged from the building. Harper noticed the long wavy hair and leather jacket and assumed it was Di Napoli until he lunged forward. He grabbed Owens around the neck and pressed a knife to his throat.

"Who the hell is that?" Harper murmured, as much to himself as to Mann. "Son of a bitch, where's Di Napoli?"

"Shit. He's going to kill him," said Mann. "We can't wait."

"Captain," said Harper. "Change of plans, we're going in."

"What do you mean, change of plans?" yelled Holloway. "What's going on?"

Harper snapped shut the phone and gripped the butt of his revolver. He pressed it close to his chest and nodded the go-ahead to Mann.

Owens kicked and yelled as he struggled to break free from the man who was dragging him across the pavement, inching him closer to the Lincoln.

Raul waved a gun at his man to hurry.

"Go. Go. Go!" Mann ordered.

"Freeze! Police," Harper yelled as he and Mann drew their weapons and charged toward them.

Raul took a poor shot.

"Put the gun down!" Mann screamed. "Put it down – now!"

Another gunshot exploded near the car.

"I said put the gun down!"

Raul jumped into the Lincoln. Tires squealed and rubber

burned as the Puerto Ricans peeled out leaving Owens bleeding on the pavement. The driver of the Lincoln backed into a cloud of exhaust, maneuvered it hard to the left, and fled.

"Shit!" Harper ran, aimed at the car, and took a shot, but it was too fast and out of range.

Owens was face up on the pavement, bleeding from the wound in his upper chest. "Son of a bitch. Ya motherfuckers! Piece of shit spics."

Harper fought back the urge to kick him. Instead, he looked down, raised his hands to his hips, and assessed the man's condition.

"What the hell ya looking at?" Owens gnashed his teeth.

"Your ugly face," Harper curled his lip. "Bad news, Owens. Looks like you're going to make it."

"Fuck ya." Owens spit at him then clenched his teeth again.

"Ambulance is on its way," said Mann as he applied pressure to the wound.

Harper turned in the direction of a siren. "Did we have one on stand-by?" He glanced back. "Look out!" The peals of sirens were close. So was the thundering sound of a car's motor. It was racing toward them; backup units' lights trailed behind it. With one sweeping movement, they grabbed Owens by the shoulders and dragged him out of the Lincoln's way.

Harper didn't have to think through his next move. Instinct and adrenaline took over. He raised his pistol, aimed at the tires, and squeezed the trigger. The car spun out of control, flipped twice, and rammed through the railing into the icy waters of Chandler Bay.

After a few tumultuous minutes, the backup units screeched to a halt. Their pulsing red lights danced across dock thirty-two.

Harper lowered his outstretched arms. "You okay?" he called out to his partner.

"Yeah," Mann said, dusting himself off. "I'm fine."

"What about me?" yelled Owens. "Ya two ever hear of p-o-lice bru-ta-lity. I'm shot – bleeding to death and ya two goddamn morons –"

"Shut the hell up!" As Harper turned away, a cat pranced out of the warehouse leaving behind sets of wet paw prints on the pavement. A wrinkle creased Harper's brow as he picked up the tabby and examined her fur and the pads of her paws. "Hey girl. What have you gotten into?" Harper rubbed the blood between his fingertips.

"Damn," he whispered. Slowly, he rose to his feet and motioned to four uniformed officers to follow him into the warehouse. They aimed their weapons and flashlights straight ahead, shining the light across the room.

Harper aimed the beam at the bloody paw prints leading around a piling of crates. "This way." He had walked only a few feet away from the door when he stopped and clenched his teeth. It felt like Gillies all over again.

43

Walt Harper rinsed his coffee mug and placed it upside down on the rack. Dawn peeked through the kitchen curtains over the sink. He brushed the yellow gingham aside and eyed the cloudless blue sky. Its color made him think of his son's eyes and the disbelief that had washed over them when he learned the truth about Police Commissioner Flanagan.

Walt never forgave Flanagan for ruining his career. At fifty-nine, he had a lifetime ahead of him and no place to go. He had pushed the hurt out of his mind, but the fury that had once consumed him was back. Sam was in charge of the investigation now. Justice was finally plausible and the risks were as high as ever. Sam would have to out-maneuver Flanagan's cunning. If he failed, Flanagan would target him just as he had Gillies. This was no time to poison his judgment. The question was would Sam understand a father's reasons for not speaking of it before?

The curtain slipped out of his hands and fell back into place. He reached for his jacket and helmet, the keys to his bike, and the newspaper clipping he had tucked into his copy of Moby Dick.

There was something about a fresh spring morning, the warmth of the sun on his back, and thirty miles of open dry road to clear his thoughts. *Time to quit licking his wounds*, he thought. Walt revved the motor of his black Harley Road King and sped in the direction of Chandler. Smooth, black asphalt stretched out before him; its dotted line quickly blurred into a lightning white streak.

Harper opened his eyes and reached for the button on the alarm. He lay still for a moment before swinging his legs out of bed. The three hours of sleep weren't enough to cure his exhaustion. Sitting on the edge of the bed, he bowed his head and prayed for the fog that clouded his mind to clear. He pressed the heels of his hands firmly against his eyes. Owens was under arrest, confined to a hospital bed. The hunt for the man he had been willing to risk all to capture was over, but his arrest brought him only a brief moment of pleasure tinged with regret. Di Napoli's lifeless stare wouldn't leave him. It stirred a familiar hollowness in the pit of his stomach. First Gillies, now Di Napoli. Two good officers were dead in as many months and both had died in pursuit of Jimmy T Owens.

He felt numb.

Harper couldn't get Flanagan out of his mind either, or what he did to Gillies – what he had tried to do to his father. He had no illusions things would ever be as they were. He too had changed. Gone were the days when someone else would shoulder the burden. There would be another Internal Affairs investigation; he was ready this time. Baby Doe was supposed to have been a routine search for a killer. How could he have known his first homicide case would churn the waters clear to the top of the ranks and cost another officer his life?

He thought back to that first day in Lou Holloway's office when the Captain had questioned his state of mind. What makes you so sure, Holloway had asked, that you won't hesitate the next time someone pulls a gun on you?

"Because. I didn't hold back the first time, damn it." Harper had proved himself last night. He had seen it in Holloway's eyes; the satisfaction in knowing that with Owens' capture, their pursuit of Flanagan was near an end.

The doorbell rang. He squinted at the red numbers on his clock. "Who the hell?" He ran his hand through his hair and wiped the sleep from the corners of his mouth.

"I'm coming," he yelled when he heard the second ring and looked through the peephole.

Walt Harper had his back to the door looking up at the sky. He held his helmet tucked under one arm while he swept back his light brown hair with the other. Harper tried to smile. He rubbed his eyes and swung open the door.

"We got him, Dad," he said. "Last night. We got Owens."

Walt hugged his son and patted him on the back. "Thank God you're all right. I heard about Tom." He choked on his emotions. "I'm so sorry."

Harper closed his eyes and allowed himself to feel the warmth of his father's affection.

"We need to talk," said Walt, placing his helmet on a nearby chair. Deanna's engagement ring was still on the dining room table. "What's going on?" he asked, giving the ring a nod.

"Broke up."

"Sorry."

"You couldn't stand her."

"Wouldn't go that far. She wasn't good enough for you, that's all."

"You didn't come here to talk about my love life. What's on your mind?"

"You," Walt replied. "You and this whole mess with Flanagan. Sam, I'm sorry. I never meant to lie to you about it. I just –"

"But you did – for seven years. Did you really think keeping it from me would make it easier?"

"You weren't even at police headquarters back then. There was nothing you could have done about Flanagan. Knowing the truth would have ruined your career. It was better this way."

"What about Gillies? Was it better to keep me in the dark about him too? You knew what I was accusing him of, and you let me. Can't you see how wrong that was?"

"Lot of things I should have done differently," said Walt.

"You had your chance to nail Flanagan. Why didn't you?" Harper growled. "Damn it. Gillies didn't have to die. You and Holloway knew what Flanagan was capable of doing and you led Gillies right to him."

"We didn't lead him into anything. Lou ordered him to stay out of it. Hell you know how stubborn Gillies was. He wouldn't take no for an answer."

Harper knew that much was true. He unlatched the patio door

and shoved it open. He closed his eyes and inhaled the light salt air. The ocean breeze brushed up against his face. He could hear the distant calls and flutter of seagulls coming up from the beach below. He liked to watch the flock's graceful drift as they hovered near the water's edge for their turn to eat whatever the low tide had left behind. Today he ignored them. "I remember that night. The way Mom cried when we heard you were shot. Did you lie to her too?"

Walt turned away.

"Jesus, Dad. How could you not tell your own wife? Flanagan screwed you over – damned near killed you. You owed us that much. You sure as hell owed it to Mom."

"Your mother worried enough about you and your brother without having to worry that another cop was trying to kill me. I figured you'd find out about it eventually; never wanted my opinion to slant your judgment."

"What about the ballistics report? You said it proved he took the shot," said Harper. "What more did you need?"

"The damned thing disappeared, so did the bullet. We had a squad of officers at the scene. I couldn't prove the bullet that hit me came from his gun without the evidence. Don't you think I would have pursued it if I would have had anything to convict him with?" Walt paced across the living room. "Flanagan always covered his tracks – just like he did with Gillies. Gillies was an honest cop, but a dead man's word won't stand up in court without proof and you know it."

"Flanagan is bound to make a mistake sooner or later," said Harper.

"No he won't. He never does."

"He will." Harper was confident of only one thing: Flanagan's arrogance. "And when he does, we'll be ready." Harper ran a hand through his hair, aware his father was watching each move he made. "Some partner, huh? I should have never doubted Gillies."

"None of it was your fault." Walt paused. "I should have taken care of this years ago, should have taken control of my life before now."

"What are you talking about?" asked Harper. "You've always

controlled your life – mine and Mom's."

Walt glanced up at the family photographs on his son's mantle. "I was never in control of a damned thing. Couldn't keep your mother from dying. I couldn't even find the bastard that ran her down. I finally came to grips with the way things are; life seemed as normal as it was going to get and then this business with Gillies happened. It all came back, like a wave right over my head. Damn it. It will never end as long as Flanagan has anything to say about it."

"You didn't have to go through it alone, you know." Harper snapped and turned away.

Walt shook his head. "I was a damned cop, for crying out loud. I was trying to protect the three of you from the filth I had to deal with." He swallowed hard. "Your mom and I, we had so many dreams. Hell, you could've buried me with her. Everything changed. You think this is the way I planned things?"

Harper knew his father hadn't been able to let her go. He watched as sorrow spilled over his father's face, then lowered his eyes.

"We were supposed to grow old together." Walt's eyes welled. "She'll never see you boys get married or our grand…" He drew in a breath, pressed his lips, and waited for the words to stop quivering. "I'll never see her again. I don't know that I could take it if anything happened to you."

The words Harper wanted to say were caught somewhere between his heart and the tip of his tongue. His mother had died the year after his father's shooting. Harper had watched his father mourn her, but he had never heard him express his grief as openly has he had done today. In spite of his anger, Harper understood his father's motives for keeping quiet about Flanagan. He also knew the last thing his father needed was to feel accused.

"Don't worry, Dad. We'll get Flanagan this time. I promise."

His father nodded and started to leave. "Oh, almost forgot. Here." Walt handed him the old newspaper clipping he had tucked into his pocket. "Maybe this can help."

Harper studied the yellowed photograph and the caption beneath it. Flanagan and his wife had posed with former Police

Commissioner Palmer sitting around a table in the ballroom of the Princeton Hotel. "That's Flanagan on the day he made captain. What's this have to do with anything?"

"I don't know. Found it in Gillies' bag. It was stuck beneath the cardboard piece along the bottom. I've looked at it a million times. God knows what he saw in it."

44

A uniformed officer was sitting outside Owens' hospital door thumbing through a magazine when Harper arrived the following morning. The officer glanced up at Harper's badge and nodded.

"Has anyone been in to see him yet?"

"Not in the two hours since I've been on duty." The officer leaned back in the chair, picked up the tattered year-old copy of *Newsweek* and returned to his reading.

Inside, Owens was sound asleep. The gauges and readings on the monitor next to the bed told Harper the patient would live. Aside from the machine's low humming sound and rhythmic beeps that measured his heart rate, the room was dead silent. The morning sun bled through the closed, heavy curtains giving the small space a warm glow; a tranquil feeling unbefitting a criminal of Owens' reputation. Harper tugged on the drawstring and drew back the drapes to flood the room with the intrusive brightness of the early spring sun.

"What the …? Harper? Should have known." Owens frowned, curled his lip, then closed his eyes again. The bandage protecting his bullet wound encircled his chest and wrapped up around his left shoulder. His arm, tucked neatly into a sling, rested on top of his chest. "Doc said I'm supposed to rest."

"You do that. You'll need it to stand trial."

"For what? That cop set me up and ya know it. Ya didn't find an ounce of anythin' on me."

"Narcotics?" Harper's laugh melted into a wry grin. "Is that what you think you're doing here?"

"What else is there?"

"Try murder. At least two counts."

"I didn't have nothin' to do with that cop or that kid gettin' killed."

"Interesting comeback. Maybe you're not as stupid as you look," said Harper. "At least you know what I'm after."

"Like I'd help ya. I don't have to do a damn thing."

"Maybe you're right. I've been told the only thing in life you have to do is die." Harper stood next to the bed and gently tugged on the IV tube attached to Owens' right hand. "You ever hear that?"

Owens kept his eye on what Harper was doing.

"That means you have a choice here. Right now, you can choose to cooperate with me or not. Either way, I'll get what I want; guarantee it. Only thing left for you to decide is how painful you want to make it."

"I know my rights."

"You should. Someone's been reading them to you since you were twelve."

"How the hell would ya know?" Owens frowned and ran his tongue over his teeth.

"I always wondered what would happen if I did this." Harper bent the flexible IV tube and squeezed it together to stop the flow into Owens' vein. "They say it only takes a couple of air bubbles in your bloodstream to screw with your heart." The monitor sounded off with an annoying set of bleeps the instant he bent the tube and blocked the flow of fluid.

"Hey! Don't. Holy shit, man. What the hell do ya want?"

"Want? The truth, but seeing as I'm talking to you, I'll settle for information. Let's start with Frank Gillies. What did you tell him?"

"I told ya I didn't have nothin' to do with him gettin' wasted."

"That wasn't the question."

Owens shook his head. "He wanted to know things."

"Like what?"

Owens turned away.

"I said, like what?" Harper grabbed him by his hospital gown and jerked him off his pillow.

261

Owens squealed. His face, contorted with pain, was inches from Harper's face.

"You scream all you want," Harper whispered. "The cop out in the hall is on my side and neither one of us thinks you're worth the time it would take to save you. But I have a dead partner and a baby's remains in the morgue waiting for justice. Your name popped up in both cases along with Chuck Toomey's. I want to know why." He gave him a shake. "Now!"

"Damn. Let go of me. Ya ever hear of police brutality?"

"File a report asshole and take your best shot." Harper shoved him away then pulled back the sheets to reveal a catheter between Owens' legs. "Well, what do we have here?"

"Hey! What are ya doin'?"

"Like I said, Owens."

"Holy shit! Get away from me."

"You decide. How much pain can you stand?" Harper eyeballed the urinary catheter secured to Owens' thigh noticing the upward direction of the tube inserted into Owens' bladder. "I hear this gadget will blow up a small balloon inside you there. Could be interesting to watch your eyes cross. Personally, if I were you, I'd answer my questions."

Owens looked as if he was holding his breath.

"Start talking or I'm going to yank every damned tube out of your body."

"Jesus, ya're crazier than Gillies."

"I'll take that as a compliment." Harper pumped the balloon at the end of the catheter a couple of times.

"Shit! No. Wait! I'm talkin', see?"

A crease wrinkled Harper's brow as he studied his prisoner and wondered if he was ready to talk. He let go of the catheter then reached into his breast pocket.

Owens cursed under his breath, flinched, and quickly raised his arm to protect his face.

"Christ, Owens. You always this jumpy?" Harper placed the small tape recorder on the nightstand next to the bed and switched it on. He read Owens his rights again and made him state his name for the record.

"Gillies wanted to know about the man."

"What man?" asked Harper.

"THE man. Flanagan."

Harper could see the terror building in Owens' eyes and knew it wasn't for fear of him. He'd have to do something about that. It had flared across his face at the mention of Flanagan's name. "What exactly did you tell Gillies that got him killed?"

"Wait a minute. Gillies told me he'd get me a deal," said Owens. "I ain't sayin' another word without one. I want protection."

Harper kept his eyes fixed on him while he slowly ran his fingers up and down the IV tube hanging from its hook above Owens' head. "The question is, who scares you more right now? This very minute. Me or Flanagan?"

Owens drew in a breath then let it out. "Flanagan's bad news, all right? That's what I told him; has been for as long as I've known him."

"Don't screw with me. That's not even worth a pat on the head." Harper ripped off the tape that held the IV needle in Owens' hand then glanced at the recorder. "Careful there, Owens. You could hurt yourself."

"Fuck, man." Shock registered amidst a frown that flashed across Owens' face. "I'm bleedin' all over the place."

"Can't imagine why anyone would yank a needle out of their hand like that." Harper pulled back the sheet again. "Here, let me help you with that."

Owens yanked the sheet from Harper's hand and pressed it close to his chest like a virgin in a brothel. "Flanagan kept the heat off Chuck and me. All right?"

"For?"

"We gave him a cut of the action."

"What action?"

"Money, man. Drugs. What do ya think?"

"What else?"

"I can't remember." Owens cringed with pain as he tried to sit up in bed. "Maybe it was the part about Flanagan blackmailin' the Mayor for that fancy job of his or the fact the guy has more than one illegitimate kid runnin' around. Maybe Gillies talked and got himself killed. Ever think of that?"

Exposing either one of those statements would have been enough to ruin Flanagan's political ambitions, but was it enough to push him to murder? Harper caught himself studying Owens. The sly bastard had always managed to slip away, but now seeing him like this; old, thin and wasted, he wasn't close to the adversary Harper had made him out to be. "Prove it."

"I gave Gillies all I know, he was supposed to figure it out."

Harpers thought back to the contents of the duffle bag and the CD files. "He's dead remember? You're dealing with me now. How'd Mellow figure into it?"

"Chuck paid him to waste Gillies. He told me so, not more than a week ago."

"Why? Why order the hit?"

"I already told ya about the blackmail and all them little bastards of his."

"Not big enough," said Harper. "What else do you know about him?"

"Hell, Chuck's the one who had his nose up Flanagan's ass. Me? I just heard what he wanted me to hear. Not Chuck. He'd do anythin' to protect the old geezer; always doin' favors for him. Seems like everyone owed Flanagan favors. That's how Flanagan likes things."

"Name one."

"I don't know. Favors. Some big, some small."

"What was so damned big this time?" Harper was thinking of Baby Doe and Holloway's mention of Flanagan's abnormal interest in the case. Maybe the Commissioner's interest was to keep his pal Chuck out of it.

Owens shook his head. "Somethin' about a cop gettin' shot. Chuck kept the bullet for him."

Owens' suggestion side-swiped him. Lines quickly furrowed his brow as his father's words rippled through his mind. Harper slipped his hands into his pockets and turned his back. "Who was the cop?"

"I don't know. Some snitch is all I know. Flanagan almost

screwed himself with that one, but Chuck was always there to cover up for him."

Harper rubbed a hand over his mouth. "Think he still has the bullet?"

"Hell I don't know. Probably. If Flanagan told him to keep it, he did."

Harper would tear the Roving Dog and Chuck's apartment apart to find it. Flanagan was his. He had Owens' statement on tape and it was admissible. He'd make damned sure of it. That's all that mattered. Stay calm he told himself. He wasn't sure how long he had mentally wondered away, but it was time to change the subject. "Where were you on the evening of June 3, 1990?"

Owens rolled his eyes, but seemed eager to clear the air about his involvement in the baby's death. His side of the story was amazingly similar to the other witnesses' statements. He had just confirmed Harper's suspicions that Chuck was the baby's killer when the sound of angry shouting filtered into the room through the solid wood door.

The yelling preceded a loud, dull thump that sounded as if someone had fallen against the corridor wall. Moments later a young man forced himself into the room.

"Hey! What do you think you're doing?" The man rushed to Owens' bedside. "Don't say another word," he ordered, brushing aside his tousled hair.

"Sorry, Detective. That's Owens' attorney," said the officer grabbing the man by the arm. "Come here, you."

"It's all right. I've got what I want." Harper glanced down at the young man. He seemed to be just out of school. The crooked knot on his tie and the shirttail hanging out from beneath his jacket reminded Harper of his playground fights. "New style?"

"Very funny." The young man quickly tucked in his shirt and straightened his tie. He stood defiantly next to his client with his hands clutched tightly around a small satchel pressed close to his side. "My client has nothing to say."

"Don't worry, junior, I've read him his rights. It's all right here." Harper grabbed the recorder and tucked it safely back into his pocket and turned to leave. "He's all yours, counselor."

"Harper," Owens yelled out in spite of his lawyer's warnings. "What about a deal?"

"Not another word, Mr Owens," said the lawyer.

Harper grinned. "Hear that, Mr Owens? Looks like you've finally bullshitted someone into thinking you're worth some respect." He had reached the door when Owens called out to him again.

"My deal, man. What about my deal?"

Harper stopped. He turned an ear toward the sound of Owens' voice. "What deal? Gillies is dead."

45

There was no resentment in Roxanne's voice. Harper mindlessly tapped his pencil against the table and caught himself staring into her eyes. Something had changed. A spark of confidence had settled into them. Her face was drained of emotion, indifferent to the consequences of her actions.

Roxanne was sitting at the metal table in the center of the room again and seemed unaffected by the charge of murder. She sat erect, her feet flat on the floor, fingers laced together, and righteously faced her accusers. The only move she made was to raise a slender finger and tuck a strand of hair behind her ear.

She was nothing like the vulnerable sixteen-year-old with whom Harper had sympathized. He wondered what had transformed her from the victim into a cold-blooded murderer. The evidence against her had unfolded like a set of Russian nesting dolls adding Chuck Toomey's death to a growing chain linked to Britni's murder.

Mann leaned forward in his chair and stared squarely into Roxanne's eyes. "How long have you known him?"

Roxanne kept silent, dry-eyed. Manicured hands remained folded in front of her.

"Answer the question," Mann growled. "How long?"

"Got a call three days ago." Her voice was clear but detached.

"From who?"

The nervous tap of Harper's pencil continued as he mentally sifted through their options. The only other two people who could have tipped her off were Alvin Quinn or Owens. In Harper's mind, it was a coin toss to see which of the two was spineless enough to let a woman do his dirty work. Which man had more reason to see Chuck dead? His dollar bill was on Owens.

"I don't know who it was," she insisted, "just a man."

"You expect us to believe some stranger called you for no good reason and told you Chuck Toomey was the guy who killed Britni?" asked Mann.

"Believe it, don't believe it. I don't care any more." She glared at him. "That's what happened. I don't know who he was, how he found me, or why he bothered, but I'm glad he did."

"And you believed him?"

"He knew too much."

"You had no right!" he yelled.

"I was justified." Her words spilled from her lips like shards of glass

"It wasn't your call."

"Whose call was it, Detective? Yours? How long would he have sat in jail before he plea-bargained himself out of a sentence? He killed my daughter with a snap to the head. Where's the justice in that? Sixteen years. I did what none of you were willing to do."

"And if you were wrong? What made you so sure he was guilty?" asked Mann.

"Instinct."

"Right. My instinct is telling me to send you to the death chamber without a trial." Mann leaned in. "Eye for an eye, Roxanne, same thing you did to Toomey."

She rolled her eyes. "I knew it was him the minute I saw him."

"You murdered a man in cold blood."

"And I'd do it again!" She slammed her opened palm on the table. "He got what he deserved."

"And you'll get yours!"

No one spoke until Mann asked her to explain how she did it.

"I didn't believe the man on the phone at first," she said. "Thought it was a cruel joke, but then why …" She paused for a moment and brushed her bangs aside. "I went to the bar like he told me. Wanted to see for myself. It was him all right." Roxanne smirked while she gave them a textbook account of the toxic powers of monkshood. Harper studied her expressions as she calmly described how she crushed the dried root into a fine powder and placed it in a small plastic bottle in her purse.

Harper envisioned her coolly gazing down on Chuck as the lethal dose of monkshood raced through his blood stream. This frail looking woman had watched him die and did nothing to help in his final moments of life. Had she given Chuck, as he expelled his final gasp, the same seductive smile that pulled at the corners of her mouth now? Harper wondered if she had bothered to tell him why she was putting him to death or did she just lick her fingers and savor the moment? He caught Mann's glance. Roxanne had just confessed to premeditated murder. It was an open and shut case. There was no reason to waste another minute of their time. Roxanne had taken it upon herself to avenge her daughter's death. A noble deed, and in spite of the fact she effectively did the state a favor, no court would ever absolve her of guilt.

Mann reached for his cuffs and ordered her to stand.

"I knew it was fast." She looked directly at Harper. "Didn't know just how fast." She had no plan, she told him. She only wanted to see Chuck's face. "But then, it came to me." She gave Harper another half-hearted smile. "I had no choice."

Their eyes locked for a moment. She had invaded his thoughts – his feelings and the uneasiness made him want to look away. Harper's thoughts settled on his hatred of Owens. A familiar disconcerting feeling gnawed at him again. Avenging Gillies' death would have been sweet. The emotional numbness between right and wrong slithered back into his consciousness. Getting Owens had been the driving force behind his tenacity to solve the baby's murder. He had been willing to risk it all, just like Roxanne, to see Owens dead. How hard could it have been to trap Owens in a dark alley in the middle of the night, raise his weapon to the man's head, and blow out his brains?

"Who would miss him?" she asked.

Her question jolted him back to reality. Would anyone miss either Owens or Chuck Toomey? In that moment, he acknowledged his understanding of her hatred and motivation to kill. *How long,* he wondered, *does a man look the other way or a victim remain a victim before either of them become so enthralled in their desire to destroy that nothing else matters?* His fist tightened and the room closed in around him. A crackling sound and the feel of the splintered pencil in his hand made him blink.

Harper felt no sense of victory seeing Roxanne Lewis in handcuffs. He watched the uniformed officers escort her out of the interrogation room and walk her down the hall. The hollow feeling in the pit of his stomach was the irony she had chosen this needless path. Chuck's blood type coupled with the three statements would have been enough to prove his guilt. They had him. He would have paid for the crime if she had only waited. The delay of one day would have kept her out of death row.

They had solved the Baby Doe case, but where was the closure he had expected? That last note in the score announcing the grand finale? He ran his fingers through his hair and was thinking of the paperwork ahead of him when a disturbance at the other end of the corridor caught his attention. Roxanne was resisting arrest. She was arching her back, refusing to take another step. She screamed and turned her head, seemingly unable to take her eyes off whatever had caught her attention in the intersecting hallway.

"But that's him!" she yelled.

Harper narrowed his eyes. "What the hell?" he mumbled. *Him who?* His steps quickened. "Hold it! Roxanne, stop." He yelled out the order and ran to her side as he swept a glance down the hall.

"Harper. He's the one," she told him. "His voice. It's him."

"Don't say another word." He immediately recognized the broad shoulders and the white band of hair across the back of Commissioner Flanagan's head. He was standing in the middle of the hall, yelling at the person on the other end of the phone. Harper motioned to the officers to take her away. Owens' words came back to him. Owens knew Flanagan was a sexual predator. All those illegitimate kids, he had said. Harper drew his weapon and called out a new set of orders.

Flanagan gnashed his teeth as he paced back and forth across the floor of Interrogation Room 2. His attorney, a man in his fifties with a touch of grey along the temples and a fresh tropical tan, recoiled at the sight of Flanagan's fist. After an exchange of angry words, the attorney gathered his things and stormed out of the room. Flanagan watched him flee then slowly turned his head. He fixed his sight on the two-way mirror. He lunged forward and landed a set of fists squarely against the glass.

It seemed there were as many reasons to put Flanagan behind bars as there were victims, but Harper's reasons were purely personal. He watched as rage burned in Flanagan's eyes and knew he had beaten the man at his own game.

"Got here as fast as I could." Kay Terrill rushed to see for herself. "Hope you two know what you're doing."

"Evening, counselor," said Holloway.

"A man in his position, no priors, not even a traffic ticket. This is insane." She frowned as she looked on, astounded by Flanagan's demeanor and tousled appearance.

"He had the priors, just never got caught," said Holloway.

"What do you have on him?"

"Rape, abuse of a minor, blackmail, extortion, two counts of attempted murder," said Holloway. "Sharpen your pencil and pull up a chair, Ms Terrill, we're just getting started."

"Whose rape?" she asked.

"Roxanne Lewis."

"I'm not buying it."

"You don't have to, but a jury will. His DNA is a match to Baby Doe," said Harper.

"Wait a minute." Kay took hold of Holloway's arm and forced him to look at her. "According to his attorney, you told Flanagan the DNA matched his son's."

"So I lied. Technically, there are only slight similarities between Britni and Patrick; they both had the same father. Beyond a question of doubt. Isn't that what you attorneys look for?" Holloway allowed himself to smile.

"How long have you known?" she demanded.

"Couple of days."

"I'm almost afraid to ask. How'd you get his DNA?"

"From a cigarette butt he left in my office. I told him those damned things would kill him."

"Get another sample," she said. "This time, make it legal. We can't afford to have him walk on a technicality."

"Someone from the lab is already on their way."

"Whatever possessed you?" she asked.

"I knew who raped Roxanne the minute she mentioned the white Mustang; had to be sure though. I remember the day Flanagan bought it." Holloway crossed his arms and fixed his eyes on him. "Patrick never deserved any of the crap Flanagan threw out to him. He certainly didn't deserve to take the rap for this. Didn't bother the old man though. How much lower can a man go than to blemish the name of his deceased son in order to save his own skin? What's that tell you about him, counselor?"

Kay remained surprisingly silent.

"Between forensics and Roxanne's statement I'd say we have him," he said.

"Roxanne? Christ, Holloway, she just confessed to Toomey's murder," said Terrill. "Hope you're not expecting me to turn her into a sympathetic defendant."

"As a matter of fact, that's exactly what you're going to do. We need her as much or more than Owens. We've got Owens' statement on tape and he backs her story as well as Quinn's. By the time we're done, Flanagan won't know what hit him. So you can start working on that long list of charges any time now."

"I expect absolute proof on the rape and you don't have it. You know damn well I'm not into assumptions or surprises," said Kay.

"Rape or not," said Harper, "Flanagan forced himself on a juvenile or did you forget that infraction?" Kay's all-business attitude would work in their favor in court, but her cold indifference wasn't settling well with him now. "The twins' DNA and Roxanne's age at the time of conception is all the proof we need to convict him."

46

Harper took a final look at the medical examiner's photograph of Britni Ewing's bones. His mind flashed back to the day they had found her. She had offered few clues, but the evidence uncovered more than the identity of Britni's killer. Harper removed the label of *Baby Doe* from her file and rubbed on a new one with the baby's full name. He stamped an imposing red *Case Closed* across the front of the folder and set it aside.

He was suddenly aware his obsession with Owens had ceased. He would never accept Gillies' murder, but at least now, he had answers. Kay Terrill had her beyond reasonable doubt evidence against Britni's killer, and they finally had proof of Flanagan's long string of crimes, including the bullet taken from his father's back. The rest would be up to a judge and jury to figure out. Harper had no desire to dwell on the case any further. He was thinking more along the lines of a tall, cool Scotch on the rocks and an equally intoxicating blonde when he heard the knock on his door.

"Mind if I come in?" asked Holloway.

"Anything wrong?" Harper glanced at his watch. He had been determined to go home early today, but the Captain didn't make it up to the fourth floor without reason.

Holloway leaned against the doorframe and shook his head. "Some case, huh?"

Harper nodded and gave him a half-hearted smile. "Has Flanagan talked yet?"

"They're still working on him. At least now, we have Owens. He'll testify against Flanagan and Chuck on all charges; the hit on

Gillies, the rape, the attempt to kill both twins, even the missing bullet. Forensics will prove the rest. He'll spend the rest of his life behind bars without parole if he's lucky."

"What about Owens?" asked Harper. "What kind of deal did you give him?"

"Reduced sentence with early parole. He's giving us everything we need. Besides, it was the only way to get him to drop the harassment charges against you."

"I figured that much," said Harper.

"Well, what does he know anyway? I'm proud of the way you handled yourself." Holloway paused for a moment. "Something wrong?"

Harper shook his head. "I don't feel as good about this as I thought I would. I was thinking about Roxanne."

"What about her?"

"I can't bring myself to blame her for wanting to kill him. Some murders are justified. Does that make me a bad cop?"

"Makes you human. What separates us from the rest is that we don't look the other way. If we did, we'd be no better than the slime we haul into this place. She had a choice. Not every case will make you feel like a winner. You do your best and move on."

Harper said nothing.

"Kay said she'd fight for a reduced sentence in return for Roxanne's testimony against Flanagan," said Holloway. "If I know her, she'll find a way to lessen the punishment."

"Punishment," he sneered. "Do you really think prison will be any harder for her than what she's already been through?"

"You religious, Harper?"

Harper mulled the question over in his mind. "I wouldn't put it in so many words. But, yeah, in a way," he nodded. "With the things we see every day, how could you not hope for something better?"

Holloway arched his brows and drew in a breath. "Maybe you're right at that. Go home. Take a couple of days and get some rest." He bounced his car keys in the palm of his hand and left.

Harper glanced back at Gillies' old desk before turning off the lights. He thought of his oath to serve and protect. *Not just words*, he thought. A conviction, something Gillies' widow would never understand nor forgive. Yet his partner had lived and died defending the rights of others.

"You and me, Gillies," he whispered. "Guess we're not so different after all." He flipped off the lights and was half way to the elevator when he heard Emma calling his name.

"Sam, wait. I'm glad I caught you," she said. "The newspaper courier just dropped this off for you. Thought it might be important."

Harper had forgotten about the article his father had given to him on the morning after Owens' arrest and the enlarged copy of the photograph he had requested from the Chandler Times.

Emma looked on as he ripped open the envelope and slipped out the glossy. "Hey, Gillies asked me about that same picture a couple of days before he died."

"This picture?"

"Yes." She gave the picture a tap. "I remember that night."

"You were there?" he asked.

"That's the night of Greg Flanagan's dinner party after he was sworn in as captain. The band didn't quit until four in the morning. Goodness, look at those hair styles," she chuckled.

Harper studied the faces of every person sitting around the table. Why had Gillies kept this particular picture? "You know any of these people? Besides the Flanagans and Commissioner Palmer, I mean."

"Most of them are his political cronies."

"Start with him." Harper pointed to a man sitting next to Commissioner Palmer. "Who is he?"

The man had been the mayor's campaign manager, she told him. He listened carefully as Emma gave him a detailed account of the man. She pointed to each of the other guests and told him what she knew; who they were, what they did for a living, and what went on in their lives when no one was looking.

"What are you looking for?" she asked.

"I don't know. We found this snap shot in with some of Gillies' things. What did he say about it?"

"Not much. Just wanted to know who the people were sitting

around the table then shot out of here like a rabbit."

"Gillies never liked the brass. He wasn't the sentimental type either. Why would he keep this?"

"He was a pack rat. You wouldn't believe the mess I cleaned out of his desk."

Harper's instinct was telling him that wasn't the case. He had discovered a Gillies he wished he had known, a shrewder man than he had given him credit for being. To Harper that meant there was a reason for keeping the picture. "You forgot one. Who's this?" he asked, pointing to the woman sitting to the right of Mrs Flanagan.

"That's Beverly. Mrs Flanagan's youngest sister. Poor woman, they took this picture shortly after her husband died. She looks miserable, doesn't she?"

"So. What's her story?"

"Well, like I told Gillies, she's something of an outcast. As I understand it, Beverly was fifteen when she got pregnant. The family told neighbors and friends she was at a boarding school that year. Truth of the matter was they shipped her off to live with a great aunt in Iowa until the baby was born."

Harper looked at her.

"The family was very private," she said. "Well to do and insisted on keeping a low profile. So you can imagine their reaction when –"

"How do you know all of this?"

"Their cleaning lady knew my mother. Small community like Rock Hill can't keep too many secrets."

"Rock Hill?" Harper immediately thought of the rape cases he and Kay had discussed.

"Yes. Does it mean anything to you?" she asked.

"No, nothing," he lied. "Go on."

"The people of the town would have crucified Beverly if they had known the truth. Mother always said the family would have been shunned from every social circle in town."

"Life's a bitch for the rich. Ain't it?"

"I wouldn't know," she said, "but forty-three years ago, most people thought any woman who was raped must have asked for it, even if she was a child. The views haven't changed much. You know that."

"She was raped?" he asked.

Emma nodded. "Can you imagine? What a horrible fright for a girl her age."

"Rock Hill must be a haven for crime. There was a string of rape cases in the mid 80's up in that area. Beverly's family ever prosecute her attacker?"

"She wouldn't ID him. I suspect at her age, a trial would have shamed her beyond belief and the last thing the family wanted was public humiliation. They swept it under the rug and let it go."

"How'd Flanagan and his wife take it?"

"They were engaged at the time; she was away at college when it happened. I supposed they were as shocked as the rest of the family."

"And the baby? What happened to it?"

"She kept him, raised him on her own until she got married a few years later." Emma shook her head. "When the Martins found out she was pregnant, they told everyone she had gotten married in Iowa but had the marriage annulled," she smirked. "They had to do something to explain why the child had their name instead of the father's."

Harper looked her square in the eyes. In that single moment, a shutter flew open, the fog lifted, and the control of the reins fell neatly into his hands. He didn't hear Emma's next words. He was thinking of Gillies, his father, Roxanne, and how every malevolent act that had crossed their paths, had led directly to one man – Commissioner Flanagan. The odds of it being a coincidence that Flanagan's wife and her sister were from the same community of the unsolved rapes were indefensible.

"Sam, is everything alright? You have that same look on your face Gillies had."

"Perfect." Harper clenched a fist. Forensics would prove the paternity, but he didn't need a lab to tell him who had raped Flanagan's sister-in-law, or the name of her son. There was a good chance the mother and child were the only two people who knew the identity of the father. The man had despised his legitimate son.

What reason would he have to look after this one if not to protect his own skin?

Owens had said it himself. Everyone owed Flanagan favors, mostly their silence. Only this favor stunk more like blackmail. He looked at the photograph again.

"No wonder Gillies kept this." He told her as he walked away. "Call down to the lab. Tell them I'll need a copy of the DNA results on the Rock Hill rapes as soon as possible and find out who's going to be on call tonight."

"I thought you were going home?"

"Eventually."

Harper couldn't take his eyes from the photograph. He couldn't be sure if Gillies had known about the five Rock Hill rape cases, but his late partner certainly understood the significance of the photograph. They had both come to the same conclusion. Flanagan was Beverly's rapist and the father of her illegitimate son. Is that what Martin meant when he called Gillies a snitch? No wonder the Rock Hill rapist had known so much about police work. He had inherited more than his father's genes. He had his father's taste for illicit sex and used the one thing he and Flanagan had in common as collateral. Therein was the blackmail.

Identifying the son would have exposed the crime of the father. That's what Flanagan had to keep quiet and that alone gave Harper a motive and enough reason to charge him with Gillies' murder. Harper felt as confident of his conclusion about Flanagan as he was about going after the Rock Hill rapist.

He reached for his cell and dialed Kay Terrill's number. The sound of her sensuous voice made him forget their professional differences. "You were right."

"Probably. About what?" she asked.

"The Rock Hill rapist – found him."

"Are you sure?"

"I'll have a match to the semen sample by sun up."

"Don't play games with me, Harper. Who is it?"

"Later. Over dinner – make it a late one."

"Is he an officer?"

"I'll be over as soon as I'm done."

"Wait. Don't hang –"

A smile tugged at the corners of Harper's mouth as he stepped into the elevator and punched the down button. He'd work through the night if he had to. Gillies would have expected no less and dinner or not, Kay would get over it. He gave his watch a quick glance and wondered what Stewart Martin was doing tonight.

Also Available from BeWrite Books

The Knotted Cord
Alistair Kinnon

The body of a naked young boy hanging in a dusty barn stirs sickening feelings of déjà vu in the detective. As he untangles each knot in the tangled cord of his investigation, he uncovers a murderous thread ... and police prejudices which may have allowed previous killings to happen ... not to mention his own guilt.

Alistair Kinnon has written much more than a tense, psychological crime novel – his twisting plot takes the reader into the murky world of child sex-for-sale ... the parent's darkest nightmare and the child's greatest threat.

ISBN 978-1-904224-12-9

The Tangled Skein
Alistair Kinnon

The loose ends of murder take crusading cop Martin Nicols thousands of miles from his home beat and into a steaming hotbed of child vice, inhuman torture and death. But this time Nicols struggles against more than evil puppetmasters with ultimate power over their helpless young victims. He must also contend with hostile and jealous colleagues and infuriating red tape that threatens to hog tie his investigation and let the guilty get away with murder. Every lead matters. All the reader must do is to decide how much. Just like in a real murder hunt, the solid evidence unfolding page by page points in more directions than a weather vane in a gale. It isn't wise to attempt to outguess Kinnon – but it's fruitless to try to resist the temptation as you're drawn into his book as a silent character.

ISBN 978-1-904224-34-1

BeWrite Books

Also Available from BeWrite Books

The Bad Seed by Maurilia Meehan

Her young daughter has disappeared, sparking a massive murder hunt, and now her husband has gone walkabout in the bush with no plans to return.

Nothing is coming up roses for small-time gardening correspondent Agatha.

So she plants the seeds of a new life in an isolated village … in the dilapidated former home of a renowned witch.

A strange new lover and mysterious visitors from half a world away will not allow Agatha's own ghosts to rest and her garden produces dark honey and poison as Maurilia Meehan's tale builds to a chilling climax.

Sinister flora and phantoms flourish in this rich and unforgettable work from the pen of the award-winning author of the acclaimed "Performances", "Adultery", "The Sea People" and "Fury".

ISBN 978-1-905202-12-6

The End of Science Fiction by Sam Smith

No matter how important your job … would YOU turn up for work knowing that you and every living being on the planet will be dead before pay day?

A beautiful young woman is brutally murdered – just as governments around the world announce that the universe will end in five days' time.

The planet Earth's 6.5 billion human beings deal with their impending extinction in 6.5 billion ways. But amid global chaos, dedicated detective Herbie Watkins stays on the case, determined to discover the killer against a merciless clock that's ticking away his own final hours.

Is he insanely obsessed, or is he the last sane man in the history of the human race?

Sam Smith weaves a unique cop story of a unique cop against a unique backdrop in a unique page-turner of a book.

No count-down novel, no disaster book, no police saga has ever been written to thrill the reader and plumb the depths of the human soul as does The End of Science Fiction. It is the last word in SF and crime … and much more.

ISBN 978-1-904492-70-2

Also Available from BeWrite Books

Sweet Molly Maguire by Terry Houston

She came walking into his office and his life with hair of spun copper, frightened green eyes and legs that stretched all the way to heaven.

Molly Maguire should never have got out of the elevator.

She was the sweetest, freshest thing that had ever blown into the jaded existence of Two Coats Mulligan, a veteran reporter with a drink problem and a great future behind him at the Daily Dispatch.

So he invited her to a party at his flat.

While in a drugged stupor she was raped. Mulligan took her in. She was to stay until the baby was born.

Sweet Molly broke the arrangement by slashing her wrists in Mulligan's bathtub.

Amid the hilarious and chilling lunacies of sleazy tabloid journalism, Two Coats Mulligan sets out to trace whoever had forced her to suicide … a death that doesn't rate a line in his own fish-wrap newspaper. But it isn't as simple as that. Drunken Two Coats is haunted by a mysterious lipstick message on his bathroom mirror … and the fact that his own name is high on his secret list of prime suspects. Staggering through a cast of clowns and killers, his investigation becomes a terrifying personal odyssey as he grapples with realities that lie far beyond Molly's death. And, in his search for the truth, he finds that fact is stranger and more sinister than even the most far-fetched of newspaper fiction.

ISBN 978-1-904224-05-1

BeWrite Books

Printed in the United States
76478LV00001B/18

9 781905 202720